NLY.150809

The Kings Circus

By

Kelston Ross

For Kitty

ANTONY ROWE
PUBLISHING

Other Titles by the author

Jack Daniels if you please

The Baron of Ancoats

The Boneheads Crusade

The Kishorn Caper

The Band on the Wall

For further information on Kelston Ross books
E. mail. fmarriott1@aol.com

Published in 2009 by Antony Rowe Publishing

48-50 Birch Close
Eastbourne
East Sussex
BN 23 6PE
arp@cpi-group.co.uk

ISBN 9781905200825

Printed and Bound in Great Britain by

CPI Antony Rowe, Chippenham and Eastbourne

THE KINGS CIRCUS is set in Georgian Bath. It is unique in not following the classic genre of this era, tales of girls from a background of either poverty or shabby gentility who struggle but who finally ensnare the young, handsome virile aristocrat and spend the rest of their lives in high society and comfortable luxury.

It is in fact an action novel and gives an insight into the true life and conditions of the time. Even the love interest is a complex three cornered affair, complicated by involvement in one of the most sensational crimes of the period.

Except for the well known historical characters and events already in the public domain, the situations portrayed and the characters are creations of the author's imagination and any resemblance to persons living or dead is purely coincidental.

In the process of writing this book I want to give my heartfelt thanks to my wife Kitty for her support and her meticulous proofing throughout this work. Also a big 'Thank You' to my good friend Bill Chislett for his invaluable help in researching this project and for introducing me to the Bath City Chief Archivist, Mr Colin Johnston who gave me superb factual information, providing such a clear deep insight to the social life, conditions and property values in Georgian Bath.

Cover design Kelston Ross & Bath design. Photo Louise Ball 2003

THE

KINGS CIRCUS

By

KELSTON ROSS

SYNOPSIS

After living abroad Frank and Kitty return to England and take an apartment in a neglected old house in the heart of Bath. In the process of its restoration Frank finds himself transported back in time to Georgian Bath where he sees at first hand a tempestuous three cornered love affair between a hard bitten Marine Captain, a young girl at a Bath finishing school and a stunning Portuguese beauty and witnesses one of the most audacious robberies of the century, when the Army payroll is stolen on its way to Ireland

Famous for its hot springs, this old Roman garrison town was first patronised by royalty but rapidly became known as a notorious lawless playground for the rich who came in droves to sample its hedonistic pleasures in one of the most notorious cities of Europe eclipsing even Venice. Here were found the ruthless property developers, crooked financiers and the hot-headed 'Bucks' who spent their time and fortunes gambling and duelling in the new parks, Famous musicians packed the vast concert halls and in the elegant glowing stone mansions in the new squares and crescents some of the most beautiful courtesans in Europe plied their timeless trade.

Behind all the affluence cheap taverns huddled on the riverside marshes where assassins could be hired and wanted footpads found refuge and a brisk trade flourished in stolen goods and kidnapped children who were sold as slaves to uncaring factory owners and chimney sweeps or to one of the many brothels.

Dramatis - Personae

Alexander Coulston	Captain of Marines (Lord Trandon)
Jessica Pennington	Admiral's daughter at school in Bath
Janet Hobba	Jessica's Cornish maid.
Captain Brooks	A notorious highwayman
Rob Dacarius	Boat man and former gang member
Rachel Dacarius	Rob's sister
Bradley Thomas	Alexander's military clerk
Lady Trandon	Alexander's great aunt, Miriam
Ezekial Barnes	Trandon House farm manager
Jeb Martin	Wagon Boy at Shires Yard
Cyrus Newton	Bloodstock breeder and dealer
Melody Watson	Tavern barmaid and crack shot
Elias Stuckey	Alexander's banker
Maria di Sienna	A famous Bath courtesan
Aimee La Blanche	Maria's West Indian friend
Florence Edwards	A well known Bath hostess
Major Kurt Mahler	Hanoverian cavalry officer.
Ellis Starkey	Wealthy rake and gambler

Preface

The Circus, Bath. December 20th 2008

Dear Patricia

First let me thank you for your good wishes and the wonderful bouquet of flowers welcoming us back to the old country.

Kit is at the moment visiting family in the north but is due back in a few days. This will be our first Christmas here in many years and we are really looking forward to it.

We are settling down very well and our new home in the Circus is exactly what we were looking for. However having been empty for some time, there is quite a lot of renovating and decorating to do. But we are overjoyed to be here and look forward to you visiting us soon, which will have to be after the holidays which we are spending with family in Cornwall. Bath is a far cry from St. Malo but after living so long in France it is wonderful to be back home and living in this elegant, beautiful and fascinating place. Right now the sun is streaming in through the tall windows and I would like to think that our globetrotting days are over.

However there have been a few bizarre events. The other day whilst stripping off some old wallpaper I came across an old rusted tin box in a hidden recess, which after much struggling I forced open to find a small blue bottle and a yellowing scrap piece of paper bearing a scribbled note with a small bright green feather through it. It read.-

Stranger,

I beg thee harken ye to my tale of mizfortune.

For near three months have I labour'd on this fine mansion a-digging of ditches , drains and culverts and putting to rights the bad work of others before me. But now I am told as how that evil Devil, Silas Carrick (Mr Wood's factor) says that he cannot meet his hobligashions and he will not now pay me my wages due. I do curse him and his family most strongly.

And if in later times some stranger would wish to know how tis to be so used by such a rogue and spekulator , then let him take but one draught from this bottle which my brother Adam (who was bos'un on the packet Orion) bringed back from the Levant.. Then shall he come witness to all the wickedness of these times at first hand. And dwell as the owner of this abode.

Should he wish to observe the tyranny and calumny abroad in this satanic place unseen he should carry about his person this green feather. Then so shall it be. And if said stranger in this Satanic place should wish to return to his own tymes then another draught will return him thence... So I be told. Stranger... May God be with Ye

Jebidiah Rustage.   Master Builder and Plumber.

Bridwell Lane Bath.   October 12 1778

10

Well, I cautiously accepted the challenge and took a drink from the blue glass bottle ..... And things really did begin to happen!

Feeling a little peculiar I took a seat in the window and as I watched the lengthening shadows of the winter afternoon, the impressive vista of the Circus began to change. The bushes appeared to wither and the massive central clump of plane trees shed their leaves and became young wispy saplings... Then they disappeared completely and the crown of grass was buried under a slowly advancing tide of flagstones. In the houses opposite oil lamps appeared at upper windows and in the ground floor rooms huge sparkling chandeliers bathed the lavish saloons in warm candle light.

Then I heard a clopping of horse's hooves and a closed carriage rolled into view from nearby Brock Street, the muffled driver on his high seat blowing his steamed breath onto his cold hands and gently 'chuck-chucking' encouragement to his high stepping horses. Inside two bonneted and fur caped young girls took their hands from their muffs to wave graciously and giggled at two sweating red faced Sedan chair-men carrying an older lady swaddled in white towels from the Queens Bath to her house in The Royal Crescent.

Somehow I felt strangely uncomfortable and then realized that I was no longer attired in my black Jack Daniels T shirt, scuffed Nike trainers and fashionably distressed jeans... Even my seat had

11

changed... The big squashy Ikea sofa was now a tapestry covered high backed wing chair and I was dressed in the high fashions of two hundred and ten years ago... A frilled shirt with a tight white cravat, dark green satin knee breeches, and a buff embroidered frock coat... I felt a bulge in one of the pockets. It was my blue bottle and I realized then that my journey had begun.... And strangely, I felt quite at home!

I may be gone some time but when I return (hopefully!)) I will tell you a tale of genius, evil deeds, decadence and debauchery and give you a true picture of Georgian Bath.

With Love and every good wish from your old friends

Frank & Kitty

1

THE DUEL

A dawn mist was slowly clearing from the river meadows and the elegant frontage of Mr. Wood's Royal Crescent slowly began to take form at the top of a gently sloping bank as nature's sounds of morning broke the virgin stillness. The squeal of small creatures as bigger denizens of the dense undergrowth and the pruned rhododendron bushes sought there welcome breakfasts. Somewhere nearby a tawny owl hooted a final triumphant farewell to the velvet night and retired with a full belly to his hidden roost. On the lower meadows indistinct lumps began to take shape as lowing cattle groaned to their feet and sniffed disinterestedly at the dew soaked grass

A little further to the east in a hidden grove behind the sculpted gardens and pristine roofs of Brock Street, other less pastoral sounds disturbed the morning. The metallic click of a brass ramrod... The ratchet rasp of pistol hammers... The stamping of riding boots on the damp ground and the jingle of spur chains and as the bushes parted in the fresh river breezes they revealed two groups of men in tall hats, and ankle length caped greatcoats. At one corner of the copse were several horses and three dark carriages, dripping with rain from the overhanging boughs.

Such a sinister tableau was not by any means unusual in this setting at this time of day because it was a favourite location for the settling of scores from the previous evening, whether the insults were real or imagined in the brittle egos of the affluent wasters who crowded the brothels, gambling halls and low taverns of this most debauched and sinful of European cities.

Suddenly there came the sound of marching feet and the group looked inquiringly at each other and the muttering and clinking ceased as the men moved to calm the horses and dampen the jingling of harness brasses. A sharp word of command rang out and the sound of the marching cadence became louder as the mist cleared to reveal a platoon of militia on the gravel road fifty yards away heading for the city centre. This was the western section of the night patrol returning from guard duty at the public buildings and river crossings on this side of the city. The young Officer of the Watch sat tall and proud on his magnificent chestnut Arab mare, his grey riding cloak with it's gilt lion clasp still showing dark patches from the earlier rain. Behind him trudged his men to the accompaniment of curses and vicious thumps from their grizzled veteran sergeant. This was his last posting as he worked out the final few months of his thirty year career and he took great pleasure from his sampling the last dregs of his privileged bullying power, for after this he faced the prospect of his twilight years on a meagre pension.

As the tall shakos and glistening bayonets on the Brown Bess muskets faded into the mist again and the river meadows returned to silence, the group of watchers gasped a sigh of collective relief and without further comment, carried on with their sinister preparations. They knew it was likely that one of those present would not leave this cursed dell alive.

"Gentlemen, to your places, please. Time is of the essence." The duel-marshal's command was crisp as he consulted his watch.

By tradition the choice of weapons rested with the challenged party and he had opted for a matching pair of beautiful walnut stocked .58 calibre Argviano pistols with gold engraving supplied, as tradition demanded, from a neutral source. In this case from the well respected shop of Mr Beresford in Broad Street.

Both parties having expressed their approval of the choice, the duel-master again took command. "I understand, Gentlemen that twenty five yards is agreed by your seconds, so please take your mark and be at my command"
For a moment the opponents faced each other then turned to stand back to back... They could not have been more different in that diffused morning light. One was a tall slender Hessian officer with an ugly scar across the bridge of his nose and a heavy blond moustache. He stared coldly ahead. The other, the challenger, was a young thick set, powerful country squire with a bull's neck and arms

15

bursting from his fine cambric shirt. The expression on his russet face was pure hatred. This challenge was definitely serious not just a sham where both parties fired wide for mutual satisfaction. As they stood back to back, their cocked pistols hanging at their side, waiting for the order, differing thoughts came to mind about their reasons for being in this situation. This morning killing was in the air.

For Major Kurt Mahler, a thirty six year old German from Flensberg in the much disputed border province of Schleswick, was a newly arrived aide on the staff of the Duke of Brunswick stationed at Warminster. To him the situation was nothing new... He had no axe to grind. He had been challenged to a duel and that was that. The rest was up to The Fates. His fourteen years of mercenary service in the armies of Hesse and Hanover had given him a fatalistic view of life's lottery and he treated this occasion as just another incident in his colourful career. His opponent however thought much differently.

The Honourable Ellis Starkey was a brutal and powerfully built man of twenty six. The son of a minor Irish lord, he had inherited a large estate on the Somerset Levels which he ran with an iron hand. He was quick tempered and was prone to hold grudges and to spend money wildly, character flaws that had led him to his present situation.

It had all started a month previously when he had been unceremoniously thrown out of the Assembly Rooms for trying to stab one of the card room staff with a hidden dagger after a long losing streak at the tables. Still seething from his three weeks exclusion from the venue, he had returned last night and deciding that he would like to play hazard had demanded brusquely that Mahler give up his place at the table. Mahler flatly refused to move and had made some remark in his native tongue to his companion about this presumptuous drunken boor. At this Starkey had flown into a rage and threw down the gauntlet. Mahler turned to see if the man was serious and seeing his glaring red face, accepted the challenge, coolly saying that his seconds would be in touch directly... And now here they both were.

They were shaken from their thoughts by an order from the duel master. "Gentlemen, at my command you will take thirteen paces forward, turn and fire at will. Are you ready? ... March!" The seconds held their breath and the drivers whispered to the horses, keeping a firm grip on their bridles as the ground between the duellists was covered swiftly and both parties turned and fired almost simultaneously. There was a deafening roar and as the powder smoke cleared a body could be seen writhing on the damp leaves while the other stood stock still holding a smoking pistol.

Both combatants differed totally in style... The farmer had turned about full face, closed one eye and sighted his weapon along his outstretched arm but before he could draw an exact bead his adversary, the veteran of a dozen battles, had half turned and in an almost reflex action, had raised his gun and fired. The shot was clean and the heavy 15 millimetre lead ball passed right through the farmer's shoulder below the collarbone before clipping the top of his scapula and leaving an ugly gaping exit wound gushing blood. There was also blood oozing from the right eye where a hard fragment of wadding had also scored a hit.

The doctor and his assistant rushed forward trying to staunch the blood and the seconds stood back aghast but Mahler did not even glance in the direction of the groaning farmer but calmly handed his pistol to one of his seconds and walked away. At the coaches he reclaimed his coat, donned his hat and riding cloak, mounted his horse and rode slowly back to his lodgings at the Bell Inn in Walcott Street for a hearty English breakfast. .. He thought no more about the incident than he would have about shooting a horse with a broken leg or a rabid dog.

As he left the grove the rider overtook a gardener on the way to his daily toil in the nearby gardens. As the soldier passed, the worker raised his crumpled old hat and wished him a good morning but the arrogant horseman ignored him. The only thing he did find a bit strange was that the artisan was wearing a small bright green feather in his hat.

2

West Wiltshire. Winter 1798

High in the clear cold blue sky above Lackham House on the rolling land south of Chippenham a hawk scoured the white landscape for his dinner... For three days now he had circled these wooded rolling West Country plains but at a time when there should have been rabbits and lost sheep in abundance nothing moved. Even the small creatures like the voles and corn rats had not left their shelters in the deep black woods. Ahead he saw a snail like trail winding through the white wilderness and dropped lower to check on it hoping to find a food source.

As a bell in the tower of Laycock church tolled it's dismal peal, a side gust from the south east lifted him high above Bowden Hill and he launched into a gentle dive heading for the creature making the trail hoping that it would be food at last but as he levelled out he found that it was in fact a twisting serpent of white humpbacked creatures heading for some distant smoking habitation.

It was far too big for him to attack so he wheeled high again to watch for smaller prey. Far below at the edge of a copse a hare peeped out of the undergrowth looking carefully around twitching his nose, seeing no sign of earthly predators he shot off across the snow covered meadow to his burrow at the far side but he was not alone. The hawk caught the sudden movement and banked easily in his steep dive.

He had found his dinner.

As the lumbering wagon train topped the hill before Corsham the snow flurries hit it cruelly and the leading driver cursed the decision of the wagon master to push on instead of letting the blizzard blow itself out while they sheltered in the warm confines of the Angel Inn at Chippenham. As he tamped down the plug in his corncob pipe Sam Carr recalled grumpily how Marcus Harris had said that the storm would soon pass and as it was only five leagues to Shire's Yard at Bath they could be there by nightfall. But he'd been wrong hadn't he? And this damned blizzard had not blown itself out, if anything it seemed to be getting worse and now it looked as though they would not be sleeping in their own beds that night. The snow was already up to the horse's knees and tough as they were, even these Suffolk punches were finding it hard going. In fact, just at that moment Sam thought he had heard the leading mare cough as she struggled to keep the traces tight and he flicked the reins sideways to stop the straining beasts.

"Whoa. Whoa there Dolly." He called above the howling wind and the lead pair dropped their heads with fatigue, blowing clouds of steam from their dripping muzzles...Still cursing profanely, Sam threw off the layers of tarred sacking that sheltered him, stiffly clambered down from his high seat and waded through the drift to check out his charges. From behind his seat another pile of tarred sacking erupted slowly and a tousled blond head appeared. "Whatcha doin' Uncle Sam?", Cried a small voice. "Are we there yet?"

Sam spat a brown glob onto the white snow and wiped his nose on the worn cuff of his heavy blue greatcoat as the caped shoulders fluttered in the gale like angel's wings.

"Nay, Jeb lad. Get thee back under the burlap. Twill be the death o' ye out 'ere. I were jus' about to look at Dolly's left hoof. I could swear she were a-limpin' back there."

"Oh no, not Dolly!" Cried the boy and he kicked aside his protective canvas and jumped into the snow, wading through the wind blown drifts until he was at Dolly's muzzle. Sam tried to push him away but he dodged the slow moving carter and stroked the huge horse's nose.

"Wassamatter then, my girl, you'm gorra a nasty stone in yer 'oof 'ave you? Lemme 'ave a look my beauty, tha knows I would never hurt thee."

Dolly looked mournfully at the young ostler and snorted a shower of saliva as she responded to Jeb's gentle touch and lifted her massive haired hoof.

21

"Oh aye!," He shouted above the howling wind, "I got un. Tis jus' a flint she's picked up. I'll soon get un out."

Sam tapped his shoulder and handed the boy his knife to free the stone. Regardless of the icy wind blowing through his hair Jeb wiped the hoof clean, and for good measure freed a lump of hard packed snow from inside the shoe. Dolly shook her head showering them again but she seemed more settled and turned to nuzzle her son who shared the front traces with her before settling into her collar again. Sam looked on with approval and Jeb was reminded of one of the first lessons the grizzled carter had taught him. That the best combination for a lead pair of horses was that of mother and son. It made for tranquillity. He was just clambering back aboard when he heard a coarse voice shouting at someone.

"Yeer, Samuel Carr. What you fink you'm a-doin'? Ye got the whole bloody train stopped!"

Sam turned to see the sinister figure of Marcus Harris mounted on a huge black stallion, with his tricorne hat tied firmly to his head by a long scarf making his bloated red face look like an overcooked plum pudding. "Tis Dolly," He grunted, "gorra flint in 'er 'oof. Jeb's fixed un."

Marcus's face turned darker and he spat out a string of obscene curses "Well, then, get 'er goin' again. Mr Tarleton's a-waiting' on us at Broad Street an' I told the post boy to tell 'im that the train would be there by nightfall. They'll be heads a-rollin' if he don't see us tonight, I'll tell ee, so gerrem movin' directly!"

With another spout of profanity he dragged the stallion's head round and headed back to his place under the protection of the leeward side of the third wagon which was already looking top heavy from the piled snow on top of its canvas covered load of furniture.

The twice weekly run to Holborn Bridge, London usually took just under three days if the weather was clement... In fact Sam had once done it in two days and four hours but that had been in a cold March when the roads were hard and the convoy had only been three wagons; but in this kind of thick snow they would be lucky to make the trip in less than four days.

Harris was furious. He was assiduously courting Tarleton's daughter Sarah, a dumpy spoilt woman of thirty three who so far had made no impression on the Somerset gentry and whom Marcus considered to be the key to his destiny; albeit that he had a wife already in Norwich. He had decided that one day he would become master of this freight company even if did mean servicing Sarah's bloated body and putting up with her inane self-centred whining! Tarleton himself had come to control the company by much the same ploy when he had wed the founder's dull daughter Bessie.

Walter Wiltshire had become the Mayor of Bath in the 1740's and started this cartage company at the urging of his friend Thomas Gainsborough the famous painter who lived just up the hill from Shires Yard. They were both great gamblers and were regular patrons of the infamous Assembly Rooms where fortunes were lost and won playing high stake games like hazard. In fact, one evening

Thomas had lost even his horse and Walter gave him one of the big carthorses to take him home, a gesture that the artist repaid by featuring the animal in his painting 'The Hay Waggon' which he then presented to his friend.

By the 1780's the freight line had become well established across the West Country extending a delivery service to Bristol and even Taunton. In fact, one of Old Walter's last ventures was a tentative service to Exeter, which however failed in the face of the regular packet service by sea to London docks. It was around this time that his service began to be plagued by highwaymen, usually discharged soldiers with no other way of scratching a living. Walter countered the threat by sending his wagons in convoys of up to six or eight providing as they did an element of collective protection. This system rapidly discouraged the highway men and such outlaw gangs as the feared Pewesy family, which dominated the roads from their stronghold in the depths of Brandon Forest and the equally sinister Night Raiders who ranged the Marlborough Downs and they began to prey on softer targets like travelling traders or the lone mail coaches. So, Walter Wiltshire's venture continued to prosper even in the face of the busy river Avon Navigation to Bristol and the Severn Estuary, the whispers about the almost finished Kennet and Avon canal and a man made iron road with steam engines. Walter strongly dismissed these speculations. "Boats?," He would tell his drinking cronies, "Waall, mebbee one day, but railways? Pagh! ... Never."

Grey clouds banked upon the hills to the north and as the sky grew darker, now even Marcus had reluctantly accepted that they must rest and get the horses under cover for the night. With a contemptuous sniff he directed Sam to make for the Cross Keys Inn near Corsham Court. The drivers could bed down in the stables there and he could pay his compliments to Squire Tracy at the hall where he might get a bed for the night and a glass of fine brandy. Forty minutes later Sam rolled the creaking convoy to a halt in the vast cobbled yard behind the rambling old coaching inn and the crews began to unhitch the steaming horses and lead them into the long warm stables where they wiped them down carefully with handfuls of soft straw before the joyful jingling of nosebags made them whinny with anticipation of their evening meal. Harris made provision with the innkeeper, giving him a note on Mr Tarleton at Shires Yard to cover the night's stopover and a hot meal.

"No need o' beds for 'em," He sniffed "they'll soon be a-snorin' along the nags. They'm well used to that!"

Satisfied with himself he called Sam outside to join him in checking out the vast wagon park and as they stood warming themselves at the big beacon fire that was always lit at night to keep the wolves away, he told Sam that due to the inclement weather there would be no need to mount an overnight guard as they usually did, it not being likely that even highwaymen were out on such a night let alone the wagon robbers.

For the second time that day Harris's judgement proved faulty, for barely half a mile away behind a wooded knoll a sinister

25

group of riders watched the wagon train bed down for the night. As the distant night watch fire flared it showed the hard faces of the men and weapons they carried, revealing just who they were and what was their night's purpose. The leader, a tall thin man with greasy grey hair straggling from his tricorne hat and a constant twisted scowl that struck terror into his victims was a notorious highwayman known across Wiltshire and South Gloucestershire as Captain Brooks. With a grunt he removed the leather-covered telescope from his eye and turned in the saddle to address his companions.

"Nay Lads, 'tis not a venture tonight there be too many o' em and I've spotted a line o' Wiltshire Yeomanry bays 'neath one o' they open sheds. That could be a patrol o' militia out a-seekin' us." Another gust of snow blew up the hill powdering the riders and their steaming nags. The horses instinctively turned their rumps to the storm and stamped impatiently tossing their heads almost unseating the rider who had again turned his glass to the smoking chimneys of the inn. "Whoa, Blackie, stay still ye evil bastard! Ye'll 'ave me in the bushes yet." He snarled viciously as he pulled the mount's head round and kicked its ribs. Cramming his hat further onto his head as the storm gusted he turned to his lieutenant.

"Listen Rob, ye take the lads back to Brandon while me an' Dickon will head 'cross Westbury way to spy what's adrift on the Warminster Road. I believe that the Bath Mail do run up from Poole on the morrow, so we'll bed down at Mother Clayton's out Blanford way tonight and then we'll see jus' what pickin's the gentry can provide us with next day. Quick now, off ye go. Move quietly and keep separate. See you at the camp tomorrow night."

With a nod of approval Rob led the nightriders back to the inns of Chippenham while Dickon and Captain Brooks stayed on the ridge watching until the gang faded into the snow flurries before moving south toward Salisbury.

Some distance away, under the cover of the tempest, a rider at the rear broke free of the robber band, turned back and followed the pair, watching them carefully ... From his pocket he took out a green feather and slid it under his scarf and as another snow flurry hit, he disappeared from view.

3

GENTLEMEN OF THE ROAD

In the early morning light a battered but sturdy fishing boat had just unloaded the night's paltry catch onto the quay at Poole harbour and the two grizzled fisherman paused in their customary bickering to check out the big 74-gun frigate and the lumbering troop ship, which were just rounding the Isle of Purbeck heading for the Quay. One of them spat into the water and snarled at his companion

"Oh gerrout of it, 'Arry, tha'll never warp them nets clear loik that! Let me 'ave a go, us'll be yeer all day if yon Man o War drops 'er chains across th' 'arbour mouth."

Harry looked up startled "Oh aye? Don' yew tell me to 'urry up Tommy Briggs! Tis yore fault that we got back late.. I tol' yew twice that that jib sail were torn but would yew listen, oh no?.. An' the bloody thing ripped out didn't it, eight mile beyond Purbeck, so we got back after all the rest an' got nowt for the catch."

Finally they stopped all the squabbling and with a shower of salty curses they cleared their berth and scuttled to raise the dirty brown sail and headed out into the basin just as the warship, still a half a mile away, announced her arrival with a boom from her starboard fo'c'sle swivel gun and commands could be faintly heard across the low swell…

"All hands Mr Travis. Bring her head round. Main chains Mr Garrick. Steady now, steady…. Mr King. Get the Marine guard on deck!"

As the frigate came closer the name on the bow became clearer revealing that she was HMS Furious. She carried the evidence of a hard and difficult passage on her hull in the form of long scrapes from rough harbour walls, chipped gun port lids and worn bulwarks, confirmation that she was overdue for a full overhaul. Inboard however told a different story where all was crisp and shining with the poop holystoned to a smooth pristine cream surface and ropes neatly coiled on deck, testimony to a tightly run ship.

Her captain, Commander Horace Worton leaned a little into the freshening inshore breeze and sniffed as he snapped together his brass telescope and addressed the port pilot.

"Think you'll berth us both Master? Don't seem a lot o' sea room to me. Yon trooper's a wallowing old sea cow at the best o' times and I can see her pitchin' on the ebb tide already. You'd better make haste, my man!"

The pilot, who had spent the past twenty years guiding ships through the rocks, shallows and sandbanks of Poole Harbour, just sniffed and signalled the grey bearded helmsman to pull three points to port.

In the big cabin beneath the quarterdeck a young girl of about sixteen was chattering on excitedly to her chubby round faced maid as they bustled about packing trunks and putting bonnets in boxes.

"Ooh. Janet, we're here in England, is it not wonderful? There were times that I had my doubts that we would ever get here, even though Papa told me over and over that this ship was the best in King George's Navy. He said that he would go anywhere in the world in a hull of English oak."

It had been over six years since Janet had left her Cornish home to take service overseas with the Admiral's daughter and she made no bones about her current state of mind as she folded a Kashmiri scarf.

"Well, Missy, sooner 'im than me!" She sniffed." I've seed me 'nuff waves an' Jack Tars to las' me a lifetime, an' painful tho' tis, I mus' tellee Missy, I won't be a-doin' it no more. Even if I 'ave to take service elsewhere! God knows, child, I love 'ee like a daughter but bringin' me breakfast back each mornin' b'ain't my idea of an 'appy life! So don' you be in any 'urry to finish school in Bath. Let's feel God's good earth 'neath our feet for a while!"

In the soft morning drizzle it was another half hour before the pilot had both vessels safely alongside the Town Quay and securely warped in. Aboard the salt streaked East India Company's troopship drums began to roll and the deck became crowded with hard looking, deeply tanned red coated soldiers. Officers stalked imperiously on the quarterdeck as wild, raging be-medalled sergeants and corporals bellowed and punched their charges into rigid ranks. Chains rattled as gangplanks creaked down to the damp dockside cobbles and the troops looked forward to finally being able to disembark, thankful that their long journey was over. It had been the best part of four months since they had left their base at Bangalore, with only a four day stop-over at Cape Town and two more at Gibraltar as they waited for the troopship to pick up supplies and a returning draft from the Rock's garrison.

Staring through the big stern window of the frigate at the mist shrouded buildings Jessica was also on pins waiting to get ashore but the captain insisted that they should wait until the troops cleared the quay. By her side her father Admiral Singleton put his hand on her arm and looked at her fondly. She was his only daughter, in fact his only living child and parting with her was most painful but her social education was of paramount importance.

For this reason he had enrolled her at Mrs. Blundell's famous finishing school for young ladies at Bath, a move that he hoped would facilitate her entrée into Regency society. There was always the hope that she might find a wealthy husband in that much talked about City. Jessica herself was just glad to be finally getting off the ship. Her education was much further from her mind than the excitement of the shops, balls and coffee houses of one of the most fashionable and infamous cities in Europe...Why even that Austrian

Countess they met at Gibraltar had fluttered her fan and rolled her eyes when she discovered Jessica's destination.

Aboard the troopship there was the sudden roll of drums and a piping of fifes and the Marine guard presented arms to greet their Commanding Officer as he emerged from the poop hatchway spitting and coughing from the cold morning air.

"Ah, there you are Captain Coulston. How nice of you to honour us with your presence in your own good time. Stand to your post, sirrah!"

It was patently clear that Captain Thomas was not pleased at the red-coated officer and he stared pointedly at his unbuttoned tunic and unshaven face before turning to the Flag Officer.

"Away now Mr Valentine, break out the Jack an' the pennants. Tell 'em we're here to stay awhile...and now, bandmaster, our Royal anthem if you please!"

The drums rolled again and the piping fife and timbales trilled the 'Regents Prayer' as the newly re-designed Union flag broke free from it's white lanyard and fluttered in the fresh breeze...There was another sound like the rapping on a window blind as a succession of signal flags snapped alive to announce that both of the ships would be staying at their berths until the fumigating and repairs had been attended to. Orders rang out and the troops began to disembark while urchins and painted doxies called to the tough veterans as the raging, cursing sergeants bellowed and thumped their charges into a solid silent column before marching them to the dock gates to await the baggage carts before continuing to their barracks at Ringwood.

Two hours later Jessica and her maid were being helped aboard the Bath Mail, a four-in-hand closed coach with the latest springs and the new loose coupling system that, so it was said, gave the horses more freedom and the driver more control. As she climbed inside Jessica sniffed at the musty smell of the damp worn yellow velvet seats but settled into a corner while Janet sat stiffly opposite her. There was banging as heavy portmanteaux and boxes were piled on the roof behind the outside seats and Jessica blushed at the imaginative cursing of the grooms and stable boys that turned the air blue but Janet just pursed her lips and sucked in air in that quaint Cornish manner, pretending that she understood not a word!

The guard sounded a fanfare on his post horn as the coach boy banged the door closed and ran alongside as the vehicle started to lurch across the yard cobbles, shoving his greasy cap in the window for the customary gratuities from the passengers. Jessica gave him two pennies while the old dame in the far corner snuffled and then tossed some small change his way but the other passenger, an emaciated old clergyman, just waved his hand in some vague blessing, which was returned with a much clearer gesture from the boy. Everyone had just begun to settle and make themselves as comfortable as possible for the bumpy journey, when having cleared the hostelry's stone arch the coachman reined his team to a halt while the three unfortunate outside travellers climbed onto the roof. Once again the horn sounded and with curses ringing in the air and the

33

driver's whip cracking, they rolled off down the Poole's dung spattered Quay Street and headed for the Bournemouth turnpike and on to Salisbury. As they halted at the next corner to let a brewery dray pass there was the sound of more loud curses outside and the offside door was suddenly thrown open and two swearing tapsters bundled in the drunken and dishevelled Marine officer Jessica had seen on the ship. With an exaggerated bow to the company, he proclaimed airily.

"I wish a good morning to you one and all. I am Captain Alexander Coulston of His Majesty's Marine Forces at your service." His voice was slurred with exaggerated vowels in a forlorn attempt to impress these stuffy civilians. Losing his thread, he grinned at them vacantly but finding no welcoming response, he let go a great gust of rummy breath, wrapped his cloak around him and slumped in the corner. By the time they were rolling through Talbot Village heading north to Warminster, he was snoring loudly and incoherently mumbling in his troubled slumber.

At the Pheasant Inn in Blanford Forum they halted to disembark one of the roof passengers, with the coachman muttering under his breath as the stiff client got down and his luggage was thrown into the roadway. Spitting into the frosty air and without a word of farewell the coachman cracked his whip and they were off again while he regaled the guard with his usual complaints.

"See 'im, Nobby, why didn't 'e 'ire a private diligence or even a van to get 'ere instead of delaying his Majesty's Mail? These bloody roads be bad enough 'bout havin' ter pull over every few miles to drop off coves like 'im. I'll 'ave to give these trotters red arses now, if we're going to make Warminster afore evenin', wot's more," he added grumpily, "the ungrateful rascal didn't give us a tip or nuffin."

The Guard just nodded, confused as ever at his companion's attitude whilst the driver in deep disgust clucked the horses into a gentle trot through the flicker of the sporadic gusts of sleet. A further six miles passed on the rutted road until it narrowed and curved into a thick wood forcing them to slow to a walk and as they lurched round a bend they were halted by two masked horsemen who emerged from the shadows and blocked the coach's path. The bigger of the two reined in at the driver's box and shouted roughly.

"Hold fast there, driver!... An' ye there Guard, touch not that there blunderbuss or I'll put a ball into thee directly! Now, thou get up easy and toss His Majesty's mail pouch down, quick now!"

He glared fiercely at the frightened guard who scuttled onto the roof while the two outside travellers sat petrified with fear. The driver just sighed and let the ribbons drop across the horses' backs as he looked at the two highwaymen with bored resignation. Today was definitely not going to be his happiest day because this was the fifth time he had been held up on this Warminster road and he had seen it all before. Luckily, he mused, they were carrying the Royal Mail, which is usually all they wanted so he offered no resistance. Casting a quick glance in the driver's direction, the footpad turned to his companion and said quietly.

"Dickon, thou keep thy barkers on these dull jakes while I find what Dame Fortune has sent us in the rig."

Inside the coach Jessica and Janet suddenly realised what was going on and clung together in fear wondering what would happen next and the old dame opposite rolled her eyes anxiously chewing her gums while the threadbare wide eyed clergyman hugged his bible closer.

In the corner, wrapped in his creased grey sea cloak, the rumpled Alexander opened a bleary eye and looked warily round the fuggy coach wondering what was happening. Suddenly he seemed to grasp the situation and shook his head to clear the last of the rum fumes just as a horse's muzzle passed the door window. There was the rap of a pistol barrel on the frame and a masked face topped with a dirty tricorne hat came into view and a gravely voice rasped.

"Good mornin' to ye Gentlefolk... Cap'n Brooks at thy service. Now, jes' pass thy purses out o' the window an' no harm will become ye ...Quick now!"

As he reined back, his horse's head again came close to the open window and in a flash the Marine threw off his grey cloak and lunged with his short sword, sinking the blade deep into the animal's neck just below its ear. The horse screamed and reared violently throwing its rider heavily into the road and before he could recover the officer was out of the coach and on top of him, scrabbling for the pistol he had dropped.

Dickon looked on with horror, undecided whether to take his

36

aim off the terrified guard or to fire at his partner's assailant. Alexander struggled with the highwayman but being unable to find enough clear space to use his blade, he hit him heavily on the side of the head with the hilt of his sword and just as he swung his opponent round Dickon's pistol roared. The ball hit his companion just below the shoulder blade killing him instantly but before he could wheel his horse away Alexander found the highwayman's own pistol and fired point blank into Dickon's side. His horse clattered a few steps along the road and stopped, confused by the uneven load as its rider slumped to one side held by his stirrup strap, his lifeless head banging against the horse's hind leg. The girls shrieked and stared wide eyed at the bloody scene of carnage while the dusty preacher shakily began to incant some obscure prayer from his corner seat. The Captain whirled round to check that there were no more gang members around to attack him and shouted to the open mouthed guard.

"You, you useless dolt, get thee down here and help me get him 'cross the saddle. Lash 'im down while I grab the other nag...Quick now!"

He grabbed the shivering horse's bridle and stroked it's nuzzle and wiping blood from it's wound before taking the weight of the dead rider and lifting him across the saddle. Soon they had both of the bodies tied down on the back of the wounded horse which they tethered to the rear of the coach while the guard mounted the other and galloped off to take the news to the Town Beadle at the

Warminster way station and the coach resumed its ponderous progress across the crisply frosted hills.

Alexander settled back into his seat and disdainfully brushed off the slush and mud from his uniform before honouring the company with a sardonic smile. He turned his gaze to the smirking clergyman.

"So Pastor, thy prayers were answered then and thy Lord called two souls to his bosom, eh, just glad I was not one of 'em. Tho' to thee it would make little difference would it? The Lord provides for and guards his children eh? Very well then Pastor, but forgive me for not being over impressed. Too many times I have seen men dying in the Indian sun calling for Him and not being heard!"

He spat out of the window and turned to address Jessica and her maid.

"Do pardon my hard soldier's ways Ladies. I have not yet quite adjusted to polite society. You see I am no longer shocked by death. In any other place I would have left the bodies for the wolves and wild dogs but here in England it seems that we must give even scum like this a Christian burial. For if not, what else would this simpering cleric here have to do to justify his stipend?"

He concluded his caustic comments by hawking and spitting again into the light snow that was beginning to dust the hedges.

Jessica looked at him disgustedly then lightly clearing her throat she addressed him with an exaggerated courtesy.

"Not withstanding our deep gratitude for your brave action

38

sir, I think that you will have to learn to control your strong opinions or at least keep them to yourself if you are to find any comfort in society here. This is not some fly blown colonial outpost but England and I for one, am grateful to be here where life is comfortably regulated with each in his own destined place!" She sniffed and stuck her small hands deeper into her fur muff while Janet pursed her lips and nodded her silent approval.

Alexander bridled at this pompous outburst and stared at her. "And who mistress, are you to presume such airs and graces? We were informed aboard the troopship Calcutta that our frigate escort carried some precious cargo and that we were to mind our manners if she ever came alongside but I had expected some thing more than a flibberty-gibbet school girl!

"I sire," She retorted feistily, "Would have you know that I am the only daughter of Admiral Sir George Singleton and you may be sure that I will have him write to your superiors about your despicable conduct and insufferable disrespect!"

Alexander smiled cynically. "Oh would you really mistress? Well just be sure to tell him also that my despicable conduct at Blanford Forum probably saved you and the rest of your companions from a much crueller fate. Believe me; I have seen such things happen!"

Jessica stared him in disgust and with a toss of her head she stuck her nose back into her book.

The rest of the journey was passed in an uncomfortable silence.

At the Rising Sun Inn in Warminster a large crowd had gathered round the town beadle and his men were waiting in the yard to take charge of the bodies and to identify them. One of the bolder spirits stepped forward and lifted the dangling head from the horses flank and shouted to the crowded inn yard.

"Eh, Lads, jus' look who we got 'ere! Tis that there Cap'n Brooks. They say there's a bounty out on 'im, dead or alive, 'undred guineas or so I yeard. I dunno who t'other one is though."

The crowd surged round Alexander congratulating him and poking at the dead men with their sticks. A few coins fell from one of the corpse's greatcoat pockets and the stable boys scrabbled across the cobbles after them. The pompous beadle brushed them roughly out of his way and asked the Captain to follow him into the inn where the magistrate's parchment authorising the reward had to be signed and forwarded to Bath Court House where the captor could claim his reward.

At the back of the chattering onlookers, holding his weeping sister close, Captain Brooks' lieutenant Rob stared with hatred at the red coated centre of attention and whispered.

"Hush now, Our Rachel. People are watching us. Just ye note yon redcoat's face. Tis not a fizog I will forget in an 'urry an' ye can be sure I will avenge ye. Tis what Brooksie would 'ave wanted. So don' ye fret none!"

The girl just nodded miserably and sobbed deeply into his coat. "You do that for us, Our Rob!" She whispered. "If only for 'is child I'm a-carryin'. Devil's curse on 'im an' them evil bastard beadle's men too"

She lifted her head and tossing her thick black hair she looked hard into Alexander's eyes before walking quickly away.

In all this hustle and bustle Jessica and Janet moved into the inn's warm parlour where they took tea and a small glass of brandy each until the coach was ready for the last leg of their long journey to the Saracens Head Hotel in Bath. Finally a blast from the ostler's whistle informed all and sundry that the fresh team of horses had been put to the traces and the passengers took their places again. The new leaders responded brightly to the driver's whip picking up a crisp trot but making a cautious descent down the twisting hill to the village of Limpley Stoke where a group of sinister looking labourers were digging a new canal for the carriage of coal from the mines at Radstock. With a loud sniff of disgust Janet blurted out.

"Oh my, lookee there, Missy. Them's they Irish 'Navigators'. Very rough men they do say. I should surely not like to meet up wi' one o' them on a dark night."

Jessica looked up from her book of poems and glanced out of the window "They do not seem to be much disturbed by the inclement weather. Their skins must be as thick as ox hide. Turn your face away. Do not let them see you watching them for it would be most distressing should they approach us!"

Whilst feigning sleep Alexander watched them from the corner and cynically tried to visualise the protected upbringing of the

41

genteel young girl. It was probably vastly different from his tough upbringing, he mused. He pondered on her confident attitude and haughty pride thinking that he would certainly show her a thing or two about life's ups and downs if they were alone for half an hour! An Admirals daughter indeed!

He compared his own background with such a product of wealth and privilege. Born in Devon he was the youngest son of a gentleman farmer distantly related to the Trandon family from Gloucester, his father had been a drunken waster but fortunately still had enough money and influence to send his youngest son to a naval academy at the age of nine. Alexander was a good student and passed out with honours to become a midshipman and joined his first ship the day after his sixteenth birthday. After two dull years aboard an escort frigate he transferred to the Marines in search of adventure. Now at thirty one and one of the youngest senior captains in the regiment but he had become tired of the constant fighting and bloodshed and disenchanted by seeing good companions dying, not in the service of King and Country but simply to line the pockets of greedy East India Company nabobs and shareholders.

This bold trading adventure that started in 1612 with the establishment of a small trading post at Surat north of Bombay and was now based at Calcutta where it had become a huge commercial empire eating up all before it, with the Royal Navy providing protection for its ships and logistic support across the globe. It was the impeachment of the Governor Warren Hastings in the 1780's

42

which had finally brought out into the open the vast sums of money and priceless antiques that were being illegally misappropriated. At his trial Hastings quite coolly stated that he was actually surprised at the modesty of his gains when compared to those of his fellow directors! This statement added greatly to his Alexander's disenchantment and he was hoping that this summons to Bath by his great aunt would provide the change of life he was seeking.

He tried to sleep but then another image presented itself. Who was that striking girl with the black hair who gazed at him with such hatred in the yard of the inn when he brought in the highwaymen? Her eyes had never left him for a moment and when he ventured a simple smile the stony gaze only hardened. But, by God, stone-faced or not, she was some beauty! Remembering that there was a new militia barracks at Warminster he decided he would ssgo there on some pretext and spend a little time combing the taverns for her. After all, he consoled himself, what else had he to do? This matter with his aunt's lawyers would be settled in a few weeks after which he would have time to indulge his fancies until it became time for him to rejoin his ship at Poole. And who knows, if his portion proved to be big enough he might even resign his commission and try his hand at trade ashore. In a bustling vibrant city like Bath there had to be many opportunities. Under the disgusted gaze of his fellow travellers he turned his head into the grimy velvet and snored.

4

AQUA SULIS

The weary wagon train finally arrived at Shires Yard at nine at night after almost twelve hours of struggling through the drifts, some of them over four feet deep. Dolly the Suffolk Punch had survived the packed snow in her hoof but was limping badly by the time the train had reached the tollbooth near the site of the old North Gate of the city. Jeb and Sam sat on the driving seat of the leading wagon and patiently waited for the self important Marcus Harris to fill out the excise document of entry required from every commercial vehicle wishing to enter. Jeb was gnawing on a carrot as were Dolly and her son while Old Sam puffed his pipe and read the freshly painted board giving the customs rates for livestock, asking the young boy next to him questions on the meaning of certain words. Not for the first time Jeb looked on in awe as the grizzled old waggoner explained the details of the notice, board and marvelled at the depth of his knowledge. How could a simple carter know so much? He could read, write and talk like a lawyer about mathematics or building or any subject you cared to mention when he chose to but seemed quite content with his lot in life.

As a young man he run away to sea and on the long voyages across the Southern Atlantic had taught himself to read and write and to speak Spanish but in his early thirties was arrested in Hispaniola on charges of trying to smuggle out church artefacts. Only his ability to speak the language and the crucifix he wore round his neck saved him from slavery but nevertheless he spent almost two years in jail eventually escaping by stealing a small boat and rowing out after dark to a British frigate on patrol duty. The experience soured his enthusiasm for life at sea and arriving home in Bristol took a job as a carter. That had been twenty years ago and he had never regretted it, finding the hardy outdoor life and the long journeys to his taste. In the orphan boy Jeb he had found the son he never had and passed on his thirst for knowledge to him on the long journeys together.

Eventually Harris emerged from the office and officiously waved the receipt in the air to signal the convoy to move off. As they passed through the barrier the watchman peeped out of his box and nodded a chilly welcome. He had had a few drinks before he came on duty and was desperately waiting for his relief to come so that he could get home to his warm bed.

The first thing Jeb noticed was that tonight there was no smell... Usually as soon as you were past St Michael's Church the stench of the small densely packed town hit you like a blacksmiths hammer but now, after a day of heavy rain, the snow had been

45

cleared away and the place smelled clean, almost fragrant, even though the open street sewers still ran with slush and rubbish. As the convoy trundled up Broad Street to Shires Yard, Old Sam said that the stench was one of the main reasons all the rich folk were moving out to the high land north of the town

"But don' you be a-goin' up there Young Jeb." The old carter warned " Th' higher up ye go the more these new houses cost. I yeerd 'bout one place in Brock Street as cost a certain Lady Parkstone two thousan' pound an' I knows fer sure that t'was built fer nine 'undred pound. I wuz up there one day helpin' Toby Darkle deliver some furniture when we overheard Mr Wood's factor talkin' to a lady. Oh, aye Jeb, things is a-changing, you know! There's some moneyed jades up there as would eat yore 'eart out.. You'm jes' the kind of young flesh they harridans do crave!"

There was a lot of truth in Old Sam's earthy warnings. The approach to the new century was an exciting time. The revolutions in America and France had been unexpectedly successful and even in a well ordered land like Great Britain there were serious murmurings of discontent. The radical Whig Party particularly was watching the actions of Napoleon with favourable interest. The mood was one of progress but here and there the talk was of a different kind of revolution; an industrial one. Already steam power was in action, as Watt's huge pumps drained and brought to life once abandoned mines. In far Cornwall Richard Trevithick had already produced a steam powered road vehicle whilst in Scotland steam driven boats like the 'Charlotte Dundas' were about to become a practical reality, although this was not a new thing in Bath, .

Development here had started in the early years of the eighteenth century by the fateful meeting of two new arrivals in the area and the fortunate discovery of a natural source of material. The talents of architect John Wood and his son, quarry owner Ralph Allen and a convenient deposit of soft building stone that hardened with age when exposed to the air all came together which made the dream a possibility. They found open land beyond the crowded airless streets and hovels clustered round the ancient abbey and the crumbling sections of the old Borough Wall with its deep rubbish filled ditch that once stood as a stout defence of the mediaeval town and this was where John Wood and his son were creating an idyllic suburb of elegant classic buildings, squares and spacious parks.

The first masterpiece had been Queens Square and following it in quick succession came the breathtaking Royal Crescent and then Brock street and the stunning Kings Circus attracting architects, artisans, craftsmen and greedy speculators from all over England to join in the building frenzy. Adams, Palmer, Baldwin, Pulteney, Lowder, Harvey, Jelly Goodrich, Pinch, and many others followed. Fortunes were made and lost as some men prospered and some were ruined but the boom and bust continued for almost a century until the finance ran out due to the ruinous Napoleonic Wars. These men were not easy going personalities. They were dreamers who ruthlessly made their dreams reality often at a ruinous cost to

47

themselves or their backers. Baldwin was notoriously difficult to get on with and his feuds with Pinch and other contemporaries were legend.

A particular case in point was his ongoing disputes with Sir William Pulteney the Bathwick landowner during the building of his masterpiece Great Pulteney Street, which became and still is one of the most famous streets in Europe. This elegant boulevard, 1000 feet long and 100 feet wide, was lined with terraces of magnificent houses made of glowing Bath stone, each doorway having a graceful wrought iron overthrow with a large lantern.

Over the years many famous people stayed here including the future French Emperor Louis Napoleon and his architect Baron Hausmann who saw the street as the inspiration for his new design of Paris years later.

Meanwhile day to day life was a continual grind and for young Jeb the end of the tiring journey only marked the start of his real job, as he scurried around the stables getting his charges fed and watered and finally bedded down. It was after midnight by the time all was finished and Old Sam had taken him to Mr Cherry's Chop House just near the horse bath on Horse Street. Sam didn't hold with the practice of washing the horses down with water from the outlet of the hot baths. It was all right for the gentry and their prancing, glossy thoroughbreds, but for the heavy shires and punches it weakened their resistance to the harsh weather conditions they all had to work in. As it was, he continued, Bath with its steep hills was a Hell for horses anyway. There was no flat building ground left on this side of the river and the land on the other side was marshy and prone to flooding so all these grand new Crescents and Squares were going up on the hillsides and the stone and timber had to be dragged up there by nags!

They bustled into the smoky tavern and threw their heavy coats onto the pile in the corner. Behind the plank bar a huge man with heavy shoulders was tapping a spigot into a cider barrel. At the sudden draught from the opening door he turned and greeted the newcomers. This was Fat Jim but nobody had the temerity to call him that to his face for he was as strong as a lion and very quick on his feet. He had originally been a butcher so he was quick with a knife too. Sam ordered up their supper of beef bone broth and oysters. It was the cheapest meal available but it was the most nourishing and Jeb ate himself to a standstill. As he dozed before the roaring fire of river driftwood Old Sam sipped his hot rum and reflected on the trip from London, cursing Marcus Harris' bad judgement of the weather which had forced them to spend two nights in the stables when they could have been home in their warm beds. Finally he checked his turnip watch and coughed signalling to Jeb that is was time to be moving.

As they left the tavern Fat Jim, shouted a hearty but distracted 'Good night, Gents," as he kept a close watch on a dice game that showed signs of getting out of hand. Outside in the cold wind Sam patted Young Jeb on the shoulder, mumbled a gruff

"G'night, young 'un," and headed to his cottage in Avon Street while Jeb made for the bridge and his home in the slums of The Dolmeads on the low lying flood plain across the river.

Still feeling replete from his hearty supper and the hot rum toddy that Sam insisted he have to keep out the cold and still wondering what a harridan was, Jeb clumped across the new bridge and found it strange too that in daytime the musty smell of the river pervaded the South Mead and even the Kings Mead but at night there was almost no smell at all.

Although it was called the New Bridge it had been built about fifty years previously by public demand as a replacement for one that had stood there since 1326. The legend was that there had once been an unreliable ferry at that point which foundered in the fast flow, losing overboard a church courier carrying valuable Abbey documents which so incensed the Abbot that he ordered a bridge to be built.

This increased the traffic across the South Mead and led in turn to the reconstruction of the South Gate in 1363. This in turn was declared redundant in 1755 and demolished; an action that was a point of great annoyance to Beau Nash in his declining years. It was later said that the stress of it all started the decline that led to his death six years later!

Although the crossing was solidly built on the five semi-circular stone arches of the old crossing it was barely eleven feet wide and was further encumbered by a small chapel and a statue of

50

the unfortunate King Edward the Third plus smaller edifices of Prior John and Bishop Ralph from the Abbey at each end. Just to add to the problem it also had a tollgate. Jeb's grandfather used to tell him about the narrow bridge that was just about wide enough for one horse and cart and the violent arguments that often broke out when two obstinate tinkers happened to meet in mid-stream. Apparently Southmead had always been a controversial area!

Jeb leaned over the parapet to gaze at the reflections of the dull lanterns on the rat-catcher's boats in the muddy lagoons and rivulets on the low banks of the Avon. Occasionally one would hear a splash and a cry of triumph as another rodent was speared and stuffed into a canvas sack. His Uncle Alf was a ratter but even though he lived with him and Auntie Beth, Jeb didn't know him at all well as he was out hunting most nights and Jeb was either away with the convoys or tending his equine charges during the day.

He made his way along the potholed slippery Widcome High Street and down one of the alleys that passed Terry Blight's old warehouse where he could hear the pitiful cries and moans of the chained up runaway boys of eight or ten that he kept as virtual slaves and hired out to chimney sweeps and factory owners for distasteful jobs like bone milling or making shoe blacking from soot and animal fat. Jeb shuddered, remembering hearing his Uncle Alf telling his wife about a twelve year old waif sold by Blight being trapped in a mill chimney in Walcott for four days. In the end a steeplejack from Chippenham had to be brought in to get the traumatised starving child out. Due to his local connections Blight escaped without charge but the chimney sweep that had used the boy got three months in Grove St. gaol.

Jeb hurried on to where the cobbles ended in the marsh and headed for home across the rickety planked causeway over the mud to the compound where the crumbling old house stood. Splashing through dirty puddles he kicked open the rotting plank yard door, holding his nose as he passed the stinking shed where Uncle Alf, often helped by two old crones, processed his nocturnal haul.

This bountiful catch often included several snared feral cats and the occasional scavenging dog as well as the rats. The skins were sold to the hatters and glove makers mills down river at Twerpington, (or Twerton as it was known to the locals.) The flesh was sold to the rough cook shops and pie makers who boiled it in vinegar and water until it was bleached white. After which it was minced and liberally laced in pepper, sage and ginger with a pinch of gunpowder added, then passed it off to their unsuspecting customers as spiced veal or devilled chicken. The bones and offal were boiled into a swill and fed to the two porkers being fattened for Christmas in the brick pen at the end of the yard: In these hard times nothing was wasted.

Yawning, Jeb lifted the latch and shuffled into the tumbledown house. There was a charcoal glow in the old fireplace where the big black pot quietly burbled above the embers and Spot the big old hound just managed a sleepy growl and a couple of tail thumps before resuming his snores. Jeb stood for a minute warming his chapped hands before the fire, and wondered for the hundredth time why Uncle Alf called the dog Spot when it was all black. Finally he kicked off his clumsy shoes and shed his patched and tarred canvas coat and kicked it into a corner before flopping on his truckle bed under the stairs. Laying his head on the greasy tick pillow and snuggling deeply under the old rug he was lulled to sleep thinking about what Old Sam had told him about the fascinating new town appearing north of the city He was also still wondering just what a harridan actually was!

5

THE NEW BABYLON

Oh what an elegant set, what a bustling of rumps
What a sweet toe to toeing of slippers and pumps
At the sight my old drumsticks are ready to prance
There is nothing I love so, as watching folks dance.

Lumps of Pudding by Henry Bunbury. 1789.

"Ye Gods, what a din!" Alexander shouted as he and his companion pushed their way through the crowd of rough looking, stinking, sedan chair men milling around the entrance to the Upper Assembly Rooms where a pockmarked and bewigged doorman gestured with his stout staff of office to the garish ticket booth. Tossing their entrance fee onto the table the two young bucks made there way across the broad foyer and on into the main salon and stopped at the palatial carved archway to take in the scene. On there left was the vast ballroom where, on a large a balcony twenty feet above the polished hardwood floor, a huge forty pipe, four consul organ gushed out it's complex chords and as the infectious heavy rhythms thundered through the vast hall, the muslin clad, be-ribboned society belles (and those who were only ladies for the evening,) whirled to it's musical spell with their elegant partners.

Ahead of the two Marine officers lay the yellow walled oval card room with it's strategically placed card tables and wheels of fortune where elegant young bucks, powdered and perfumed posed and postured. Their tight fitting exotic satins and silks showing off every curve of their trim muscular figures while they gestured effeminately to their equally peacock clad cronies. In spite of the law forbidding duelling, the atmosphere around these self-centred dandies was one of tense suspicion and menace. At the slightest hint of a perceived insult they would demand satisfaction and on the morrow often would fight to the death in the early morning frost of the cultured meadows on the north bank of the Avon.

These gently sloping cow pastures were now overlooked by Mr. Wood's newly built Royal Crescent where an army of artisans still laboured to transform the beautiful facades into elegant houses, each one an individual reflection on the buyers taste and budget. Once it was finished, crafty John Wood had sold only the Palladian front elevation and the plot of land behind it and although it was said to have been completed 1775, quite a few of the houses were still unfinished and were not fully occupied for another five years. One, in fact had no occupants for twelve years until its purchaser returned from his government service in India.

The bulky doorman indulgently bowed his massive head as Alexander slipped a further half crown coin into his horny palm to find them a place at one of the gaming tables and he led the way through the dance hall into the vast gambling salon where dealers slapped pasteboard cards onto the polished oak tables and loudly declared their odds. At baize covered tables games of Hazard were in progress. It was a dangerous, high stakes dice game and fortunes could be won or lost in minutes as the odds were doubled at each round. It was a game for desperate men or very rich ones and the strain showed on some of the pasty white faces under the bright chandeliers.

At a far table there was suddenly an abrupt disturbance. One of the gamblers, a young obnoxious farmer, well into his cups with his stained satin waistcoat bulging open over his beefy body and a tight fitting tail coat, shouted in drunken anger at his losing streak and lunged at the dealer but before he could strike with a hidden dagger, (all short swords having to be left at the cloakroom on entry,) the security staff were on him and he was hustled outside and into the tender care of the sedan chair men.

These bully boys had been known on many an occasion to lock such objectionable clients into their chairs and carry them down to their lairs in Walcott, a riverside settlement below the Paragon cliff outside the North Gate. Here, hidden among the foreign immigrants and drifters who were not allowed to settle inside the city walls, they could hold their prisoners until a suitable ransom was paid. Any application to the Beadle or the City Magistrates proved useless as the chairmen would simply say they were waiting for their hire fee to be paid. After all, it had been the honourable client himself who had requested to be taken to the stews and cheap brothels of the riverbank, as all their chair carrying brethren would swear. At other times when a client had refused to pay the outrageous fee or even presumed to insult the pole-men in some way, he would be locked into the chair and left with the roof panel open to the elements until their demands were met.

As things returned to normal, the two Marine officers strolled around checking out the tables and eying up the diaphanously clad beauties who hung around the gamblers and posing fops. Suddenly there was a second moment of excitement as a tray full of glasses shattered on the polished hardwood floor and a heavy circular silver tray rolled into Alexander's shins. The whole of the salon stopped what it was doing and turned to check out the scene of the disturbance, while the dealers and table masters quickly slipped their stake money and cards into secret table drawers, acutely aware that such noisy diversions were often staged by gangs to cover some theft or violence.

Alexander looked up as he rubbed his bruised leg to find himself caught in the violet eyes of a black haired beauty whose face he was sure that he had seen before. She was not smiling and did not appear to be even distressed by the situation but simply stood above him staring with an almost rabid hatred. Then it hit him! It was the girl he had first noticed in Warminster when he had brought in that dead highwayman. Picking up the still spinning tray he handed it to the sullen serving-girl.

"I believe this is yours, my dear ...but wait, do I not know thee? Thy face seems somewhat familiar to me."

Biting her lip the girl stared him full in the face, her eyes glittering and replied coldly as she took in his expensive apparel.

"Nay, sir, I doubt that our paths have ever crossed but I beg forgiveness for the bruise to your leg. I, er, musta tripped or misjudged yon doorway. Ye can be sure it will not 'appen again for the Cap'n will be rid o' me after tonight."

"What's that ye tell me, dear maid, surely not?" Alexander said warmly. "Twas but a simple mishap, and what are a few bits o' glass anyway. I shall tell him 'twas my fault and that I will pay for any damage. Just say that I bundled thee."

She curtsied and briefly mumbled her thanks but the eyes showed no warmth at all.

Just at that moment a tubby figure wearing an expensively trimmed, though ill-fitting yellow silk coat, the shade of which exactly matched the painted walls of the gaming room, came waddling through all the confusion. This was Captain Warmley, the Assistant Master of Ceremonies followed by his factotum, who was frantically signalling the dealers to restart the gaming and for the organist to strike up a jolly air for the dancers, as such disturbances gave the gamblers time to think about their game, which in turn affected the takings.

"Ah, good evening, Sire." He gushed, his ample jowls quivering with suppressed anger to "Do please accept our deepest apologies for the clumsiness of the wench. She is a newcomer here, straight from the country. But she will not bother you further because...."

Before he could finish Alexander disdainfully waved a languid hand saying. "Oh, marry sir, tis naught of importance. I fear that it was all my own doing so please do not blame the maid. I just turned and trod on the hem of her skirt by accident. I shall of course pay for the breakages of thy crystal. Pray let us consider the matter closed."

Reluctantly the official forced a smile and accepted the explanation, waving the serving girl away. He could have sworn that the girl had dropped the tray from shock on seeing the Captain's face, but he shrugged and moved back to his post at the raised top table.

This time just the hint of a grateful smile lit the girl's face.

Alexander and his friend Sheldon moved back to the gaming tables but after his meeting the fascinating black haired serving girl Alexander could not concentrate on the fall of the cards. After loosing four times on the run he decided to cut his losses and find out more about the girl from Captain Warmley.

The Master of Ceremonies was ensconced in his yellow walled office at the rear of the big hall, the door guarded by a burly steward.... It cost another half a crown to get past him and to be announced to his master. Warmley looked up apprehensively as Alexander entered; silently preparing his defences in case the client was seeking financial recompense for his brush with the silver tray.

"Ah, Captain Coulston, what may I do for you sir?"
Alexander hesitated for a moment and then plunged in.

"I was, er, wondering Captain Warmley, about yon maid I just met. I would like to know a little more about her. Not a local by her accent I'd say but I am not familiar with the patios yet. I seem to know the face but cannot place it."
Warmley sensed money in the enquiry and smiled smarmily

"Oh you know how these maids do come and go, sir. Though I might say that they may well be maids when they arrive but a goodly number are not when they leave here. Ho, . ho, ho!" He guffawed loudly and the steward at the half open door aped his master while Alexander gave an indulgent smile.

"Aye, true enough I do suppose but how did you come by such a beauty. I am in need of a maid or two up at the manor."
Warmley raised his eyebrows.

"Oh, and which 'Manor' might that be, Sire?"

"Why, sir, Trandon House on the Bitton Road. We are just below Cleave House, about half a mile upstream from Crapper's place. You know Kelston Hall I presume? Well Trandon House is the country seat of my great aunt Miriam, Lady Trandon. You may know her physician Mr Jennings. He's a regular patron of yours I believe and a cousin to Mr Tarleton of Shires Yard."

Warmley was impressed and his demeanour changed drastically at the realisation that he was in the company of "Old Money".

Miriam Trandon had been one of Beau Nash's patrons and had caused a family scandal by going to his funeral. Warmley was surprised to find that she was still alive... She must be well into her eighties now and there was no one left to inherit her vast holdings. True, she had a younger brother but he had never married. On top of that he had been in India for over forty years and was reported to be senile and unlikely to ever return to England. So it looked like this sunburned marine would be the next Lord Trandon...He had best tread careful!

"Ah I see, sir... The young wench in question came to us on the good offices of Mrs Edwards from Gay Street. On her return to this Georgian Gem after her Italian wedding, she opened a marriage bureau and as a sideline found employment for her charges where wealthy young men would come seeking wives, (or perhaps just company for the evening) and where better to be seen and admired than in her establishment or at the New Assembly Halls?... So naturally, we came to a mutually satisfactory arrangement."

"I do not think that such a wench would find any difficulty in finding company."

"Ah Captain, that is the rub and the reason that I would feel relieved to get rid of her... but I cannot offend Mrs Edwards."

"And why would you want to lose her? Such a beauty can only adorn this place."

"Aye, truly it would if she could be more, shall we say, amenable, to the advances of our clients…Young men of good family and fortune seek her company it is true but she will not tarry with any o' them. She simply does her duties to my satisfaction and then is picked up by her elder brother to stay somewhere in Widcome village with his family. I have the Devil's own job to convince some o' my more ardent patrons that I am not condoning such actions to increase her value on the marriage market! In fact Mrs Edwards has spoken to me on that very subject more than once." Before continuing he sniffed self pityingly and took a pinch of consoling snuff, blowing his nose loudly on a large blue handkerchief. "So truly, I can only suggest that you pay your respects to Mrs Edwards yourself and perhaps she can enlighten you. If you will leave me your card I shall tell her to expect you at her soiree on Wednesday next…I am sorry but that is the best I can do. Perkins here will escort you back to the salon. Good night to you sire."

Feeling somewhat rebuffed Alexander wound his way back to his companion who was deeply involved in a hectic game of hazard. By the look of things he was doing rather well with a neat pile of golden guineas growing by his left hand. Thinking that a game might put his mind at ease he sat down heavily at the table, threw down a guinea and signalled the dealer to give him a hand but it was all to no avail. He just could not concentrate on the fall of the cards he decided it was not his lucky night and told his friend that he was leaving. Sheldon just waved him an impatient goodbye saying that he would catch up with him the next day at the Star, a popular tavern in the Vineyards where many of the young bucks about town would regularly gather for a liquid lunch and a post mortem on the previous night's happenings. Alexander just nodded his acceptance with his mind in a fog. The one thing he was sure of was that he must arrange an early visit to this mysterious Mrs Edwards.

Deep in thought he made his way through the milling crowd and as he entered the foyer he found himself suddenly confronted by a group of stunningly beautiful young women, one a slim tall blond and her companion a voluptuous brunette, just behind them, feigning a kind of boredom, were a sensational dark skinned woman and a fresh young beauty with worldly wise eyes who exuded class and confidence. It was the blonde who spoke first.

"Good evening to you sir," She said confidently. "I am told that you are Miriam Trandon's nephew. Is that true sir?"
At any other time Alexander would have been flattered by the attentions of such sophisticated beauties but after his discussion with Captain Warmley his mind was on the mysterious serving girl and something made him cautious. This meeting seemed too well rehearsed to be as casual as it appeared.

"Aye, Madame that is true, and whom may I ask, wishes to know?"

She fluttering her fan and glanced at her companions. "It seems they were right then … If he had been here a little longer I would consider such a question to be an insult to me." Turning back to face him she heaved her impressive cleavage and flashed her brown eyes.. With a shallow mocking curtsy she announced. "I am Lady Henrietta Lamb and I am a friend of your aunt, or perhaps I should say, she is an acquaintance from my early childhood and these are my dear friends. May I present The Honourable Caroline Sinclair and two foreign ladies who are newly established here, Signora Maria di Sienna and Madame Aimee La Blanche from Martinique. We are all pleased to meet you sir. Miriam was ever boastful of your dashing adventures... It is good to meet such a legend in the flesh at last."

Then, eying him over disdainfully and fluttering her fan she murmured. "Well at least you look the part... We would have to get to know you in more intimate circumstances to be able to fully appraise your abilities."

"Yes, of course." Enjoined the Honourable Caroline, who's beauty at second glance was not as impressive as it first appeared, being somewhat marred in profile by a rather large hooked nose and a pointed chin which reminded Alexander of a Welsh witch.

Assuming that his stare was one of awe rather than curiosity, she continued unabashed. "I am holding a soiree at my house at Paragon Buildings on the twenty fourth. You really must come, sir. I am sure that the evening would be to the taste of such a man of the world like you. I will see personally that you and your companion receive an invitation."

Alexander was taken aback by the forwardness of the

exchange and resented being treated like some piece of meat to be bargained over. What was it Miss Lamb had said? 'To fully appraise your abilities?' as though he was some Italian macaroni gigolo seeking a patroness?

Containing his resentment with considerable restrain he ignored the invitation and replied bluntly that he looked forward to meeting them all on some future occasion when his duties allowed and with a brusque. "Goodnight, Ladies." inclined his head and walked off without even a bow, leaving them open mouthed.

In one case however the effect of this minor social skirmish was shattering. One of the 'Foreign ladies' so casually presented by the brash Henrietta was left dumbstruck. As she turned to watch Alexander weave his way through the revellers Maria di Sienna (as she was now called) felt a shiver go through her. It had shocked her to the core. She, who had built a prosperous life for herself using such men as mere stepping stones, was now quivering like a sixteen year old milkmaid. Astounding, but there it was! That man had stunned her and she would have to find out more about this fascinating stranger....And she would!

After Alexander's abrupt departure the quartet of beauties continued on their nightly trawl of the tables seeking some fresh diversion but Maria was still pre-occupied by the earlier events and consumed with a strange curiosity about the handsome officer.

She vividly recalled that as the idle flirtatious banter continued she felt suddenly as though she had been hit by a

65

lightening bolt. Never before in her entire life had she felt like this but this stranger had unbalanced her. The brief inclination of his head and the curt 'Madame' when they were introduced had stunned her. It was as though she had been waiting all her life for this moment. She shook her head in disbelief and clung on tightly to her friend Aimee's arm. He was a man, just another man, wasn't he? She had known dozens of them. So what was so special about this one? She stared again at his broad back as he weaved his way through the crowded casino; and she knew in her heart that she had to find out more about this mystery man. Looking round she beckoned over a footman and whispered her request to him, slipping a half crown into his horny palm.

In the foyer Alexander knocked at the doorman's lodge and reclaimed his hat, cloak, sword belt and pistol which he tapped on the muzzle to make sure that the ball was securely tamped down before slipping it into a leather lined pocket in his cloak.

"Hope it won't be long afore we see ye again Y'r Honour... I noted earlier that your companion was on a lucky streak. P'raps twill be your turn tomorrow night, sir." The bulky doorman smarmed "As my old mother used to say, you never know when lady luck will give you her blessing, sir!' Knowing what was expected from him and not wishing to listen to any further homilies Alexander slipped two shillings into his horny palm and asked him to find a link boy to light his way through the dark streets, glad to leave the din and the bustle of the building behind.

He found the night air crisp and pulled his cloak close as he walked round the northern side of the Kings Circus in bright moonlight. Just at that moment a church bell somewhere beyond Queen's Square struck midnight and he stopped to check his hunter. He flipped the steel face plate and saw that his watch said five past the hour. Without a moment's doubt he concluded that the church bell was wrong. After all, this fine pocket watch had been left to him by his grandfather and it had seen him punctual across thousands of ocean miles and near twenty years of service?

As he turned to head for his hotel he caught sight of an oddly dressed man standing at a candlelit first floor window watching him and turning a green feather in his hand

Alexander sighed and thinking nothing more of it turned into Brock Street, making for the Burnt Bush Inn on Upper Church Street,

The owner Charlie Parsons welcomed him enthusiastically into the stifling, smoke filled bar parlour. In spite of the late hour was still crowded and riotously jolly. Charlie smiled and passed him a hot toddy enquiring as to his luck at the tables but Alexander was not really in the mood for barroom banter. Excusing himself he walked through to the back room and ordered a supper of Wiltshire gammon and duck eggs. For the first time he noticed how tired he was and having polished off a pint of sack wished the innkeeper a good night and headed to his room.

Awaiting him at the top of the stairs holding a candle was a cheery, buxom young chambermaid who led him to his room. She smiled at him as she turned down the bed and removed a bright copper warming pan and inquired into how he had found the seductive pleasures of the New Assembly Rooms. He answered her warmly saying that the temptations were hard to resist but he had had other things on his mind......but now he was feeling a little more relaxed. He left the inference hanging and she looked at him knowingly and responded warmly to his offer of two crowns for her services. Without further delay she helped him out of his clothes, folding them neatly onto a bedding box in the corner as he popped into bed. After that she stripped off her own few garments, unpinned her luxuriant brown hair, posed for him a moment or two and then humming a tune did a few mocking steps of a minuet just to show him what he was getting for his money before blowing out the bedside candle and joining him under the crisp snow white sheets.

In the early morning he woke to find his companion gone and his mind returned to his quest for the mysterious violet eyed beauty he had found in the card room and wondered again where they had met. Rising from the warm bed he splashed water on his face from the porcelain ewer and bowl on the side table, dressed and paid his bill but refused any breakfast, claimed his horse from the nearby liverery stables and headed home. As he clopped round the Royal Crescent cobbles he mused again about the mystery raven haired lady. He would have been surprised to find that her reaction to their meeting was completely at odds with his own!

Just after Alexander had left the Assembly Rooms the previous night and had stopped to consult his watch in the Circus, a cloaked figure hiding in the shadows at the corner of Bennett Street watched him and then proceeded to follow him, being careful to keep beyond the light from the link-boy's torch as his quarry headed along Brock Street to the tavern. Waiting a minute or so he bustled in after Alex and after getting his pot of cider leaned against the chimney breast to keep an eye on the diner in the back room. As Alexander pushed away his plate and moved towards the stairs Charlie turned to the busy bar and gave a knowing wink. Under the cover of the ribald shouts and comments the watcher slid away

An hour later the watcher was back giving his report to Maria in an ante room off the Octagon card room. She nodded quietly as he told his tale but bit her lip when he told her about the chambermaid sharing his room. Brusquely she stood up, gave the footman his coin and dismissed him...She was simmering with jealous rage. A serving wench indeed! When she, a woman who men fought over and bought valuable gifts for, was willing to share her charms with him freely?

It was insufferable and she swore to avenge this gross insult.

6

RACHEL

It was sometime after Alexander had left the casino, when a tall female figure swaddled in a long dark hooded cloak, appeared from a narrow door at the rear of the Assembly Rooms and clambered aboard a waiting wagon, silently taking her seat next to the driver in his tarred burlap cape. Without a word the driver flicked the reins and the cart moved off towards Lansdowne Road and headed down to the river. The silence continued though the deserted town until they were approaching the bridge at the end of Horse Street. Tamping down his pipe the driver turned and said quietly.

"Is you alright, Maid? You'm not said a word since we left yon den o' Satan. Is summat the matter with ee? Tha' looks like you'm seed a ghost."

Getting no immediate response he puffed again on his corncob pipe and guided the horse to the narrow river crossing.

As they approached the bridge the girl tossed back her voluminous hood and the moonlight caught her glittering violet eyes and said clearly. "Nay, t'were no ghost … I seed 'im tonight, Rob."

"Oh aye? He grunted "Someone as I should know wuz it?"

"I seed 'im, Rob, I wuz close to him as I am to 'ee!"

"Well, who was it then?" Said Rob distractedly

She turned to stare across the riverside mudflats and said coldly. "I'll tellee who 'twas.. That bastard as killed my child's father... That Devil in Red we seed at the Risin' Sun in Warminster when they brought in poor Brooksie and Dickon. That Captain o' Marines... This close 'e were.. I coulda gutted him if I'd had a blade wi' me.... Then I'd a-made 'im pay for two lives, for it was the shock o' seein' my Brooksie like a lump of dead meat that made me lose the child afore twas borned. But I tellee Rob I'll gerrim yet. Ye can wager on that!

"Ye'd better watch it a-talkin' loik that our Rachel! One o' them Satan's whores at yon 'Semblee Rooms is a-goin' t' ear thee. An' then wot'll ee do?"

She bit her lip in suppressed fury and spat back. "It's a bit late for that, Rob." She spat back. "Old Warmley has turned me off tonight... Sed as ow I was not keeping' the gen'lmen 'appy. Wot does "e want me to do, swive 'em on the Hazard tables?"

Rob sucked his dead pipe and held his peace as they rumbled into Widcome village. This long silence was not unusual behaviour for Rachel and Rob for although she dwelt under the same roof as Rob and his family, days could pass and they would not exchange a word. It was as though by some telepathy they always seemed to know

71

what the other was thinking.

Their father had been one Tomas Da Carius, a Portuguese sailor who was second mate aboard one of the Lisbon wine carracks that regularly docked to unload it's cargo in Weymouth. On his final visit Tomas had fallen from a yardarm onto the dockside and broke his leg and the generous captain had given him his back pay and lodged him with a family assuring him that he could rejoin the crew on their return with another cargo in eight weeks time. However, sadly all did not go to plan, as the Portuguese ship floundered with all hands in the Bay of Biscay on the journey home, leaving Tomas stranded.

He was nursed back to health by the daughter of the family and as soon as he was up and getting around, he asked her to marry him. Her parents objected strongly pointing out that he was a foreigner, even if his mother country was England's oldest ally. He argued back that he could speak a fair amount of English and that he was an experienced seaman. He then proved his worth by getting a berth as assistant on the pilot's cutter where his marine know-how, European languages and quick learning made him a valued member of the crew. He could read and write too but the most compelling argument for the marriage was the fact that daughter Mary was three months gone with Rachel's brother Rob.

The marriage proved to be a good one and they had four children the last being Rachel who inherited a unique beauty that mixed Tomas' dark hair and complexion with her mother's piercing violet eyes and magnificent long limbed body. Tomas, now ironically shore bound, became a clerk in the Customs Office and often spent his spare time at the docks buying trinkets and curiosities from visiting seamen and selling them in his little lock up shop in town. One day a lascar had come in and offered him some carved ivory idols which he thought his wife would like and so he took them home. Within four days he was prostrated with some unknown infection which raged through his family. In a brief five weeks it killed him, his wife and the two middle children.

Rob and Rachel were on a trip to a boatyard in Chichester when this pox took the others and were advised by the local beadle not to return or they would bare the brunt of the local resentment from other families in town. Being unable to go back, Rob lost his job at the dockyard and took his young sister to Poole, which was about as near as they dared go to their old home, where Rob got a job in a timber yard and a room in a quayside house. The job was tedious and the hours long but Rachel could go to a local school and keep house for them. Rob bore his discontent as long as he could until one night in a backstreet tavern he met up with Ralph Brooks who claimed to be a horse trader but was in fact a feared highway robber. They often met in the tavern and eventually Brooks invited the powerfully built Rob to join his gang.

Rob brought with him to the camp deep in the Severnake Forest both his sister and her friend Melody Watson. Rachel who was by this time a blossoming fourteen year old was tingling with the excitement of it all and was swept off her feet when she first met Ralph Brooks. Within two years they had become lovers and she settled comfortably into the gang's lair in the Severnake forest. Melody too had a fling with Rob but did not stay long in the primitive conditions at the camp and moved back to her father's farm at Dilton Marsh.

However she quickly found the toil of the soil was not to her taste and took a job as a barmaid in the local tavern where her charms would be more appreciated. She still kept in touch with Rob who came down to visit her from time to time.

The pickings on the road were good and life in the forest was pleasant for about a year until success in his evil profession began to give Ralph delusions of grandeur and he insisted on being addressed as Captain Brooks and taking more and more chances until his final reckoning on the Warminster Road outside Blanford Forum.

After that the gang broke up and with his share Rob bought a horse and cart and moved to a cottage in the Dolmeads of Bath where he lived with his now pregnant sister and a woman called Nan. However the shock of Brooks' death caused Rachel to abort her child and she vowed vengeance on the man who had killed both her man and her child: Captain Alexander Coulston.

7

MRS. EDWARD'S SOIREE

Two days after his next visit to the new Assembly Rooms, (where he had lost the best part of five guineas,) Alexander received an engraved invitation to one of Mrs Edwards's much-vaunted soirees. His Aunt had silently rolled herself in from her ground floor suite in her wicker backed chair with its felt-rimmed wheels and had taken the card from the footman and was perusing it disdainfully as Alexander descended the wide stairs.

Looking at him over her lorgnette and demonstrating clearly that her eighty odd eventful years had not mellowed her acid tongue or her perceptive mind, she simpered sarcastically.

"Oh, Alexander, I see that you have been favoured by an invitation to Madame Edwards' cattle auction on Wednesday next, what a fortunate young man you are." She paused and gazed at him with an air of disappointment before continuing. "I had hoped that you might find a better broker in the nuptial marketplace than a woman of such dubious pedigree as that faded harridan. She was once one of Hester Thrale's set and it looks like she is carrying on the old tradition."

Miriam Trandon had a long memory and had never forgot or forgiven Mrs Thale, as she then was, for spoiling her advances on the eminent diarist Doctor Johnson on his visits to Bath and never missed an opportunity to pour scorn on her one time rival, never failing to inform whoever was listening that. "Of course, that was before Henry Thrale died in '81 and she married her children's Italian music teacher Signor Piozzi! And ran off to Italy"

Alexander took the gilt edged engraved card from her and bowed with a gentle smile. "Thank you Aunt Miriam, (She had expressly forbidden him to ever call her Great Aunt!) but you need have no fear that any of Mrs Edwards's young ladies will hook me. It is just a matter of curiosity and familiarisation with the social courtesies of the city, on my part."

"Oh, really, Alexander curiosity indeed... And may I ask about what? Or should one say, about whom?" She gazed at him quizzically from under her plucked eyebrows. (It was a look that must have devastated many a young buck fifty years previously but somehow lost it's magic by the slightly off centre wig and the pinkish eyes.) The last thing Alexander wanted was any questions about the black haired beauty so he took the offensive.

"About Mrs Edwards, how do you come to know the lady?

"Ha! Lady indeed! Harridan would be nearer the mark for that jade! How do I know her?" She spat. "A lady you say? Well,

76

I'll tell you how I know Madame Edwards, for that is truly what she is! --- Yes, a Madame! One who provides her visiting gentlemen with overnight comfort?" Furiously waving her fan, Miriam quavered on "She and her pagan friends! Harlots like Caroline Baker, whose house at Larkhall is a notorious palace of depravity. Another one of these sirens of sin is Miss Griselda Metcalf, who calls herself by the spurious title of Lady Zelda and has an establishment on Paragon Buildings, only three doors away from that bawd of an actress, Sarah Siddons who, when she is not entertaining visiting bucks spends her time trying to find more ridiculous headwear than her neighbour!.. And now I hear that she has recruited another two whores to her circle. A certain half Italian mongrel brothel owner who presumes to call herself Maria Di Sienna... Pagh! Sienna indeed! .. From what I have heard whispered, more likely the Redcliffe slums of Bristol: And a coal black wench who pertains to come from the French Caribbean ...or was that from the stews around St Paul's!"...

(She was referring to St. Paul of All Mercies, a church just outside the old Bristol walls where a community of poor discharged African seamen and emancipated West Indian slaves, many of them from Martinique and Guadeloupe had built up.)...

Alexander thought it wiser not to mention that he had already met the subjects of her outburst and let her rave on.

"They are an evil group, believe me and they always have been, even as far back as when Dr Johnson was calling on me.

77

Whenever he came to take the water cure here in Bath, Mrs Thale was convulsed with jealousy and prevailed on her allies to make it most embarrassing for us whenever we were out to dine, whether it was at the Pump Rooms or the Concord Hotel.. Oh yes, and I remember another harlot who was jealous of my position too, …, although that was a good deal earlier. Harriett Sawyer was her name and she too was a brazen scandalous bitch, both here and in London. She died in '46, the same year that Teddy became Lord Trandon. I recall that he and Dick Nash went to her funeral but I flatly refused to accompany them. Pagh!"

By this time Aunt Miriam was lurching around in her rolling chair and going purple in the face. The rumpus brought her maid Agnes rushing from the kitchens to see just what was happening but before she could say a word Lady Trandon had thrown the empty scented envelope on to a side table, spun her chair and trundled off back to her sitting room ordering Agnes to follow her and shut the door.

At exactly six o'clock on the following Wednesday evening Alexander presented himself at Mrs Edwards's sumptuous house in the Kings Circus. Having left his horse at the livery stables in St James' Square, he enjoyed the stroll past the elegant new houses on Brock Street and round into the western segment of the circus. At his first knock the door was thrown open by the lady herself who was seeing an earlier guest off the premises.

He was quite surprised to find that Mrs Edwards was not at

all the harridan described by his vitriolic old aunt but it was quite obvious why they had never got on, even considering their difference in age and backgrounds. She was a warm and welcoming middle-aged plump woman with a round happy face and masses of curly auburn hair piled high on her head, held by a bandeau with a tall peacock's feather at the front. She was elegantly dressed in the high-waist fashion of the times and wore white stockings and dainty gold pumps.

"Ah, then you must be Captain Coulston." She chirruped in a light, singsong voice. "I have seen you out and about in our sparklingly new city and Captain Warmley has talked much about you. May I bid you welcome to my house. Alexander isn't it? Lady Trandon's grand-nephew: In fact her only nephew and, I believe, perhaps her closest living relative, for I cannot see her Brother George giving up his Indian paradise now!"

Alexander was taken aback by such enthusiasm and did not know exactly how to respond.

"Err, Thank you Madame." He dithered. "My aunt sends you her best wishes and insisted that I pass them on and that I enquire as to your health after all your travels, trials and tribulations."

"Oh I have no doubt that she did." Responded Mrs Edwards wryly "Miriam always did have my welfare at heart: You must tell her that I find her memory remarkable for one of such maturity… With her the old traditions die hard but I feel the murmurings of the changing times and wish to partake of the pleasures of our brave new world."

It was quite obvious that Mrs Edwards, with her bursting self confidence and natural charm was not one to simply accept blindly the hide bound social mores of yesterday: Her travels in Europe, particularly in Italy, had shown her another more relaxed yet still graceful side of social behaviour.

Beau Nash had originally laid down the old rules of social etiquette for both residents and visitors to this Queen of Spas and had instituted a system of well-publicised financial fines that were rigidly enforced. Any refusal to conform could and often did, result in the transgressors being barred from some of the many delights of the city. However the old rake and gambler had been dead many years now and in these new liberated times, as the century turned, the excesses of the Prince Regent exemplified, Bath had indeed become one of the most exciting cities in Europe and a new regime was needed. And who better to be the new arbiters of fashionable behaviour than Mrs. Edwards and her charming, wealthy, worldly-wise companions?

One of the first things to go was the old stiff formal method of announcing the arrival of guests. Previously Major Domo of the house had performed this function by loudly banging his staff on the hardwood floor and bellowing the names and the (often lengthy,) titles and distinctions of said guests. It was a process that brought all things to a standstill and damaged the easy ambience of sometimes quite intimate conversations.

However in the Edwards' house this archaic performance had been subtly replaced by the provision of beautifully engraved cards bearing the names and titles of her guests, which she attached to the splendid coats of the gentlemen with small pearl-headed pins. She also assigned one of her young ladies to chaperone any newcomers as a guide and to facilitate the introductions, and make a discreet disappearance once a conversation was launched.

It proved to be an excellent idea, which reduced any embarrassment and provided an icebreaking talking point. Naturally, at first a few guests were taken aback by this new social form and hid their cards inside their coats but soon the male ego surfaced as they noticed that their bolder companions were getting all the attention. The ladies of course, were allowed to keep their anonymity to preserve the feminine air of mystery, yet another example of Mrs. Edward's sophisticated understanding of the fascination of the unknown.

Casting her eyes upward to stare into his, she tilted her head to one side as though seeking his approval and as her ample bosom pressed against his chest the exotic scent of her perfume sent his head spinning and she said huskily.

"Come, my dear Captain, it is time to meet my other guests." Again there came the breathtaking smile as taking his arm firmly, she steered him through a set of ceiling high double wedding doors leading to a large salon at the back of the house overlooking a superbly maintained garden bathed in the bright late afternoon

81

sunshine. The walls were washed in a pale primrose matt with pastel panels of French blue. A huge Persian carpet covered the centre of the polished wood block floor and elegant bowlegged boudoir chairs and settees, aided by several beautiful carved and polished occasional tables were strategically placed to enhance the feeling of space and expensive casual elegance. It was apparent that the newly wealthy Burghers of Bath were taking their new image seriously!

A pair of glazed French doors stood open to the garden where the servants had erected a striped canopy over a long table with a snow white tablecloth which was already stained in places from the profusion of wines and delicacies that were being enthusiastically sampled by the gossiping guests who turned as one to greet the newcomer.

The women boldly eyed this fine specimen of a military figure with calculating gazes, appraising his upright, broad shouldered bearing, the skin-tight white breeches and the flattering dark green velvet coat with his clean-shaven deeply tanned masculine face and the fine lines around his cool, all-seeing blue eyes that told of a lifetime of experience. The strong, masterful jaw line and the high cheekbones really set their hearts a-flutter. The men however were somewhat more circumspect in their inspection, affecting to be bored with this new distraction and carried on their conversation with the affected gestures that were de-rigueur in the macho world of the young Regency Buck. In spite of their hidden curiosity not one of them expressed even the slightest hint that he should join them

In a far corner Alexander noticed a man also watching and turning a small green feather in his hand, however, when Alexander looked again the man seemed to have disappeared.

Mrs Edwards glowed as the guests gazed in admiration of her new addition to her social circle and gestured to a pretty blond girl to join them. The girl was presented to Captain Coulston as Alice and was instructed to circulate with him and make whatever introductions were required. Alice did her best but to Alexander they all remained a mystery: The one he was looking for was nowhere to be seen. His eyes ranged the vast room searching every corner and alcove and every knot of gossiping guests in the hope of seeing some sign of his phantom gypsy beauty. About the only person he knew was one of the pushy presumptuous women who had accosted him at the Assembly Rooms a few days earlier. Sensing she was about to start a conversation with him he curtly wished her a good evening and turned on his heel. Maria di Sienna glared at his retreating back convinced that the snub was a deliberate insult. Couldn't he see how much she wished to know more about him?

Finally, making his excuses to Alice he made his way over to the magnificent buffet table: And magnificent it truly was, for the reputation of the hostess was hostage to the standard of her hospitality and that of Mrs Edwards could in no way be faulted in the profusion of culinary delights. This was that most difficult of repasts to attempt and the more timorous hostesses tended to avoid it. This was the classic cold buffet where the ingredients had to remain fresh and appealing throughout the long early evening function: No hot sauces here to mask even the slightest hint of tainted meats or any not less than perfect fruits or vegetables; and although relishes and pickles were presented in abundance they too had to be fresh and sharp.

In pride of place, dominating the centre of the long table, were several large oval platters of sliced cold meats. These unique viands were supplied by Herr Gruber's White Meat Shop on the corner of The Abbey Green and North Parade Passage, a few doors down from Sally Lunn's teashop. Gruber was a Rhinelander from Lahr near Baden-Baden and his specialised refugee craftsmen presented a selection of continental specialities for the delectation of the sophisticated wealthy visitors to Bath. Here were cuts of the finest roast veal, milk-fed kid, spit-roasted goose and turkey breast, pale Bavarian style bratwursts and spicy Toulouse sausages. Ringing them in an artistic display were slices of exotic salamis and foi-gras pates and loaves of feather light French bread and robust, flavoursome Italian country rolls. About the only thing that Alexander did not like was a traditional fermented fish sauce called garum, a Roman delicacy that had been handed down from the days when Bath had been the legionary rest camp of Aqua Sulis.

"Ah, Major Coulston, I do believe?" Said a voice at his elbow "Lady Trandon's nephew I believe?"

Alexander, in the process of popping a second quail's egg into his mouth, turned in surprise to see a small chubby faced man wearing round silver rimmed spectacles clipped to his nose and a tightly curled white periwig smiling genially at him.

With another painful gulp the quail's egg was finally gone, allowing Alexander to gasp an apologetic. "Why yes, sir. And you are?

"Cyrus Newton, bloodstock breeder dealer at your service, sir." He was not in anyway discomfited by Alexander's response and breezed on. "My stables are out Lansdowne way, just across from Freezing Hill so please feel free to call anytime you are passing. I've got some fine blood out there just at the moment. In fact I have recently purchased from Ireland a matching pair of chestnut geldings that would grace the finest carriage in England. You must come and see 'em."

He suddenly stopped and his mouth became a small round *O* and he gazed quizzically over his pince-nez and said quietly. "Though I don't suppose that geldings are what we are seeking here just at the moment. Perhaps fillies would be nearer the mark, what?" The *O* was replaced by a slight tight-lipped smile as he touched Alexander's arm almost spilling his wine. Cyrus immediately apologised profusely. It was apparent that he had struck a nerve and did his best to diffuse the awkward situation but Alexander realizing that his cover had been blown, opened up to the stranger and told him of his underlying quest.

It turned out to be a road travelled by Cyrus himself on more than one occasion and they retired to one of the settees to commiserate further on the subject and soon they were well in their cups. Their noisy fun soon drew the attention of the all-seeing Mrs Edwards and she came over to see if everything was in order and what had made them suddenly so jolly but they invented some tale about one of Cyrus' livery customers and she went away content but still curious about the incident. Their hostess archly inquired if they wished to visit any of the ladies in her upstairs apartments? She smilingly added that it would be no problem and as a welcoming gesture any indulgence would be her personal expense.

However by now both men were drunk and with profuse thanks said that they must decline her generous offer. Mrs Edwards was taken aback but managed an iron smile and left them to the bottle until Alexander invited his newfound friend back to Trandon House for dinner.

On reflection it was not one of Alexander's better ideas and did not in any way please Lady Trandon or do a lot for Alexander's credibility.

8

MARIA DI SIENNA

Maria di Sienna had known about Ellis Starkey longer than he realised. Her old friend Aimee had warned her of his reputation in Bristol when she came to Bath but their first actual meeting had been early one summer morning at one of the spectacular public breakfasts presented by the Court Masters at Vauxhall Gardens, a favourite last stand for revellers after a wild night's debauchery. In spite of her friend's warning, Maria found herself intrigued by his appearance and his aura of power and danger. In place of the usual silks, satins and powdered wigs of her other suitors, he wore a plain but well cut dark green coat and grey knee breeches, cutting a sinister figure with his left arm in a sling and a black eye patch. He made Maria feel secure, a very rare thing indeed considering her occupation, and it wasn't long before he was escorting her to balls and parties and trips along the river. They got on very well but she rebuffed his intimate advances saying that she valued her independence too much to risk any further emotional entanglement. Eventually he told her that he had decided to move to Bath and leased a suite of rooms at Pratt's Hotel on the South Parade. Since then they had become quite close friends, so much so that she had asked him to accompany her on this pleasant afternoon trip to see her new house. Right now he was sitting beside her in her carriage.

From its window Maria gazed with some satisfaction at what had once been a sadly neglected property at Axfords Buildings, a small block attatched to the extreme east end of Paragon Buildings, just a few doors away from the sumptuous mansion where the celebrated actress Sarah Siddons regularly held court. At the moment the house was swarming with workmen and lengths of sawn timber and buckets of hot tar were strewn across the sidewalk in the final stages of returning the house to its former glory.

In fact, it had been at one of Sarah Siddons' soirees that Maria had met its former owner; a young rake who had inherited it but had never lived there, leaving it empty and neglected for several years. He was in some way related to the Gay family, one of the first of the landowners to lease land to the famous John Wood the Elder. The property developer and architect who had first shown the open mouthed citizens of Bath just what they're city could look like when he had built Queen Square and launched a frenzy of building in the classic style that lasted over sixty years.

To Maria the house represented the attainment of respectability; well not exactly respectability, because that was a quality somewhat at odds with her profession, but perhaps an elevation in prestige and clientele, for Maria, not to put too fine a point on it, was a prostitute... Ironically, it was also situated close to John Palmer's recently completed St. Swithins Chapel which, due to

88

financial troubles had taken thirteen years to finish!

The former Mary May Jones had come a long way from her hard schooling as a twelve year old in her Uncle Jonas' brothel in the shady Redcliffe area of Bristol where the clients had been mainly smugglers, seamen and small time crooks. One of whom had been a highway robber called Rob Dacarius.

She had been adopted by her uncle after the death of her parents in an outbreak of the plague in Clevedon who instead of giving her a convent education as he had sincerely promised the priest he put her to work as a kitchen skivvy in his evil establishment. Far from being the jovial outgoing character that he presented to the outside world, Jonas Harrison was the leader of a sinister press gang that haunted the dockside taverns and brothels looking for unsuspecting men on a night out. A night out that often ended miles out at sea for a very long time! In the course of this calling his cobblers knife and cudgel had maimed and killed several men. In short, to those who knew him, he was known as a powerful and very dangerous man and certainly not one to cross.

Within months Mary was being abused by Jonas and his cronies and at fourteen she was put to work in the brothel itself. Accepting her fate, she determined to become mistress of her own destiny and quickly learned the tricks and turns of one of the oldest professions in the world. She became popular and was soon earning her corn, caring little for her fellow workers and nothing at all for the stupid clients. She was scrupulously clean, regarding the sex act as

89

nothing more than a bodily function and simply a job, succumbing neither to the threats of the pox faced Madame or any unruly clients.

However she did make a good friend there, a black girl called Aimee from the French Caribbean island of Martinique. She had been the mistress of a Bristol sea captain who promised her freedom when they docked next in England. True to his word he had introduced her to Jonas Harrison who immediately put her to work in his brothel. Like Mary she saw no wrong in what she was doing and went about her business with a smooth detached efficiency and it was from her, and her many clients that Mary learned all the advanced positions of love making and its many perversions.

Ironically this impersonal detachment and enthusiastic co-operation put Mary's clients at ease and made her the favourite of the more selective and wealthier ones. Among these was a baker from Clifton with a taste for the depraved low life who told her she should go to Bath because that's where the real money was. For some little extra favours like flagellation and such he would introduce her to a certain house in Avon Street run by his friend Mr George, where she would find that her talents would be more appreciated.

The idea appealed to her, so on her next day off she took the London coach, got off in Bath and found her way to muddy Avon Street in the Kingsmead area. The house turned out to be the last one in the street with a side garden reaching to the river. She presented the baker's letter to the owner and as he started to enquire into her abilities she gently took his hand and whispered. "Let me show you."… Which she did leaving him breathless and weak as a kitten! The terms and conditions of her service were settled and she was installed that very evening.

Jonas Harrison did not discover that she had gone until his return from Southampton and went mad at the loss of such a high earner. In a fit of anger he fired the house Madame and the porter whose job it was to keep an eye on his charges at all times.

Mary's first moves had been to change her name to Maria di Sienna and her thick Somerset burr to a refined Mayfair accent with Italian overtones. With her new persona and her startling sexual abilities she was a sensation and was soon the talk of the district. There were no repercussions from Harrison who, she heard, had sold the brothel in Redcliffe and ostensibly had joined a group of property speculators in the new housing boom at Clifton, which was in fact a cover for his deep involvement with the sinister slave trade. Maria settled easily into the routine of the house, regularly depositing most of her earnings with a Portugese Jew called Mendoza who operated a private bank & shipping agency at Bristol.

Two years passed easily. She was eighteen now and really enjoying life in the fashionable city with its busy shops and cafes and feeling free for the first time in her life. Which is why she felt shocked late one night when the porter called her from her bed and told her that the night watch were at the door and wanted to talk with her. She felt a shiver of fear. Why? What did they want? Had Harrison found her? Though it wasn't likely he would go to the beadle. The porter said roughly he had no idea but she'd better get going before Mr George got back. Cursing all and sundry she threw on some clothes, gabbed her bag and put a warm shawl round her shoulders and went down.

Two large men, one of them carrying a lantern on a pole, were waiting in the street.

"Yew Mary May Jones, late o' Brizzle?" One asked.

"I might be." She replied cautiously in a thick Bristol accent. "Ooz it wants t'know? An' wot for? I ain't done nuffin!"

"B'ain't nobody sez as yew did." The watchman sniffed and wiped his nose on his greatcoat sleeve. "Tis jes' that some jade thaz bin assaulted give us yore name. We got both parties up at Kingsmead Square an' Beadle Morris sez you gotta come an' vouch for the girl. 'Er name's Aymee or summat Froggy loik tha'. Come along now!"

Maria followed them and there sitting on a bench in the square was her old friend Aimee from Redcliffe. When she saw Mary she burst into tears and hugged her. The pompous beadle banged his staff on the cobbles and said that Aimee was being held at the request of a gentleman. He dug into his capacious pocket and drew out a paper'

"This yeer document sez that yore black friend took 'is money an' then refused to provide the services she had been paid for."

"Oh yes" Said Mary "An' oo waz this yeer contractor then?

Beadle Norris snorted "'E's a sort o' gen'mum farmer, name o' the Honourable Ellis Starkey. We had to restrain him for breaking shop winders on Westgate Street. He put up resistance so we down'd 'im and put 'im in the lock up in Saw Close. They'd thrown him outa the Assembly Rooms earlier fer tryin' to stab one o' the dealers."

"Oh aye, an' owe much did this would be assassin pay for my friend's services then?" Snapped Mary.

"'Twas two sovs, I believe." He responded hesitatingly.

"Oh aye ? Frum wot you sayin' it sounds as though 'e was too far gone to swive anythin' an' s'not like 'is kind to pay for anythin' fore he gets it , izzit?"

The beadle shuffled his feet and cleared his throat and coughed nervously. He had not expected such spirited opposition and did not know how to handle it. Mary knew he was lying but before he could reply she delved into her purse and dropped three crowns into his horny hand.

"I reckon as that should cover any inconvenience he may 'ave 'ad." She said quietly. "I think I can trust yew to sort things out. May I take my friend home now?"

The beadle sighed and jingled the coins in hand and turned away with a brief nod and hustled his men off to the Southmead.

Mary threw her shawl around the scrawny shoulders of her old friend and hustled her back to the house. Once inside she led her through to the warm kitchen where a big black cauldron of beef stew was bubbling slowly over the dying embers of the fire. She sat

93

Aimee on a chair at the scarred deal table and poured two big measures of red wine into pewter tankards and after adding a cinnamon pod to each, she pulled out the ever-present glowing poker from the embers and plunged it into the wine. As it bubbled and settled she took down two earthenware bowls and ladled out a portion of steaming stew in each one.

Between slurps Aimee explained how she came to be in Bath. Apparently she had been picked up by Starkey while shopping in Bristol's Broadmead market and he enjoyed her company so much that he became a regular punter, often taking her away for weekends. This was her third outing to the Assembly Rooms Casino but Starkey was an aggressive and obnoxious customer and this latest outrage gave the manager a solid reason for barring him. In his frustration he turned on his companion accusing her of stealing his money and triggering off her arrest.

Later, as the girls snuggled down in Mary's bed they planned a new future together deciding that Mary would continue to be known as Maria Di Sienna and Aimee would keep her exotic name but invent a more imaginative background. It was Aimee herself who suggest the surname La Blanche as a joke. The following morning Mary introduced Aimee to Mr George who enthusiastically added her to his stable. One of the older girls was leaving to go back to Taunton to help her newly widowed mother to run the family farm so she was installed in her room.

Together they looked an absolute sensation. Even in a city

that was bursting with beautiful women. Maria was tall blond and elegant with pure white skin and an unerring sense of style in her clothes and her accessories. Aimee with her glowing brown skin, her aquiline Ethiopian features and her full figure was the perfect foil for her partner. Both women oozed a smouldering sexual presence which left other courtesans looking gauche, over painted and awkward.

Dressed in their finery, their first call had been to the Assembly Rooms to meet Captain Warmley, now promoted to General Manager but still wearing his greasy yellow coat. He was snooty and diffident when asked if they could frequent the dance hall and the casino unescorted. He stared at them coldly and reminded them that the gambling room was usually not available to unaccompanied ladies but that perhaps some accommodation could be reached as regards the dancing room. He paused and looked them over coldly: finally he said that as long as their friends spent plenty of money in the building he was prepared to allow them entrance. Of course there would be a charge for this indulgence and the sum he mentioned left them gasping. In other circumstances the girls would have offered some exciting personal service they could perform for him, like a threesome but the thought and the risk of coupling with this sweating loathsome toad was too appalling and so they reluctantly accepted his terms.

It was pure extortion but it was the best deal that they were likely to get so they simpered a genteel 'Thank you' and made there way to Mr Carrick's coffee house in Savile Row to consider their next move.

One thing was apparent from the outset. The competition was very fierce and if they were to reel in the big spenders they would need the very best clothes, a respectable address and a carriage, none of which was likely to come their way in Avon Street. In the light of this Maria decided to visit her Portuguese banker and ask for a loan. Surprisingly, Mendoza was quite co-operative. He asked Maria about her business plan and apart from tweaking it here and there he agreed to help provided that the loan conditions were met and there were regular and prompt repayments. The terms and conditions being agreed, he gave her an introductory letter to Mr Cyrus Newton a well know Bath bloodstock dealer with a stud farm at Lansdowne He hinted that Cyrus was also a client of his and would give her a good deal on a good horse and nice carriage. As Maria was shown out by Mendoza's sour faced sister she realised that their venture was well and truly launched.

The next thing the girls needed was a place to work from and they found a nice building on the Lower Borough Walls near the South Mead but on the other side of Horse Street and well away from the horse bath and the stinking open sewer that the older locals still called the Bum Ditch which still served the town and debouched into the river near the bridge... (In fact all the town sewers and streams emptied their loads of human and animal waste into the Avon including the detritus from the town's butchers and tanners too. It was a clear example of the old adage that it was 'An ill wind that

96

blew no good' but about the only creatures that gained from this river pollution were the fish and rodents which grew both in population and size. A local parson noted at the time that the fish caught down river from the town bridge were almost twice the size of those caught upstream.

This new place had once been a shop and divided up neatly into a salon to welcome the guests, an ample kitchen with out buildings including a privy in the backyard and six good sized bedrooms. The rent was reasonable, particularly so after the girls agreed to pay for the renovations and a two year the lease was drawn up and signed. They then found a housekeeper, a doorman and two more attractive girls who were glad to be off the streets. Six weeks later the work was finished and they moved in, discreetly calling the place the Paradise Gardens. Their old employer Mr. George caused no trouble and let them go without asking for compensation and they showed their appreciation by allowing him two free visits a month for the first year, an arrangement that suited everybody. The venture had proved successful and Maria extended the lease for another year but halfway through the term they realized that it was time to move up in the world and Maria went back to Mendoza who arranged a mortgage for her on the house at Axfords Buildings.

Aimee also played her part well and roped in a young architect client of her's to help. He put their ideas into working drawings for the interior which included converting the vast cellar complex, which ran out under the wide pavement and had its own separate entrance at the back, into a copy of the Roman catacombs. Maria realized the potential earning power of such a place where exotic erotic appetites could be satisfied in complete security and discretion. Called Saturnalia, it soon became an exclusive haunt for the gay and sexually liberated community and was crowded every night. However she kept it separate from the main house so that the less adventurous rich clients would not be offended.

She was about to tell her coachman to move off when the foreman came across the pavement to tell her that their work would be finished at the months end and when the decorator could start. .... He made a slight bow and doffed his greasy cap which oddly had a small bright green feather pinned to it.

As they rode off for lunch at Ellis' hotel Maria reflected on the story he had told her about his family background and how of he came to arrive in Bath

----

The Starkey dynasty had been established by Charles Reuben Starkey, the son of a successful cattle dealer from Wilmslow, Cheshires who, to the disgust of his father, had taken a deep interest in landscape gardening and horticulture. Shunned by his family as an effeminate waster he made his way to Liverpool and took a job on a Dutch ship as a cook. In Flushing he jumped ship and made his way

98

to Amsterdam where he encountered the phenomenon of tulip growing and dealing. The novelty of breeding different colours of the bloom had at first been a hobby but later progressed to an industry and then to an obsession amongst the wealthy who would pay hundreds of guilders for an unusual colour or unique design of flower. The Holy Grail was of course the fabled black tulip which was worth a fortune.

As in many other cases, quick thinking businessmen saw that as the commodity was so often bought to trade on for a profit, it was far more convenient to issue a certificate of authenticity than to inspect the item itself. It did not take long for the con men to latch on to this and soon certificates were being issued and traded for merchandise that did not actually exist. Seeing an opportunity and on the strength of some bogus aristocratic contacts, Charles offered to handle their business in England.

For a few years fortunes were made until in early 1637 when the whole thing fell apart. In that fateful year a prosperous Amsterdam draper decided to give several valuable tulip bulbs as presents for the groom's influential family at his only daughter's wedding to their son and sent one of his servants with the relevant documents to collect them from his broker. The broker was none other than Meinheer Starkey who of course having no merchandise whatever except a sheaf of counterfeit certificates, made sympathetic noises and promised that he would deliver the order personally the following week.

Two days later Charles hopped aboard a boat for Dunkirk carrying his ill gotten guilders and from there took another to Newhaven, safely away from Dutch justice. However, the news of the disaster spread quickly across the North Sea and soon many speculators in London started looking for redress from the man who had sold them the worthless shares causing Charles to quickly move on, this time to Ireland where he set up a small brewery in Cork.

By the age of fifty his enterprise had grown and he was a wealthy man with a large estate with a mansion in Dublin and large family. At his death in 1690 his son Thomas inherited the business but having delusions of grandeur, married the plain daughter of a minor nobleman from the English Pale and became Lord Garwin.

Ellis was the youngest of his five sons and like his grandfather before him soon realised that his prospects were bleak and took an agreed amount in lieu of his inheritance and moved to the English West Country where he set up as a gentleman farmer, but unfortunately, unlike his grandfather he was a selfish brutal bully.

The myriad attractions of hedonistic Bath quickly took hold of him and he became a regular (paying) guest at the many parties and spurious clubs that operated round the clock. Of course, the greatest of which was Bath's Upper Assembly Rooms where he became a regular but hot-headed punter and was, for a time, successful and added considerably to his land holdings.

However it was also here that he made one of his biggest mistakes of his life, when in a fit of pique he recklessly challenged a

German officer to a duel where he received grave injuries and was lucky to have escaped with his life.

The experience had a serious effect on his confidence and for a few months stayed away from the addictive life of the tables but it did not last. Within a year he was in trouble again and more objectionable than ever.

9

LADY TRANDON'S NEWS

About three weeks later Alexander came clumping down the stairs to breakfast. He was in a foul mood and the sight that was about to greet him would do nothing to lift his black depression. The previous night, in fact for most nights of the past week, he had again been to the New Assembly Rooms, gambling and spending far more than he had intended. Also, in the hope of finding anything about the present whereabouts of his lost raven haired beauty he had spent another boring hour with the obnoxious Captain Warmley as he rambled on about his latest conquests and the many influential contacts he had in the city. Alas it had all been a waste of time except for the glaringly obvious fact that Warmley harboured a secret desire to seduce this beauty himself!

Earlier in the week Alexander had even called on Mrs. Edwards but she said that she had not seen hair or hide of the girl herself. The only news she had to offer was that she had heard that the girl in question had been seen on the river at Kensington

Meadows sunning herself aboard the boat of Mr. Paul the Widcome corn merchant. Apart from that small tit-bit there was nothing. It was more than just the search that was getting him down. He was growing tired of the constant social round of dances, fetes, drinking and gluttony: Even of Mrs Edwards's gay evenings. He felt that he was due for a change of direction and that was exactly what awaited him this dank dull morning. As he walked abstractedly into the breakfast room his already dejected heart sank further at the sight of his Aunt Miriam seated at the table with her maid pouring the tea.

"Ah, Alexander….Good morning my dear, shall you take tea? Agnes will attend to you directly".

Alexander just grunted a vague reply and helped himself to a liberal helping of kidneys and bacon from the sideboard and took a sideways glance at her, wondering why she was up and about so early today. She usually had breakfast in her room and did not appear in public until mid-morning. Also it was rather unusual for her to be so pleasant and out-going. Such suspicious behaviour only added to his stubborn manner and he grunted again as he scraped his chair across the polished parquet floor to the table like a spoilt child, knowing that would annoy her. Again surprisingly, the expected reprimand was not forthcoming. Instead she gave him a gap-toothed smile and announced that she had some news.

Alexander perked up. "Oh yes, Aunt, and what would that be? Fat George had another fit then, has he? Prinny will be pleased!

Miriam tut-tutted at such irreverent remarks and with her

103

folded fan tapped a small pile of letters at her side. "Now, now, do not be so facetious my dear boy. It does not become you. Listen and you will learn something, for I have had a communication which I am sure you will find of great interest."

Putting aside her fan she took a sip of tea and selected an official looking letter.

"This one, my dear boy," she cooed, "is from Admiral Singleton. Do you know who I mean? As I recall, did you not travel with his daughter from Poole when you had some fracas with that road ruffian? Well I have recently been in correspondence with him and now all has come to fruition and I am free to inform you of a new development."

Alexander grunted again as he munched on a piece of toast wondering just how she could dismiss an attempted highway robbery with two dead as a mere fracas. Sometimes she was unbelievable! Completely unabashed by his surly responses Miriam presented her news.

"Well, Alexander." She gushed, "During his time in Ceylon on the Trinchomalee Station he made the acquaintance of my dear brother Timothy who has a large tea plantation there. They got on very well from all accounts and the Admiral told him that his daughter would be coming here for her social polishing at Mrs. Blundell's institution in Lansdowne.

As she paused for breath Alexander said. "Well, Aunt Miriam I do not see how that would in any way effect or reward me."

"Ah! But you see that is only part of my news, and you will soon appreciate that this connection is very much in your favour. You see, through the good offices of my dear brother the Admiral has requested that I take care of his daughter Jessica during her stay at Mrs Blundell's academy and provide rooms for her and her maid here at Trandon House." Alexander was somewhat shocked at the prospect of such prim company but held his tongue as Miriam sailed blissfully on. "We are agreed on this and his letter contains an open draft on Mr. Stuckey's Bank to adequately cover any outgoings required, including a very fair price indeed for their sojourn here. Is that not good news? But for you, my boy, the best is yet to come."

Alexander speared his bacon and wondered just where he figured in these new arrangements and muttered. "Oh, then there is something in all of this for me, after all, eh?"

Miriam demurely put her hands in her lap and cocked her head to the side and looked up at him in what she imagined was a coquettish pose and twittered on.

"Well, My Dear Alexander, I think that we will both agree that the time has come for you to attend to your future welfare, which is for both of us to realize that I can no longer continue to manage the myriad responsibilities of the family estates on my own."
Alexander began to wonder if she was about to announce a change to her will but still sat in tense silence as she explained.

"You see, my brother Timothy has indicated that he desires to live out his life in his Indian paradise and will not be returning to these cloudy shores. So as my next nearest kin, the estate is to be your sole inheritance and papers to that effect have already been drawn up by my advocate Mr. Willerby. They require only your signature to complete the changeover and give me a little peace in which to end my days."

"But I am still a serving officer. Albeit one on indefinite half-pay leave." He said ruefully. Miriam smiled at him benignly.

"Ah, that too has been attended to by the Admiral's generosity and from the next quarter day you are to be returned to the active service list and become Chief Procurement Inspector (West) at the Quartermaster's Department in Warminster with a separate office at Bath."

She sat pouting at him for a moment before announcing mischievously. "Which means of course, you shall no longer be a serving Captain of Marines but will be commissioned as Major and wear the blue uniform of your new department. Your duties will be well supported and you can continue to reside here and attend to your new role as Lord of the Manor as well. Does that not please you?

Alexander was dumfounded at the news but the growing resentment of what his aunt had done behind his back was quickly dissipated as the full implications of the changes hit him. About the only fly in the ointment was that the prissy Miss Singleton and her bumpkin maid would be residing under the same roof as him.

However on balance his appointment to the Warminster barracks might help in his quest to find his raven-haired beauty

10

WOOLEY POWDER MILLS

Alexander thought that it was all happening too quickly but after due consideration he realised the full extent of what had happened and how much his situation had improved. He was finally returned to the Active Service List and his inheritance was securely in the bag. Of more much immediate importance was the fact that his new posting here at Warminster Barracks which gave him the opportunity to pursue his lady at King George's expense. … 'Oh yes, it was all dropping into place very nicely.'

With a contented sigh he swung his captain's chair sideways and plonked his shining boots on the corner of the large mahogany table that served him as a desk, lit a cheroot and gazed out of the tall window at the pristine parade ground with its equally pristine sentries pacing their beat. Out on the road beyond the tall iron barrack gates he watched the coaches rolling by wondering if his long lost beauty might be in one of them. In fact that was one of the reasons he still spent more time here than at his office in Bath.

His work in the Procurement Department was routine and to some extent boring. In essence all he had to do was to fit in with the old established system that had been brought over from Holland by the Prince of Orange when he became King William the Third in 1689. This meant waiting until he received an approved request from the Quartermaster General and then contacting the approved civilian contractor and placing the order with him. There was no question of following up the order or inspecting the quality of the merchandise, whether it was food supplies, animal fodder, clothing or armaments. His remit did not even cover any medical supplies or equipment. These items were usually purchased by the doctors and invoiced to another government department.

On the whole, the service as originally conceived and operated by the frugal Dutch, had worked well because it had a system of checks and balances built in to guard against abuse. However, since the arrival on the throne of the House of Hanover in the shape of George the First, these controls had been steadily eroded, to such an extent that by the ascendance of Mad George the Third in 1760, the whole business of procurement was wide open to abuse and corruption was rife. A failing that became very apparent in times of dangerous active service.

Alexander made a point of reading through the original manifest of his duties when he arrived and soon realized that the whole system was a shambles. He also realized that there was nothing he could do to change things. Others had tried but had come across entrenched opposition from their superiors who were suspicious of change of any kind.

In addition, many of these senior officers were already deep in the pockets of the venal contractors and drew nice quarterly dividends. In fact Alexander owed his present elevated position to his over-zealous predecessor who had asked too many awkward questions and had found himself suddenly promoted and posted to the jungles of Siam where he could do no further mischief.

Browsing through the pile of dusty correspondence on his desk he came across a request from the Board of Ordnance for gunpowder. There was a note attached by the Quartermaster General's office informing him of the current supplier, a certain Mr Strachey and partners of Wooley Powder Mills near Charlcomb, a beautiful valley a couple of miles north of Bath.

The first thing he did was to make inquires about the firm. Firstly, because it was quite rare to find a gunpowder mill so far inland, (albeit a bare thirteen miles from Bristol) and secondly why had there been no serious soliciting on behalf of the owners to obtain military contracts? Other contractors were falling over themselves to get the security of Government money so what was going on? Judicious questioning of certain lawyers of his acquaintance produced information on the financial set up of the company: Including the most surprising confidential disclosure that dividends to shareholders were as high as twelve per cent and had been for some time. So why had they taken government contracts in the first place?

Although now run by a syndicate led by Adam Strachey under the patronage of Lord Carrick, the company had been founded in 1722 by four partners, Abraham Hooke, John Parkin, Edmond Baugh and Harrington Gibbes, all of whom were officers of the pompously named 'Society of Merchant Adventurers, ship owners and traders in linen, iron, and sugar'..... Alexander noted wryly that there was no mention of their most profitable commodity, the Slave Trade, where small kegs of powder were a major trading currency. It soon became clear to Alexander that their acceptance of the occasional government job gave the company respectability and was a good cover for their less pleasant operations.

The note from the Ordnance Office also suggested that he rode over to introduce himself as the new procurement officer. It was dated some six weeks ago on August 13th

Later that week, in the company of Silas, he found himself plodding through the hamlet of Ensleigh on the crest of the broad Lansdowne plateau and down the steep valley to the Wooley Powder Mills on the Lambrook stream. In spite of the beautiful rural surroundings there was a strange smell in the air but the riders dismissed it as animal dung spread across the fields as fertiliser but they soon came across the true source of the pollution.

On the narrow twisting lane to the village they came across a large high-sided wagon drawn by two bay shires heading in the same direction as them. The driver was a young man with a mass of yellow hair bursting from under his torn tweed cap who saluted them with his long whip as they edged by.

"Ye Gods!" Exclaimed Cyrus. "What a stink!.. What the Hell is that?"

Alexander also wrinkled his nose and informed his companion that it was raw saltpetre one of the necessary ingredients in the manufacture of the dust that builds empires, gunpowder.

"Nay, Alexander... Saltpetre ye say? Yon stench is night soil. What in God's name is a night-soil cart a-doing out here polluting the good green countryside?"

"Ah, Cyrus my friend let me explain. The careful blending of three commodities, charcoal, sulphur and lastly saltpetre is what makes gunpowder. And that cartload of detritus we have just passed is the principle source of that ingredient."

They rode on in silence as Cyrus digested this amazing revelation. Emerging from a small wood they came in sight of their destination. The mills themselves looked neat and well cared for but fields leading down to the stream were scattered with dung heaps, some six feet high, steaming gently in the morning sun and pervading the air with the same industrial perfume of the recently encountered cart.

As they passed under the aqueduct bringing water from one of the hillside ponds and dismounted in a cobbled yard they found awaiting them a heavily built grey haired man who presented himself to them as Marcus Jory, manager of the factory. He bade them

111

welcome and instructed one of his boys to take their horses. The introductions complete, Marcus led them to a somewhat stained and distressed plank table beneath the eaves of an old barn where he served them with refreshing cold fresh cider from a cracked earthenware jug. The conversation centred on the general topics of the day. The growing popularity of the Spa town and of the distinguished visitors thereto until Cyrus, his appetite whetted by Alexander's comments on the appalling smell, enquired more about the process of making gunpowder. In particular he wished to know more about the mysteries of creating saltpetre.

This often made request permitted Marcus to present his full thesis on the process, a performance that had provided him with an evening of free drinks on many an occasion in the taverns of Larkhall. He eased his apron, took a deep draught of his cider and prepared to give his distinguished visitors chapter and verse on the making of 'The Devil's Dust' but before he could get started there was a confused clopping of hooves accompanied by the jangling of harness and the rumbling of iron shod wheels on the uneven cobbles of the yard. They all turned to see who had arrived and Alexander and Cyrus caught the whiff of the wagon they had passed on the hill.

"Good day to y'all, Genmum'" Called the young driver, doffing his cap and allowing his yellow mop to flop across his face. "Goin' to be a good un too, by the looks o' things. Now, Squire Jory, where shall I be a- parkin' this fragrant load? "
Marcus smiled at the driver indulgently and shouted back.

"Ah, a good day to you'n all Young Jeb. Jes' you put 'er round the back, next to the top bed, facing the crusher if you will. Then come an' join us for a wet."

Jeb clucked to the horses and headed for the shed.

"Be thar direckly Squire... Keep the jug cool fer oi!"

Relieved to be free of the pungent aroma Jory took up the story of how he had come into the gunpowder trade. Saying that it was quite unusual for an inland town to be in such a business but that of late it had been realized that the most difficult ingredient to find in the manufacture was top quality saltpetre and seeing as how the principal source, in this country at least, was human waste well watered by the urine of drinking folk, it was obvious that centres of habitation were necessary ... But also, he pointed out craftily, as the processes of extraction were so pungent and penetrating that isolated country places in easy reach were the best locations. Hence Squire Tracey's works out here in the Wooley Valley.

Jory sat back satisfied at his explanation took a puff at his corncob pipe and quaffed his cider as the information was digested by his guests... Before they could respond however young Jeb came back from around the building.

"You'm gorra bit 'o trouble wi' yon mare Mizzer Jory, that there young chestnut. Coughing like a good 'un she were. An' by her hind legs she looks as tho' she got the runs an'all."

Cyrus started. "Ye mean the one with the white blaze on her head? That's my Maria... She was fine when we left Lansdowne.

113

What d'ye think is wrong wi' her?"

Jeb sat down and took a pull from the cider jug before replying.

"Well," He said wiping his mouth on his sleeve. "I reckon she's had some bad feed or bin a nibblin' on rosemary leaves."

"Oh, ye know a bit about horse flesh then, do you?" Asked Cyrus sniffily.

"Oh aye. I bin lookin' after nags all me life." Replied Jeb "Afore I were a-drivin' these muck carts I were 'orse boy on Mr Wiltshire's wagon convoys 'tween Bath an' Lunnon. Week in an' week out we wuz a-doin' it. But my old Uncle Tab got sick wi' the river fever an' I 'ad to find summat wot would keep me near to 'ome to 'elp out. Haulin' this stuff for Mr Perkins in Widcome was the best paid work around so I took that… Tis alright but the smell do stay with'ee all the toime ... So I don' 'ave many friends left now!" He broke off into a hearty laugh at his own misfortune.

"Wiltshire's wagons, ye say?" Asked Cyrus. "I thought that firm were run by Old Tarleton these days... Didn't he bed an' wed one o' Walter's daughters?"

Jeb looked at him cynically and rejoined. "Aye, an' a right ugly jade she were n'all! But she got tubbed up by 'im and they wed over in Brizzle where nobody knew 'em... An' when the Old Man snuffed it Tarleton inherited the bloody lot… Walter 'avin' no sons, like. So you might say as 'ow he got there on 'is cock. Mind you, It looks like he's goin' t'be paid out in kind, cos that evil bastard Marcus Harris the foreman is a-courtin' Tarleton's eldest daughter now.. An' she's about as attractive as her mother... When I saw which way the wind was a-blowin' I wasn't sorry to get out. But I am beginin' to think there must be better jobs around than haulin' this evil smellin' shite."

They all laughed at his tale and Jory got on explaining the gunpowder trade. But, before he could get into his stride Cyrus addressed Jeb.

"Listen." He said "If you're looking to change employers and y'are as good as you claim to be with horseflesh, come over to my stables in Lansdowne and I will give ye a week's trial. Then perhaps we might talk about your future. What say ye to that?"

Jeb was taken aback by the offer, he had been hoping that something might come his way since old Perkins had begun to hint that if there was a lull in carting the drivers usually give a hand at digging out old privies and cesspits to obtain the saltpetre sources and Jeb did not fancy that at all! On top of which he had recently heard that Perkins had bought an old building in Milk Street that had been empty nearly eight years since an outbreak of cholera had killed off all the tenants.

It turned out to be a gold mine to someone in his line of business when he discovered that the inner courtyard, which was also backed onto by two popular taverns, had been used as a privy and dumping ground for household waste even before the plague struck. Apparently there had once been a cesspool there, with an open sewer that ran down to the river but somehow a sheep had drowned in it

115

and blocked the exit, so the detritus had just kept building up until it was higher than the ground floor windows and had solidified into a black mass with a silver crust of crystallised nitre. Realising just what Perkins had in mind for him Jeb had decided to move on.

His life was horses and although he didn't mind the rancid smell so much, digging out vintage excrement from dark dank cellars was not his idea of a good job. With the result that he jumped at Cyrus' offer and assured him glowingly that he would be there the following morning to show him what he could do. Marcus Jory topped up his mug and looked benignly on as though it had been his influence that had put this fine opportunity Jeb's way.

Deciding that it was time to change the subject Alexander asked Jory how long the mill had been operating.
Jory rubbed his chin and tamped down his pipe to give him time to think.

"Ooh, must be well over eighty year I'd say... As fer I can remember the fust mill 'ere wuz built from some old farm buildings around 1720... An' after that they built the Littleton Mills near Chew Magna an' then came another at Moreton nearby. Oh aye, an' there wuz another mill below the weir at Bathampton as well but 'ere at Wooley they 'ad a bad explosion in '45 so they put up a proper purpose built mill with a race from the Lam Brook. Then they sorted out the water supplies by diggin' out the big holdin pond. Oh aye an' 'bout the same time, they moved the main Brizzle magazine house from Tower Harratz mills in town to a new dock down river for easy loadin' of the ships."

Satisfied that he had dealt fully with this enquiry he creaked to his feet and without further ado shepherded them all towards the factory building to demonstrate just how gunpowder was made... Whether they wanted to know or not!

"I trust that it is not dangerous Mr. Jory?" Said Cyrus looking aghast at Jory's smoking corncob pipe. "I mean to say, that pipe o' yours 's a bit risky ain't it?"

"By George no, Mr Newton, sir! There is naught to be cautious of till we get to the dryin' sheds. All the mixin' is done wi' water and even when tis caked up there is little danger.... That's if you'm careful, loik!"

Cyrus was not really assured that it was safe and made sure to place himself behind Jory when they were in the sheds.

"Well Gents, ere we are." Announced Jory as he kicked open a rough plank door "This is where we make The Devils Dust. Jes' you follow me an' I'll explain it all as we go."

"Nuffink's goin' to go bang is it, Squire?" Jeb asked anxiously.

"Naw... There's nuthin' like that Jeb lad, till tis powdered an' dried. Even then you've gotta 'ave a flame or a spark to set it off. An' that's not likely ere is it?"

Jeb also looked at Jory's still smoking clay pipe and wondered if he was hearing things!

"Mind you," The smoker added. "We 'ave 'ad the odd

117

misfortune, as you might say.. There wuz an explosion a while back that killed old Arthur Price and took an arm off Jerry Carter... but 'e survived that …. Well, for a while 'e did, 'bout a year in fact…But there's bin nuthin' gone wrong this year……. Mind you, it's only early days yet!" He chuckled

He turned away from Jeb's open mouth and winked at Alexander and Cyrus

"Anyway, lookee 'ere," continued the puffing Jory "this be one of the drainin' beds. Y'see as 'ow the night soil drains through to the tray in the bottom? Well, when we pour off the spare water and dry out the tray we get our precious crystals of sparkling nitre.. thaz wot we call saltpetre 'ere… and we can start the mix... But we don' do that in ere… Jes' you follow me next door."

In here the noise was deafening as the big room was bisected by a twelve foot high water wheel being driven by a narrow, fast moving stream of water in a brick channel. A thick round shaft pierced its axis to drive huge twin millwheels on either side through a system of creaking and squealing gears.

Jory had obviously given this tour a hundred times before and revelled in the attention he was getting and ushered his latest crop of visitors into a long low shed where six men in stained leather aprons were busily mixing the ingredients in short wide tubs. There was the pungent dry smell of sulphur in the air from a yellow pile in the corner and large barrels of charcoal placed along the wall of the shed at regular intervals but the precious saltpetre was in one large barrel on a flat, iron wheeled platform that was rolled along to each team as they called for it. Alexander looked curiously at the tubs and asked. "Well, Mr. Jory, how do they know how much of this stuff to mix?"

"Oh, Eric, the foreman has a chart with the amounts on it." He replied with a harsh dry cough. "These days the demand is for wot we call the French mix... Twelve parts o' saltpetre to two parts o' sulphur and two an' 'arf o' charcoal... Oh, aye, an' two parts o' water. That be for the main mix but sometimes we get an order for fine sporting powder or even a coarser, heavier mix for the Navy guns... Tho' strictly speaking we've not bin gerrin many Government orders these past few years or so."

Alexander was curious at the man's seeming reluctance to accept a government contract. "Oh, and why is that then Mr Jory?... Was it not a profitable venture for you then? I know that the treasury are slow at paying their bills but with my influence as Procurement Officer I can speed that up for you by giving your company wartime priority status.. In fact I am empowered to do just that in this time of National Emergency."

Jory stroked his chin thoughtfully before replying "Nay sir, 'tis not just that, we'm runnin' at full capacity already now. The private civilian trade is most demanding here in the sportin' shires, what wi' game keepers and stewards in constant need and we have new contracts for our small 'Black Trade" kegs from Mr. Collier out at Hatton where his factory makes cartridges for the Navy and from

119

Mr Beresford's gun shop in Bath. He has a highly specialised trade in custom made shotguns and repairs throughout the West Country. He also imports Continental products as well. Very 'ighly thought of is Mr Beresford."

"Well," Said Alexander. "I'm here to see if we can change that situation... It's about time that we started getting a steady supply from a local source and I intend to put in a memorandum to War House to that effect. And in the meantime, I have brought with me a contract for your perusal and a copy for your patron Lord Carrick. So you can expect some changes very soon."

Jory touched his forelock in gratitude and proceeded to lead them through to the drying room where racks of cowpat-like brown cakes with daubs of yellow paint on them were ranged on racks around a large cast iron dome protruding from the base of the wall.

"See, them are French mix. They got that yeller mark on 'em. Next thing we do is powder and barrel 'em but that's done outside, away from 'ere"

He led then through another door into a room with a large fire in the chimney, the fire-back being the inner side of the dome they had seen in the drying room, then out into the yard and across to an open sided barn, judiciously tamping out his pipe on the way much to Jeb's relief. Here several wheelbarrow loads of dried cake were being milled into powder and packed into barrels which were then tightly capped and bunged.

The whole operation struck the visitors as astoundingly

casual and they were only too glad to reclaim their nags and say a fond goodbye to the dangers of the powder mills, leaving a few guineas as a gratuity for the workers... Most of which ended up in Jory's pocket as his fee for the unsolicited guided tour. On the way out of the reeking valley Alexander announced that he had some good news for Cyrus too. He produced a contract for him to supply remounts to the Cavalry Depot at Warminster Barracks. Cyrus was overjoyed and invited Alexander to dinner and stay the night which he accepted gracefully. It was certainly better than having to put up with Miriam's incessant moaning every morning. He would probably face an inquisition on his return anyway, so he stayed for a fine dinner and some good French brandy.

11

SALLY LUNN'S

Jessica and Janet sat at a table in the window of Sally Lunn's teashop gracefully buttering their buns and sipping China tea. It was only mid-day but day bt they had already been to their morning's lessons on etiquette and deportment at Mrs Blundell's Academy for Young Ladies and now, feeling the need for a pick me up, had followed a bright shaft of sunlight from Orange Grove down the gentle slope towards the Abbey Green to the already famous teashop.

"Oh, this is lovely Miss." Janet gushed. "Much better than bein' on one of your father's ships, no matter 'ow big it be!"

Jessica smiled brightly sipping her tea as Janet rattled on...

"An' that there Missus Blundell do know a thing or two 'bout society, don' 'er? Showin' us 'ow to hold a champagne glass an' to respond to a toast...and 'ow to do a proper curtsy when we meets the Queen."

Jessica had allowed herself a secret smile at her maid's inclusion of herself in the morning's instruction in etiquette but Janet charged on.

"An' wot about that there Ralph Allen, eh? A very famous man, she said 'e were... All these yere buildin's is made frum stone frum 'is quarries up top o' that 'ill. An' fancy 'im a-comin' frum Cornwall loik me. A proper 'Oggy' 'e wuz an' all, borned at St Columb 'bout 1695 she said but later 'e moved to St. Blazey near Sen'Ozzel. Thaz where Oi cum frum! Thaz 'mazin' innit?"

A bubbly waitress came bustling over with a fresh pot of tea and Janet fussily tidied up the table until the girl moved away. After a check to see if the she was coming back Janet asked eagerly.

"Any'ow, tellus, who waz this yeer Sally Lunn, an' where'd she come frum eh? Tidden' as tho' she were borned yeer, not wi' a name like yon,"

Jessica sipped her tea until the storm had passed and as Janet sat back with her hands in her lap took up the tale.

"Well, from what I've read, it seems that she was the daughter of some French Huguenot refugees who came over here from Nantes over a hundred years ago and set up her shop here in an old disused bakery that nobody wanted: In this very shop in fact."

Janet sucked her gums and made her typical Cornish whooshing sound, an intake of breath that denoted that she didn't quite believe the story.

"Oh yes?" She queried "An' 'ow old was this shop then?"

"Well it's not the oldest one in the city but according to the register of tithes in the Abbey it was put up in about 1480. Apparently it had always been a place where food was prepared, even back in the Roman times. In those days it was probably just a stone hearth at the edge of the mud surrounding the hot spring."

It was all getting a bit too deep for Janet so she brought things up to date by stating bluntly." Well, Missy, I think that Sally Lunn is a daft name anyway. It don' sound very French to me." Jessica sighed, tired of all these questions when she was trying to remember her morning's lessons.

"Oh Janet, it's not sure that Sally Lunn was her name; people just called her that. Many folk think that it referred to these famous buns baked here called Sol et Lune because underneath they were dark from the oven shelf and the top light with the golden honey. You see that is French for the sun and moon."
Janet just nodded but still eyed her mistress warily.

"Oh aye?" She said doubtfully "Well worra 'bout all these yeer big Roman lookin' 'ouses and baths? When did this all start to 'appen then?

Jessica replied wearily. "Well, the hot springs here and the baths have been known about for along time but lots more people took notice of them when Queen Anne came here I suppose."

"An' when wuz that?" Janet demanded..

"Oh, about 1703 or so, I think, at least that's when some people got the idea to build this new town."
It was all too much for Janet to take in and as usually happened when she became confused she suddenly lost interest in the conversation and sat gazing at a man coming out of a house on the corner opposite

124

and suddenly blurted out

"Well then, oozat there a-comin' outa yonder house, looks like a man wots not short o' a few guineas, don't ee?"

Jessica was still taken aback by her sudden changes of mood and odd questions but fortunately she knew the answer to this one

"Ah, that, my dear Janet, is Mr John Palmer. He is the man who launched that very necessary contributor to modern life, the Mail Coach! Before he instituted that service there was no certainty that a letter package would arrive on time, or even at all! I for one am very grateful for it. "

Janet, who could barely write and almost never read anything just shrugged her shoulders and slurped her tea as Jessica continued her comments.

"Not only that. He was given fifty thousand pounds compensation when the government took it over. He's a very famous man, as was his father. He was called John too." The only response to this detailed explanation was a yawn!

Janet still appeared confused and just sat in silence looking at her. Anxious to defuse the tense situation, Jessica changed tack and chirruped gaily "Ah, Janet there is some important news that I forgot to tell you."

"Oh, an' what be that then?" Replied the maid sulkily.

Jessica took a sip of her tea and folded her hands in her lap before announcing

"I have the date for our moving to Trandon Hall. A rider

125

came this morning with a letter from Lady Trandon to tell us that she is sending two men and a carriage for us and our belongings next Friday morning. What do you think about that?"

In spite of her mood Janet admitted that she felt a little excited at the prospect but still seemed doubtful about the accommodation there but grudgingly said that... 'It would certainly be better than going back on one of the Admiral's ships again.' Jessica assured her that everything was going to be fine and they got back to discussing the ribbons that they were going to buy at Mr Hetherington bazaar on Pulteney Bridge but Jessica wasn't listening as she was full of uncertainty and had misgivings about the move.

In the end it fell to Janet to console her by pointing out the advantages of the new situation – A comfortable private apartment in a fine country mansion with all its amenities and even a carriage for their trips to town.

"...And as for that nephew of 'ers that we've already 'ad experience of " She added tartly. "Well, Missy, as far as I can see he spends most of 'is toime in Warminster doin' summat fer the government. He most certainly will 'ave a very different social circle than ours!" She ended her comments with a touch of Cornish homespun philosophy. "An' tidden as 'ow he'd be under us trotters in such a big house, izzit?

Realizing that Janet was in one of her more obtuse moods, when almost nothing would please her, Jessica sighed and signalled to the waitress for the bill leaving Janet to assemble all their shopping bags.

As Jessica paid their bill and as they made ready to leave
they noticed a tall figure lounging in the doorway. As they passed he
stood aside and graciously raising his tall hat wished them a good
afternoon. Jessica bobbed a shallow curtsy in return and noticed that
the black hat had a small green feather in the band.
Janet just sniffed and muttered that she thought that all these Bath
folk were a bit daft!

There was much more to their relationship than just mistress and maid. They were more like old friends, almost like mother and daughter though each came from contrasting back grounds. On this long journey from India they had become closer than ever, exchanging opinions, hidden fears and intimate opinions and confidences.

Jessica was barely ten when Janet had come out to India to be her maid and there were few secrets between them. They lived comfortably in the admiral's spacious, colonial mansion overlooking the Bay of Bengal but rarely saw Admiral Singleton who had a smaller house up in the hills where he lived with his exotic Indian mistress. At times Janet felt that she had only been engaged to provide a veneer of respectability to the admiral's social set up. She had no particular talent or quality to recommend her except her unquestioning acceptance of her position and blind loyalty to her charge. Her background had been a tale of misfortune and events beyond her control not unknown to the rural labouring class of the time.

Janet Zemelda Cobba was born at St.Blazey in Cornwall on a cold winter's night in 1760. She was the third child of tin miner Walter Cobba and after the usual childhood and scanty education available to girls of her class became a kitchen skivvy on a large farm near Bodmin.

Her first love was Edmond Grey, a baker's boy from St Columb but at 15 she met up with Gypsy Jacobs, a 35 year old fairground fighter at Bodmin fair and travelled with him. What had promised to be an exciting life on the road turned out to be a nightmare and a difficult pregnancy at 16. The birth was handled so badly that it prevented her having any further children. As he grew older Jacobs lost many bouts against younger stronger men and took to the bottle until he became a stupefied wreck. Abandoned with her four year old daughter in Bridgewater, Janet met and married a farmer who treated her equally badly and after her daughter died of smallpox at the age of nine she took service with various wealthy families until she saw an advertisement in a Devon paper for a ladies maid and companion willing to travel to India. In a moment of madness she got a friend to write a glowing application and after an interview with a solicitor in Bristol, much to her surprise she was accepted and put aboard an East-Indiaman bound for Calcutta the following week.

Jessica's background was also somewhat bizarre. Her prim formal manner and apparent respectability was some way from the actual truth. Before the arrival of Janet she was raised mainly by a retired Indian teacher who found her to be an intelligent, ambitious pupil and her father's mistress. By the age of eight she could do advanced mathematics and read, write and speak the difficult Indian script along with English and French, while as her teenage years began the Admiral's mistress instructed her in the exotic temple dances and all the arts and womanly wiles of love. By the time she had reached fifteen Jessica was putting her learning to the test in the most overt way with a group of riotous young officers!

It was then that Admiral Singleton heard the alarm bells ringing and packed her off to Bath where he imagined she would forget all this foolishness and emerge a polished English lady.

To Jessica however, the news of her imminent change of residence was not at all that welcoming. She had always had a wild streak (which had been the main reason that her father had sent her to Bath!) and enjoyed this rare unsupervised independence. Her accommodation as a boarder at the school, which was actually two large houses joined together, was airy and pleasant and her room mate, the daughter of a wealthy Bristol merchant, was another equally adventurous young lady and they got on very well. Along with seven other girls she studied French, deportment, dancing, singing, dressmaking, fashion, make up and table setting: But not cooking which was not considered a subject for young ladies of

129

quality to study. They were also expected to study a musical instrument (Jessica chose the flute) and singing and dancing at which she already excelled but in a somewhat more exotic style!

Janet was also well settled there and had become the perfect companion, sharing a large loft in the roof with Edwina's servant with whom she shared the cooking (The two girls usually ate in their rooms) and cleaning. In spite of the grandeur of there future accommodation they were somewhat reluctant to move but Jessica's father had made the arrangements so they would have to obey his instructions and they would have to adjust to their new lodgings as best they could.

12

TRANDON ON HOUSE

Jessica and Janet arrived at their new home on the following Friday around lunch time. The coach had turned up at the academy at 7 a.m. as Lady Trandon had arranged, bringing an extra man to help load there boxes, a task that the coachman somehow thought beneath him and he sought every chance to avoid the heavy lifting and carrying. Mrs Blundell was wise to his sly ways and set her porter to watch him closely and spur him hard if he caught him slacking. When all was loaded the coachman, still puffing loudly with false fatigue, clambered aboard while Mrs Blundell summoned the other man into her parlour and slipped him a half guinea and a shilling , instructing him to tell the coachman, if he asked, that she had just wanted to check that they had everything and give him the shilling. Finally Jessica thanked Mrs. Blundell profusely for her care and kindness and assured her that she would be back bright and early on Wednesday morning for her lessons.

    At Trandon House Alexander was on the brink of leaving for

Warminster and had just mounted his horse when the coach rolled up the drive. Curiosity drove him to tarry and see just who had been so honoured by the dispatch of the vehicle to collect them. He edged his mount to the verge and sat casually watching as the manservant jumped down to open the emblazoned lacquered door. To say that he was surprised to discover just who was arriving would be putting it mildly and he was even more discomforted when Janet performed a gracefully sarcastic curtsy and greeted him with her Cornish burr.

"Mornin' Y'r honour, zur. Tis 'andsome day, idden he?"

Completely left footed Alexander replied with a hesitant gruff. "Er, yes... Yes it is...er, is your mistress with you, then? And what ..." Before he could finish Jessica joined her maid and adjusted her bonnet. "Ah yes, Major Coulston. " She cooed." ... A very good morning to you... How nice to see you again. No doubt you are as pleased to see me as I am to see you. However it seems that we are about to see a lot more of each other for the next few months... May I hope that we find it mutually enjoyable?"

Alexander still did not know exactly how to respond. He had known that she was coming of course but he had not expected the confident manner in her speech. Where had the timid little mouse from the Poole mail coach gone? It disturbed him considerably because like so many military officers his experience of women was very limited and certain prejudices were ingrained in his social consciousness...

Unsure of what else to say he spluttered a gruff, "Ah, yes, of course... Jessi'.. er,.. Miss Singleton," and trotted off down the drive where an escort of four troopers waited to escort him to Warminster Barracks.

Lady Trandon wheeled herself to the grand entrance, gushing a warm welcome to her new guests while her maid Agnes had the servants bring their boxes and portmanteaux indoors and take them to the assigned rooms in the eastern wing of the house facing the river and its landing stage. The girls were very happy at their new home and Lady Trandon told them to take a tour of the house and grounds while Agnes would see that all was attended to.

The Trandon estate consisted of a big red brick Queen Anne style mansion, and several outbuildings on about an acre of riverain pasture with the home farm buildings and barns further up on a plateau high above the river where a fresh brook filled a big iron reservoir with clear water. From there a clever system of pipes diverted the waters down to a dairy and scullery behind the vast main house kitchen, from where the constantly running water was channelled on to the privies and then back into the old stream bed before debouching into the river below. Above Home Farm, across the Bitton Road, their farmland ran as far north as the outskirts of Weston Village and its western boundary was marked by a copse of trees on the summit of a hill known as Kelston Round just above the hamlet of North Stoke. To the south was a beautifully manicured lawn leading down to the landing stage on the river where a large boat with a single mast was moored along with two or three skiffs and rowing boats. This exquisite semi-rural paradise had been

Miriam Trandon's home since her marriage to the Honourable George Trandon in the 1730's

The rooms allocated to Jessica consisted of a neat sitting room, a larger bed room and a smaller annex for her maid. The place was well furnished and Janet's room was also home to a large copper bath (An arrangement that somehow made her feel uncomfortable!) The big windows were bright with southern sunshine and had the scent of pine from the polished mahogany tables and chairs. It seemed that they were going to be well looked after.

Lady Trandon warmly welcomed them back downstairs and insisted that they all took tea in her private sitting room where she told them a brief but somewhat embroidered version of her colourful life... About her visits to Court, her quality background and education and her blissful marriage followed by a reclusive dignified widowhood... It was all very neat and delivered with just the sort of superior modesty of a truly aristocratic Georgian Lady... The girls appeared to be suitably impressed but Janet's shrewd Cornish insight made her a little doubtful. The story was just a little too perfect and it seemed a well rehearsed performance..: And she was right because the truth was somewhat different... It was actually more interesting and eventful than Lady Trandon's fairy tale version of events!

Miriam Trandon was actually christened Mary Jane Besant in 1713. The third daughter of John Besant a successful Bristol coach builder, she was educated at an exclusive ladies college in fashionable Weston-Super-Mare and much like Jessica, she had been sent to Bath to add the final polish to enable her to enter Georgian society.

But here her father's plan faltered when, during an illicit visit to the Lower Assembly Rooms, she met up with hell raising rake and property speculator The Honourable Edward George Trandon , younger son of the Marquis of Staverton, who in the company of his friend Richard 'Beau' Nash, gambled and wenched wildly through the Spa town. Within a month, the precocious seventeen year old Miriam had moved in with Edward at his house in Kingsmead Square.

They were inseparable and deeply in love, she matching his every reckless move. One of her unusual talents was fencing, which had been taught to her by her brother, a noted Bristol duellist and people gasped in wonder to see her majestic figure dressed in frilly shirt and tight velvet breeches demonstrating her prowess with foil against the most capable of the men and she was not above fighting seriously if pushed. As evidenced when she challenged one of Nash's mistresses, the notorious courtesan Fanny Murray, to a duel with horse whips on the river meadows. Some months later she acted as a guide and companion to another famous courtesan Anne Bellamy a mistress of the Leader of the Parliamentary Wig Party Charles James Fox and who was described by one court observer as 'One of the most amorous and lascivious women of her age'.

Surreptitiously advised by the family solicitor that his father did not view his son's lifestyle favourably and realizing that it might affect his future prospects, Edward legitimised the liaison and married Miriam in 1738

Relieved to see his son was at last showing glimmerings of respectability and to anchor him more solidly to the family, the old Marquis bought him this unsold Queen Anne house that he had seen while inspecting the newly built crossing at Newton Ford on the Western borders of Bath. This single span stone bridge was built in 1735 by the ubiquitous Ralph Allen, who seemed to have his hand in every new development, for £800; a good deal cheaper than The City Engineer's estimate. It was Bath's second bridge and provided the affluent Upper Town gentry with direct access to the Bristol Road without them having to go to the centre to use the old crossing.

The Old Marquis did not actually like the house very much but he got it at a knockdown price from the bankrupt builder which made it more attractive. This was what became Trandon House though it was some years before it was fully finished. In truth, its main flaw was that it was built in brick, which was sadly out of favour at the time, everybody being seduced by Wood's Palladian masterpieces being constructed of the beautiful local golden stone.

A year later Miriam responded to her father-in-law's generosity by presenting Edward with a daughter who they called Chloe and eighteen months later a son they called Miles. By now even the wild living Edward had begun to appreciate the joys of family life: Not that it slowed him down so much as to give up his voracious partnership with the shady 'Beau' Nash and for the following two years the pair prospered from the fever of speculation which had grown in Bath.

Tragedy struck in the fateful year of '44 when Chloe contracted smallpox and died at the age of eight. Two years later in 1746 the Old Lord died of apoplexy after a heavy night on the amontillado and Edward became the 5th Lord Trandon, his elder brother George, who was making a fortune on the Pacific coast of Canada in the timber trade simply refused to come back to England to stake his claim. With his new found wealth Edward bought up the surrounding land and put the finishing touches to his riverside home which became the epitome of good taste and invitations to his outrageous parties there became like gold, featuring the most fashionable beauties of society and the pursuing fortune hunters and debauchees known as macaronis, due to their outlandish mock-Italian style costume.

However, Trandon's fortunes, like those of his fellow debauchee Nash, took a turn for the worst in the late 1740's during the first recession of the wild fever of building speculation but by ruthless sharp practice the pair engineered some dubious land deals with innocent greedy speculators and managed to stay afloat until a double tragedy hit Miriam when in the March of 1752 Edward was killed. It was his ninth duel and this time fate let him down: His pistol misfired and his opponent put a ball through him. This sad event was followed closely by the death of her son, Cornet Miles

Trandon at a minor skirmish in Brunswick. Beau Nash hit rock bottom too and was finally called to account by his creditors and spent the last few years of his life on a niggardly pension from the Bath Council in a rather grudging appreciation of all he had done to put the city on the map. He died in 1761.

As the clouds of her private grief gradually lifted, Miriam realised that, now at the age of forty she had become a prosperous independent widow. She also realized that there was no one left in a position to question her version of events and she could weave any fantastic version she chose of her past life.... Which she did with some enthusiasm!

Once more Janet's Cornish intuition had proved correct.

As the girls clattered back upstairs to their room they passed one of the servants who bowed and bade them welcome and hoped that they enjoyed their stay here. Jessica smiled graciously but Janet, ever conscious of her mistress' status, just sniffed and brushed past him with her nose in the air. Behind her back the servant pulled a face as he twirled a small green feather

13

ALEXANDER'S NEW REMIT

Alexander was a little annoyed to be summoned to the barracks so perfunctorily and without explanation by the Regional Commander. The dispatch rider had brought him the package of orders telling him to delegate the overseeing of the powder deliveries from the Wooley Mills to one of his subordinates in the Bath office and make haste to a special meeting with a government official from the War Office concerning a matter of great urgency and national security. To be honest though, he was not all that put out because he was duty bound to spend the week at Warminster on procurement matters anyway and the latest development at Trandon House made him glad to be away from all the upheaval.

Ten o' clock the following morning found him in the General's office in the company of Sir Everard Johnston and two senior officers from the War office and a ruddy faced fat civilian from Westminster. Beyond a brief introduction there were no further pleasantries or the usual formalities that protocol demanded and the

Government minister opened the proceedings directly.

Briefly he told them that recent persistent action by French privateers from St. Malo had become a serious risk to commerce in the western English Channel and it had been decided to transport the treasury money to pay the army in Ireland from Bristol instead of the usual route via Portsmouth. This meant that a military escort would have to be provided for the convoys from London. The route was well covered by garrisons along the Thames Valley as far west as Swindon but the escort from there to Bath would have to be provided by Warminster Command. Alexander could see that such an unexpected development would stretch his garrison to the limit as the depot was manned mainly by a battalion of one of the newly formed fast moving Light Infantry regiments and a few hundred Hanoverian dragoons, quite unsuitable for plodding escort duties. The Minister finished outlining the project and some of the logistical problems involved saying that his principle function was to find out how the plan could be implemented.

General Johnston said that The War Office had foreseen the same problems as Alexander. The open country along the River Kennet and over the Marlborough downs could be adequately provided for but the narrow winding roads through the often hilly villages between Bath and Bristol would be difficult for such a large convoy of heavy wagons so it had been decided to load the gold into a vessel at Bath and ship it directly to the Bristol docks along the safely navigable River Avon. It was to be Alexander's responsibility to procure vessels and secure storage for the valuable cargo in Bath: The scheme had to be up and running within two months! Not easy to set up in such a short time frame.

Although the meeting had been held in strict secrecy a young clerk had been present at some of it, bringing them coffee and refreshments and taking away the used items… and the subject of the discussion had become plain to him. Such information had a high value in the back street taverns of the town and it was not long before he found a willing buyer. As he returned to the kitchen two of the scullery maids were washing dishes and swapping barracks gossip. Hearing him come in, one of them turned and sneered at him.

"Oh aye, Bradley Thomas. An' jus' where you bin all this toime eh? Ad yer ear to the keyhole, did yer? Wocha find out then? Which 'orse to back, or oo's a-swivin' oo in Bath these days?"
She looked at her fat faced mate and they dissolved into shrieks of inane laughter. Curious as to the source of this merriment the yard porter popped his head round the door to see what it was all about... Just in time to catch another outburst from the vampire at the sink.

"Oh, aye, an' jus' what do you want in 'ere then, Tom, you nosy bugger?....An' ave ye any idea jus' 'ow daft ye look wi' that green feather in yore cap?"

At the end of his long day the clerk handed in his docket at the guardroom and scurried past the stone-like sentry and out of the sally port of the big gate into the busy evening thoroughfare outside. As a decoy move he made his way into a tobacco shop just in case someone from the barracks might be trailing him and dallied a few minutes over buying a cheap clay pipe. Sensing that he was in the clear he left the shop and headed towards the rough taverns and bawdy houses at Cold Harbour on the old Dilton Marsh road. The dusk was quickly drawing in when he saw the light of the lantern above a rusting and faded sign announcing the Ram's Head tavern. At the door of the tumbledown inn he was almost bundled to the ground by a struggling group of drunks who were being ejected by the irate bulky landlord and two of his barmen. Having given the last of them a hearty kick up the backside to help him on his way the publican turned to greet his new customer.

"Hello there Young Bradley... Jus' finished then, 'ave ee? Th'art workin' 'late at yon barracks.. Mus' be payin' well, eh? C'm'n in an' tell us all the news about the war... Tha' must 'ear a lot o' things in there."

Bradley shuffled through the low door into the smoky interior and up to the plank bar where he ordered a mug of ale and a gill of gin to keep out the evening chill. He saw that there were several pork knuckles roasting on a tin tray at the kitchen fire behind the bar and ordered one of them too.

Taking a seat at a wobbly wooden bench to await his supper

142

he took in his surroundings. It was the usual scene in this shabby tavern as in all the others: A log fire was glowing in the blackened chimney with wisps of smoke leaking out of the ill fitting bricks, with a selection of scarred tables and rough stools against the walls and the usual crew of early evening drinkers leaning on the bar or playing a desultory game of Penny Jack in one of the corners; Some of them had been there all afternoon and were now showing signs of wear as they bravely tried to stick it out in the hope that somebody they knew would flop in and buy them a drink.... But the man that Bradley was hoping to see had not yet arrived.

"Yew see anythin' o' Rob these days, Leonard?" He asked. Leonard straightened up from the cider barrel he was tapping and looked at the questioner. "An' which Rob might that be then, Bradley?"

"That there Rob wi' the foreign name, Carrus or summat... Y' know, 'im as used to run wi' Brooksie afore 'e got topped on the Blanford road. 'Im wi' the good looking sister wot Brooksie tubbed up!"

"Oh that Rob... Dacarius you mean? Naw.. Not a lot really... But he does come in from toime to toime... Usually when 'ee's got summat on offer, know worra mean? Lives down in Bath these days...Set up 'ome in Widcome Village wi' Susan Blythe, ye know, that blacksmith's daughter from Frome. I think 'is sister is there an' all but she lost the child, I think t'were the shock at seein' Brooksie dead. Why d'ye ask?"

Bradley weighed his answer carefully.

"Oh, nuffin really... Jus' that I 'avent see him around much lately. If yew do see 'im tell im that I wuz a-lookin' fer 'im, thaz all." This time it was the suspicious landlord who was cautious.

"Oh aye, jus' that eh? Well, Bradley, jus' you remember. If you got summat goin' on I'm allus on the look out fer a good thing to stand in on. Y'eer? Don' you fergit that!

"Oh, right on. O'course Leonard, I wont fergit ye. That's if I 'ear of anythin' of course." Anxious to get off this tack he changed the subject.

"Anyhow, what's he doin' these days, still gorr' is wagon?

"His wagon?" Scoffed Leonard. "He's got three of 'em now... an' a big trow on the Avon. He works for that Ralph Allen, shiftin' buildin' stone all along the river to Canesham an' beyond. Goes as far as Brizzle sometimes! They say that when the new canal's done Mr. Allen will be sendin' stone to Lunnon as well. Oh aye, He's a busy lad now, is our Rob!"

As an after thought he added that Rob sometimes got in on a Tuesday night after Market Day and that he would mention to him that Bradley was looking for him if he saw him. Just at that moment a serving maid came bustling in with a wooden platter loaded with Bradley's smoking pork knuckle, cabbage and roast potatoes causing much comment from the topers at the bar. Bradley just smiled at their ribald shouts opened his clasp knife and got stuck into the feast. He had got the information he'd been seeking.

14

THE CONVOY

Two ruddy cheeked grizzled sergeants of the 35th Regiment gazed through the window of the Tudor beamed Stork Inn on Marlborough's high street at the leading elements of the bullion convoy as it passed by. One of them, a powerful, corpulent red faced brute wiped his mouth with his sleeve and commented.

"That young Cornet seems to know how to handle his mare... He's up an' down that there column like a mother hen... And Old Albert is makin' the lobsters step it out an' all... Does bloody well 'e does, considerin' that thigh wound 'e got in 'olland 'cos they wuz a-goin' to saw 'is bloody leg off but lucky fer 'im the surgeon sobered up just in time.

His companion just grunted and stuck his head out of the door to review the marching troops and decided that they could manage another mug of ale before they were going to be needed to take over the rearguard and he signalled the innkeeper to fill 'em up again.

So far it had taken them four days from the depot at Reading where they had taken over from a company of the Thames Valley Yeomanry and there was another day to go before they reached the Warminster barracks where they would hand over responsibility to an escort from the North Somerset Militia. That's if the road stayed dry... Any heavy rain would delay the convoy by a couple of days or more. Three heavy high sided wagons rolled by and the soldiers appraised them with knowing glances.

"Ow much would you say they've got aboard then? Tis a bloody 'eavy load by the look of them shires. The sweat's a-rollin' off of 'em."

George ran a practiced eye over the road, noting the deep wheel ruts.

"Reckon there's a good two ton on each of 'em... at least. And that's a lot of back-pay money. Reckon there'll be a bloody mutiny if owt goes wrong. Tis bad enough being stationed in Ireland at the best o'times an' I'm glad that we're not on the draft, I can tellee!"

As the last wagon rolled clumsily by the veterans drained their drinks and stomped out to join the rearguard, thumping and cursing the marching soldiers as they passed.

Quartermaster Sergeant George Torrens was wise to have doubted their estimated time of arrival at Warminster barracks because the rain did fall and they were delayed. All had gone well along the Bath road as far as Calne where the convoy had to change direction across country towards Warminster via the poor second class roads. It was here that the clouds opened up and they were

146

forced to bivouac in the town square at Melksham, the troops having to bed down under the wagons with just a quart of ale and bread and cheese for supper. It was late in the afternoon of the following day when the weary convoy rolled through the majestic iron gates of the Warminster barracks.

The Guard presented arms and the garrison's drums and fifes piped up a welcome to the soaking footsore escort companies and the steaming draft horses as they passed into the main parade square and were directed to their respective destinations. Garrison troops took over the security duties and the escorts crowded into the massive drill hall where a meal of steaming mutton stew was awaiting them.

Three of the wagons which were loaded with supplies for the depot were detached from the column and formally handed over by Sergeant George to his opposite number in the garrison, after which he joined some of the other NCOs in their mess hall. The Convoy Marshal checked that the other wagons and carts were in good condition and that their loads were correct and well stowed before he signalled two of the drivers to move to the opposite side of the parade ground where a fresh escort awaited them. These heavy vehicles each drawn by two powerful shires, contained the six iron banded oak chests of money for the Army of Ireland and were driven through the wide open gates of the inner citadel to await forward transport to Bath the following day.

All this activity was avidly noted by the prying eyes of Bradley Thomas from his vantage point in the Commanders Office...

It did not take him long to identify the person who could supply a little more data on the bullion cargo. A sudden noise from the hall and the click of riding boots on the polished parquet made him realize that Major Coulston was returning from the parade and he scuttled down the back stairs to make the acquaintance of Sergeant George Torrens and invite him to join him in a drink and a little willing feminine company at a welcoming tavern on the Dilton Marsh road later in the evening.

By nine thirty Sergeant George and his mate Sergeant Topping were firmly ensconced in the Ram's Head tavern, quaffing ale and cider at Bradley's expense and warming to the charms of Melody Watson a dumpling breasted barmaid, well known for her enthusiastic indulgence in carnal pleasures. She had also been one of the girls who attended to the off duty requirements of Captain Brooks' robber gang. The redcoats took one look at her and thought that their Christmas goodies had come early as she swayed to the table to take their orders.

"Evenin' Bradley. Oo's yore 'andsome friends then?" She cooed.

Bradley took the bait and introduced the two NCOs glowingly saying that they were on a special mission of national importance. Melody's mouth sounded a round admiring ooh and said that she loved soldiers and guns too. At this the men looked askance and Topping said scornfully "Guns? Wot d'yew know 'bout guns, lass?

148

Melody proudly answered "I can tellee Mister Soldier Boy that I know a lot about 'em. An' I can use one too! My father wuz a keeper down at Longleat an' he taught me to shoot when I were thirteen, an' when he died 'e left me his gun."

"Oh aye?" Said George doubtfully "An' wot kind of a piece is it?"

At this remark Melody bridled, saying "Well if'n yew must know, 'tis a German 'untin' rifle called a Jaeger an' I've won prizes wi'it. You ask Bradley 'ere. Captain Brookes used to say as I wuz the best women shooter wor 'eed ever seed. "

Not knowing who Captain Brookes was and not wishing to sour the evening the Redcoats questioned her no further.

An hour later they were well into their cups thoroughly enjoying themselves and spouting off happily about the secret nature of their convoy. Bradley pretended to be fascinated by this confidential information but in fact by now, thanks to the gossiping drivers, it was a well known fact. However Bradley was seeking more detailed information on the load and judiciously timed his questions.

The ordered food arrived at the table. The large platter of boiled gammon and spinach with roast parsnips on the side was served by the luscious Melody, who caused the fascinated redcoat sergeants to gasp as she artfully flashed an erect dark pink nipple from the low neckline of her peasant blouse. Bradley saw the distraction and took his chance.

149

"Well, Sergeant, 'ow you goin' to get all that coin to Brizzle, then?" George's eyes were following Melody's swaying hips to the bar and answered absently.

"Er.., y'wot? Oh it's goin' down the river by barge under escort direct to the trooper a-waitin' at Avonmouth. S'not goin' to Brizzle at all, see. Clever that, eh?"

"Oh aye, Oi see now. Right smart move that is, 'specially if you gorra good escort wi' it. But won't some of the river men hear them chests a-rattlin' an get suspicious…; Y' know, with it bein' all secret, like?"

George saw the bar girl returning with a platter of bread and straightening up to catch her attention, he said loftily,

"Oh no, Lad, that's all been attended to. The coin is packed tight in tarred canvas bags. That makes 'em easy to manhandle an' no noise, see?"

Melody had arrived at the table with tankards of ale and moved the big platter strategically opposite George so as to give him another flash of her charms and leaned admiringly on the table as George continued to try to impress her with his knowledge and his important duties.

"'An' as for escorts," He said "We've got a special squadron of Hanoverian Dragoons in charge of that detail. Red hot they are, bloody big brutes on big 'orses. Iron disciplined an' they only speak German… And their commander, Major Mahler is a right bastard so there's not much chance o' them givin' owt away, is there?"

150

Puffing up with self importance he gave Melody a gap toothed smile and helped himself to some gammon. She in turn served him some potatoes saying how much she would like to hear more about his interesting life later when she got off duty…: Perhaps in the privacy of her room? George gulped!

While this intimate exchange was taking place, a scruffy tavern handyman was at the nearby hearth raking the fire. As he dusted off his grimy hands on the seat of his breeches, a small green feather peeped out from his waistcoat pocket.

15

THE PREPARATION

"So Bradley, when did you find out about all o' this?"

They were in best room of Rob's house on the edge of Widcome Village where he had brought his visitor, the mysterious meeting having been arranged by his sister Rachel when she had returned from a visit to a friend in Warminster where she had found a note waiting for her from the landlord of the Rams Head.

Bradley Thomas looked warily around him and told Rob about the convoy and how he had overheard it being discussed in the adjutant's office in the barracks. A little unsure of Rob's lack of enthusiasm for the project he went into the further details he had found out from the two sergeants. Rob did not interrupt him but sat puffing on his long church warden pipe taking in the information and carefully weighing up the possibilities.

"An' where, might I ask, do you fit into this yeer adventure? Are you jus' selling me information or what? "

"Oh no, Mr Rob, if'n you'll get summat goin' Oi wants to be

part of it wi' you. Jes' fer me fair share, y'know. Oi'm fed up wi' bein' a dogsbody fer them ooray 'enrys at the soddin' barracks. Wanna to 'ave a bit o' excitement in me life an'I'll be withee all the way."

Rob had a final puff on his pipe and said cautiously

"Well, Brad me lad, the fust thing you've gotta learn if you fancy coming along-a me, is to keep your gob shut, right? 'Ow many others 'ave you told about this already. Who else knows?"

"As for who knows about the load, well, ye know wot them drivers are loik. It don't tek long fer them t'get the whisper, do it? But nobody but me knows the full score 'bout where, when an' ow its bein' shifted. Lionel at the pub thinks that I'm jus' lookin' fer cheap drink by bringin' 'im customers from the barracks an' Melody can't remember the difference between one cock or another so long as she get paid right. Speakin' o' which….."

He left the question floating in the air and looked steadily at Rob who smiled and said quietly.

"Ah, I wondered 'ow long t'would be afore you got round to that. Tellee worra'll do, I'll give ee four crowns for yore trouble an' the news you bring. If it proves to be correct, well, there's a lot more to come..,. But if'n it's not true or if'n you blow off yore gob to anyone, I shall be a-looking for redress, know what I mean?"

Bradley gulped and nodded as Rob continued.

"It's too late now to catch the mail coach home so you can bed down in the stables. There's fresh straw an' plenty of 'orse

153

cloths to keep ye warm but I want ye gone by mornin' an' no mention o' this visit to anyone. Call in 'ere afore yew leave an' I'll give ye further instructions, right?"

After his guest had gone Rob bolted the door then, drawing his candle nearer he began to sketch out his plan. When dawn came his sister found him asleep, slumped across the scarred kitchen table with a blanket round his shoulders and a broken quill in his hand and an untidy pile of crumpled paper on the floor. Under his elbow rested his carefully prepared plans for the new venture that would change their lives. He was ready to make the move.

Rachel had known for some time that her brother was becoming restless in spite of his relative prosperity. The stone carrying contracts with Mr Allen and Sir George Pulteney's factor brought in good money. So good in fact, that Rob had been able to buy two more broad-beam trows to carry building stone to Bristol and beyond. Then there was also the new canal. Construction there was going apace and it would not be long before there might be loads as far as London too. To her the future looked bright and secure but somehow it just wasn't enough for Rob. He missed the excitement of the old days but she definitely did not. She remembered all too vividly the life with Brooksie and although there were the highs, most of the time it was a constant battle to keep ahead of the law… And she didn't want anymore of that life, thank you! But with Rob it was different.

She used to think that they had a close bond but these days you never knew just what he was thinking. She decided that the best thing to do at the moment was to leave him to plan his new adventure.

Barrels! .... That's what he needed to get hold of and he remembered a wine importer at Sea Mills who had just such merchandise for sale. They were big old tuns that had been used for the storage of sherry and were now too old and leaky. On his next trip to Bristol he had called in and bought eight of them. On the same trip he called in at the Saltford lock where he sought out a retired sail maker he knew and giving him the dimensions ordered sixty tarred canvas bags with drawstring necks. And some three foot squares of the same material. The old man was grateful for the work and Rob paid him half the money up front.

The next thing was to check out the place where the bullion chests were to be held in Bath before onward shipping to Bristol Docks. According to Bradley's information it was a riverside building on the right bank of the Avon just below fashionable South Parade where the ferry crossed. There was a landing stage built on wooden piles and an area of hard standing on the bank itself. The building, which was used as a drill hall and depot for the militia, stood back from this. It was brick built with a locked and barred gate opening direct onto the loading dock. There was also an under croft for storage with a side door and it was here that the chests were to be kept. Further information supplied by the mole in Warminster revealed that for security reasons, it had been decided that the chests would only be moved two days before the trooper was due to sail to Ireland which gave them two weeks to execute Rob's plan.

Bradley called in two days later saying that Rob's instructions had been carried out and handed over the soap impressions of the four padlock keys sealing the chests and the date they were due to arrive in Bath. He also confirmed that the old gang members that Rob had selected were available and would be arriving the next day. A locksmith in Keynsham was instructed to produce a set of keys from the impressions and to supply six new padlocks and keys. The five gang members duly arrived and were accommodated at Rob's riverside compound in a hut used for overnight accommodation by crews returning to Bristol.

The Avon Navigation project had been finished in 1727 and the river had been regularly dredged and constantly up-dated with new locks, bridges and loading docks all along the route to Bristol and Rob remembered a certain clause in his stone carrying contracts. He carefully perused his documents and came across the clause he was seeking in the small print at the bottom of Mr Allen's agreement. Although couched in flowery legalese and designed to cover any possible public liability due to neglect of the riverbank, it stated that if any contractor became aware that the bank should be crumbling or in general need of repair he was to attend to it directly.

'Well,' thought Rob. 'That ferry landing stage looks a bit neglected so I am duty bound to see to it directly, as the contract requires.'

The following morning his gang began to earn their corn by filling the tarred bags with broken stones and loading them into the barrels leaving about nine inches of space at the top filled up with loose chippings and the lid tamped on and tacked. As each barrel was filled it was rolled aboard the trow. When they were all loaded Rob told them to put a couple of empty ones aboard too and warping the trow across the current to the landing stage they heaved the cargo ashore using a block and tackle from the sail beam. There was some grumbling and moaning about the manual labour involved but the thought that they each would be over a hundred guineas richer when the project was finished kept them going. It was a very impressive sum indeed for the times... it was more than they ever saw working the highways with Cap'n Brooks. In fact, for some of them it was more money than they had ever seen.

Once more Rachel was dispatched to rendezvous with Bradley to get a progress report and give him further orders regarding the temptress Melody Watson. She returned with the news that the convoy would be arriving at Bath five days later.

News of the coming arrival went round town like wildfire and innkeepers got in extra supplies while beggars, peddlers and street entertainers jostled for position on the sidewalks. Bluff red faced fairground men set up whirligigs and boat swings in the squares and parks, even on vacant lots of land beyond the old walls, while sweetmeat and pie sellers pitched their stalls in the busy streets causing severe traffic problems. Also there were the quack herbalists selling their miracle cures and a few Gipsy fortune tellers who also doubled as agents for the back street abortionists so much in demand these days. (The most favoured at the time being the Carew sisters in Milk Street.) On the riverside green of Norfolk Crescent a prize ring was roped off and a large hoarding set up announcing the big fight between the local champion Ben Harper and 'Crusher Curbishley' a tough ex coal miner from Bolton who was travelling the country challenging all comers. It was a grudge match as the two had met once before but the Watch broke it up when violence exploded with the supporters. The book makers too were anticipating a big crowd.. It was Carnival Time!

A detachment of the Bath Militia complete with its drum and fife band was waiting to escort the colourful parade from Claverton on the Warminster Road. As it rumbled along above the village of Bathampton cattle rushed about the river meadows startled by the rasping trumpets of the Hanoverian dragoons. Finally, with the band playing patriotic airs they turned majestically into the splendid new boulevard of Great Pulteney Street in a colourful and impressive cavalcade, the proud cavalry chargers prancing and tossing their manes while the beautifully uniformed troopers sat rigidly upright in the saddles their brass helmets and the silver buttons on their pale blue tunics sparkling in the sun. Supply wagons and equipment carts rumbled noisily by while the drivers cracked there whips and shouted to impress the young girls in the crowd. At the centre of the parade were the three high sided wagons carrying the bullion chests closely escorted by the tramping red coated militia.

All went well until they reached Laura place and the Argyle Street approach to Pulteney Bridge where the column lost some of it's cohesion on the muddy ramp leading up to it. Two different architects had been involved in construction of the bridge and with the later development of Pulteney's Bathwick Estate and there was a difference in the levels roughly closed by a muddy potholed ramp and further constricted by a couple of iron bollards.

Luckily the confusion had managed to sort itself out before the parade turned into High Street where the Mayor and a deputation of City Fathers stood on the Guildhall steps to take the salute. Standards and lance pennants were dipped, officers flashed their sabres in salute and even the shuffling part-timers of the Militia smartened up as they passed by and on to Kingsmead Square where they were dismissed and stormed into the rough taverns of Avon Street. The bullion wagons however, escorted by the dragoons turned into Orange Grove and made their way to the riverside Militia depot where the precious cargo was to be held until the next move. A gang working on the landing stage watched the arrival with interest.

Everybody was caught up in the euphoria including a bunch of drunks who marched along behind the cavalry led by a shouting shabby tramp waving a stick with a green feather tied to it.

159

16

ACTION STATIONS

Thomas Pennington snored gently next to his pleasantly plump young wife under a mound of quilts and coverlets in their vast curtained bed in the large house on the river bank west of Bath. They had had a wonderful supper of roast goose rounded off by Burgundy wine and French Brandy and had come to bed tired and happy. She was in that delicious state of mind when one wakes in the middle of the night from a pleasantly carnal dream and hoping to prolong her arousal she slid a warm hand across the ample rump next to her. Thomas stirred and turned towards her and gently sought out her full young breasts as a growing erection brought him to full consciousness. She sighed and pulled him close, easing herself into a comfortable position to receive her husband. God knows, she thought, it did not happen all that often these days so she wanted to get the best from his response... but before the situation could move to the next stage there was a ferocious banging on the studded oak front door.

They froze and a look of frustration and resignation passed over her face... After all she reasoned, he was getting on a bit...And she had married him for his money but she did expect a bit of conjugal pleasure now and then. As for Thomas, he immediately forgot about the developing trip to heavenly bliss and sat bolt upright listening to the dogs and his servant thundering up the stairs. The bedroom door burst open and they all came crowding in, the dogs barking at the excitement of the hammering at the door and the general atmosphere of the emergency. Leading them was Walter their manservant

"Fire, Master!" he yelled, his nightshirt covered by a tattered blanket and his hair wild, his face still puffed with sleep. "The mill's afire, big un' too!" He shouted, "That big shed on the landing dock is blazin' like a good 'un!! You'm better come quick!"

Pennington shot out of bed and pulled back the heavy window drapes to be greeted by a bright orange glow which lit the room as the fire roared through the wooden warehouses on the river bank. As he opened the window the sweet smoky smell of burning sugar filled the bedroom.

"Good God Almighty!" He raged "How did it start and when?"

He stood for a moment dumb-founded at the sight. Nothing like this had ever happened before. The big shed was usually empted once a load had been landed but this time the barrels of molasses for processing had been left there for a week or so while a subsiding part of the landing dock was being repaired.

He dressed rapidly, throwing on anything that was to hand and hurried outside while his disgusted wife roused the housemaids, noting sourly on the big case clock at the foot of the stairs that it was just after midnight

The blaze was now consuming the riverside buildings one by one and was increasing as more combustible barrels burst, further spreading the flaming molasses over nearby property. The servant looked vacantly at Thomas as though expecting some kind of miracle.

"Oi sent Dickon fer the fire engine Massa, soon as I yeerd the fust bang...T'was loik started by a hexploshun or summat. You could smell the powder in the air. Fust one to go was the boat shed. Blew up, he did!"

While they were waiting for the fire engine to arrive the few servants and younger maids were marshalled into a bucket chain from the river to try to prevent the conflagration from spreading. It was only partially successful as there were so few of them but soon gawping Twerpington villagers began to arrive on the scene and the men were pressed into the bucket chain. The main riverbank commercial sheds were now too far gone so the chain concentrated its efforts on the outbuildings of the big house and the equipment sheds while Thomas pondered the mystery of it all.

He had inherited the business from his father who had managed to get a contract to supply the Navy with rum and had

162

imported large amounts of sugar cane waste to process into molasses, a prime source of the navy grog. The product he made was far purer than the imported kind and he then began to supply it to several Bath bakeries as sweetening agent. It was in short, a very successful enterprise and Thomas could find no reason for what he now considered an arson attack. He had no competitors and was a respected member of the Bath Chamber of Commerce and a Masonic Brother to boot... So who would do such a thing and why?

By now the word had got around and there was a crowd on the far bank of the river, shouting and hooting wildly, some of them boarding boats to get across the river and the courtyard of the house was becoming crowded with locals and more than a few outsiders bent on seeing what they could glean from the chaos. Somewhere a window was broken and a fight erupted between the servants and two men who were trying to force their way further into the yard. The mob was getting excited and there was a feeling of looting in the air. Thomas moved fast to dispatch one of the stable boys to alert the military camp at Albion Warf on the Western Riverside. (Ever since the cloth worker's mobs had attacked the Bath mills back '97 and almost overpowered the local militia, a company of regular light infantry had been posted there to suppress any further riots.)

There was also a detachment of the Hanoverian Dragoons posted there too for just such an emergency

Watching it all from the stern of an old battered rowing boat was a vermin hunting ratter who was bringing his batch of skins to a riverside glove factory on Locksbridge Island. The small green feather in his cap could be clearly seen in the light from the roaring inferno on the far bank.

Half a mile to the east, three men and a boy sat in a boat hidden in the reeds at a bend in the river and noted the blaze with satisfaction. A man with a smoke-blackened face tapped the boy on the shoulder and told him to get ashore and unhitch the grazing bay pony. "Tell Rob that it's goin' like Hades! An' that the fire engine on the Brizzle road has just passed by us... Unerstan', Lad?" With nod, the boy jumped out of the boat and flung himself on the pony and galloped back across the flood plain meadows to Widcome. The two galloping boys reached their respective destinations at the same time.

Rob had been waiting impatiently and as soon as the messenger arrived with his news Rob sprang into action. He roused his disgruntled crew and hustled them aboard a boat and warped across the river and moored up just below the landing stage awaiting the signal to go ashore. For several days now they had become a familiar sight on the right bank spreading stones and gravel and checking the oak piles supporting the landing stage. The keys had arrived and been tested by Rob and Melody had been briefed about

164

what was expected of her. She asked excitedly if she should bring her gun but Rob gave her a firm no and just do what she was being paid to do!

The beating of drums and bugle calls from the river told them that the militia were being called out and the clatter of hooves and rattle of equipment accompanied by the guttural German commands on the road nearby confirmed the fact. This was the half battalion of Hanoverians, the only regular cavalry in the city, acting as a quick response unit to hold back the rioters at the fire until the Light Infantry arrived from their camp.

It was time to go. The under croft gate was silently unlocked and Melody went into action with the gawping watchman at the front door of the building. Having made his acquaintance in his local tavern in Horse Street in a casual way, she had told him that she was visiting a sick sister and needed to get away from the gloom of the house and relax with a few drinks now and then. A passing kiss and a warm embrace had fired him up and they had met in the pub on a couple of occasions since.

"'Ello, Percy, me lad." She said sidling up to him under the portico. "Wocha fink's a-goin' on then? Wot's all this clatter an' noise fer?"

Percy couldn't believe his luck.

"Oh... Evenin' Helen." He gasped. "Fancy a- seein' you 'ere. Oi niver 'spected that. Bin a-visitin' 'ave yer?"

Melody liked being called Helen, she thought it suited her better than her birth name; it gave her a bit of dignity and poise so she played the part with conviction.

"Oh, Percy," She said, wiping a tear from her eye. "I jus' 'ad to get away.. Drivin' me mad she is! Wot I need is a few gins an' a bit o private company, I do… But go on, tell us."

Percy's jaw had gone slack at the prospect of a private rendezvous and slobbered a garbled explanation. "It sounds loik a riot or summat. Oi yeer'd 'em drummin' up the militia 'bout ten minutes ago an' now them Germans is streamin' down the Brizzle Road an' there's a fire glow o'er Twerpington. Reckon it's serious."

"Oh, sounds excitin' don't it! Shall us go an' ave a look? Or shall us jes' go down to Avon Street fer a jar or two? Nobody's goin' to be a-missin yew wi'all this excitement 'appenin."

Percy looked up and down the deserted street and said breathlessly. "S'pose it'll be alright... The sentry went off duty an hour back, so you jes' wait ere while I get me keys an' check that the under croft gate's locked and I'll be wi'thee direckly, alright?"

Bradley who had been watching the exchange gave a hurried whistle of warning to the waiting robbers who huddled behind the tall barrels in the trow. Percy came down the side of the building and shook the under croft gate to confirm it was securely locked and the crew held their breath as he looked over the tranquil river and he relieved himself on the brick wall before hurrying back to his promised evening delight. Melody grabbed his arm and whispered in his ear and hustled him off towards Kingsmead. Bradley was glad to

166

see them finally tripping off down the road arm in arm. As they disappeared from sight he hurried back and gave a low whistle to start.

Rob led some of the team ashore, through the gate and down to the under croft where the chests were lodged while the others rolled a barrel into the landing stage gate behind him. The keys worked well and with only the faintest creak from the hinges the heavy oak lid opened smooth as silk in a fitting tribute to the skill of the master locksmith. He opened the drawstring on one of the bags to find that this chest was filled with Maria Theresa dollars, which he marked on the lid with a MT. The sovereigns obviously being in the other chests

By now a human chain had been formed and the bags were passed from hand to hand to be stacked in the empty barrel. A second barrel was rolled alongside the first and forced upright, the lid levered open and a bag of stones passed back down to the chest. The process was then repeated with the next barrel until the full load had been exchanged. At this point Rob opened up the next chest and locked the first one with the new padlocks that would delay any inspection before their arrival at their destination across the water.

He was fortunately alone in the under croft when he opened the fourth chest and found on top of the tarred bags ten square canvas covered packages bearing the Treasury seal. Feeling the weight of one he realised that they were gold ingots and quickly hid them in a darkened corner before anyone came back in from the river bank,

167

intending to retrieve them later. The fewer people who knew about them the better!

By the time Melody and Percy returned in a gin and brandy fog to put the final touches to their intimate evening the whole operation was finished and the scene looked totally undisturbed with gates locked and the barrels of stone still in the places they had been. The militia came marching by to Grove Street gaol, thumping and cursing a few unhappy captured looters and the dragoons clopped slowly back to their barracks, somewhat disappointed at not even having drawn their sabres. The fire was out and the riot had been successfully quelled. Everybody was happy.

All, that is, except Percy, who somehow in all the excitement lost sight of his beautiful Helen!

Three days after all the excitement Rob was sitting on the wall of his compound having his mid-morning drink and keeping a watchful eye on his barrels across the water when he heard the sharp bark of orders and looked up to see a neat naval cutter heading up river. As it pulled in to the opposite bank he watched its progress with keen interest. On the side of the prow HMS Columbia and a number six were emblazoned in white and above on deck stood a red-coated marine with his musket scouring the approaching bank for signs of trouble as did two others at the stern.

The crew, six tough looking men with tarred pigtails in tight striped jerseys and broad brimmed black straw hats, were at the sweeps and went about their business with smooth efficiency while in the stern sheets a young midshipman in a reefer jacket and an older officer with two gold rings on his sleeve were watching the approaching shore. Next to the mate, who was also acting as helmsman, stood a tall, sinister, hollow cheeked figure dressed in a long black tarred canvas coat and a broad brimmed hat low over his eyes that Rob recognised instantly as Jim Hornsby the head river pilot on the Avon Navigation. He was pointing to the bank as the young officer's voice rang out

"Bring her in handsomely Mr Norris if y'please. Easy now."

The grizzled mate clenched his teeth and muttered a sullen.

"Aye, aye, sir. Steady as she goes, lads"

One could sense his disapproval. He was a deep sea sailor who hated this inland traffic. What did they think he was a bloody river rat or summat?

The oars were shipped smartly upright then slid into the gunnels as the boat eased to the landing stage. While one man jumped ashore to tie up, the others bent a block and tackle to the yard arm and then jumped neatly to join him. Waiting for them with keys to the barred gate was Percy the watchman who stood aside as the chests were trundled forward on rollers and swung aboard. Percy was astounded to see such efficiency while the mate stood by with his Malacca cane to maintain the pace. An hour later and the cutter had been warped round and with the crew pulling easy, headed off back

169

downstream to her mother ship waiting at Avonmouth. Rob watched them leave with satisfaction and wondered just how long it would be before heads started rolling.

At the main British military base in Ireland just outside Dublin, Lieutenant Colonel Moran-Cooper, Head of the Fiscal department of the army in Ireland, stood staring out of his first floor window at the incessant rain pounding the parade ground. His face was white and he was biting his thin lips in fury and frustration.

Barely an hour ago he had been elated to see the escorted convoy arriving... At last he thought, here was the money he had been desperately waiting for. And just in the nick of time too! The troops were on the fringes of mutiny, tired of waiting months for their back pay and only yesterday the Oberst of the Hessian mercenaries had hinted that they might be recalled if they were not paid soon. On top of which, the civilian contractors were also threatening to suspend supplies unless their bills were met. Yes, an hour ago he could see the cloud lifting from him. But now things had changed.

His Chief Clerk had come to his office with a problem. Apparently the purser of the troopship Columbia was insisting on a signed Certificate of Acceptance for the chests before he could hand over his precious cargo.

"Well then, just check the contents and bring me the document to sign... What is the problem?" The Colonel asked

170

The clerk shuffled his feet in embarrassment and replied that he could not do that as the keys sent with the trunks did not fit the padlocks sealing them. He cringed at the Colonel's outburst but went on to explain timidly that also as the chests were actually Crown property he could not damage them by force either. He said that he would have to have the proper keys which must still be at the Treasury and scuttled out to escape the further outburst.

"Oh Good Jesus! I don't believe it!" Moran-Cooper shouted to the empty room. "Who the bloody hell was responsible for this fiasco? This means that it's going to be at least another two weeks before we get the keys; even if they can find 'em!.. Just what am I supposed to do now?"

As calmer thoughts took over, he decided to drop the whole problem onto the lap of the Governor and poured himself a large brandy,

----

Back across the water in the back room of the Ram Inn in Widcome a group of rough looking men were enjoying the contents of a small keg of Navy rum. Rob Dacarius held his pot high and addressed the assembly.

"Well Lads, 'ere we are then, 'appy as sandboys wi' a job well done, eh?"

Rachel and a couple of village girls finished clearing the tables of their supper of boiled beef and cabbage and left them alone with their pipes to talk... Rob waited until the girls had closed the door before

171

continuing

"But jes' afore I divvy up yore dues I gotta word o'caution for you." They all perked up at this and paid attention. "Any o' you lot remember Charlie Burns? 'Im wot got on the wrong side o' Brooksie?"

"Oh aye... Recall 'im well, I do" Chimed a big bruiser in a crushed tricorne hat and a dirty yellow striped waistcoat that was living out it's last days in a losing battle to confine his belly. "They found 'im in the Severnake Woods, chained to stump, 'e wuz. The wolves 'ad 'got to 'im. Why wot's 'e got to do wi' owt?

"Well," Continued Rob, sipping his toddy. "As you said, 'e fell foul o' Brooksie. Talked too much 'e did. One o' them dockers at Poole saw 'im comin' out o' the customs 'ouse there and three o' our lads got lifted, so Brooksie called in the Redemptors and left it to them to sort out. You've all 'eard about them, aintcha? They don't tek no prisoners I can tellee that!"

A silence descended on the smoky room as the gang looked at each other.

"Y'see I wuz Brooksie's right 'and man in them days an' 'e introduced me to one o' the Elders, thaz wot them Redemptors call their parsons, though they'z more than jus' preachers. They 'ave awesome powers and their people obey them without question... Well, to cut along story short, I still pay my tithes to 'em and they are sworn to 'elp me in any difficulty I may 'ave with the law. Or even outside of it." He added.

172

As the hidden content of his message became clear to them they gulped and sat in silence waiting to hear what Rob had to say next.

"But we don' wanna put a damper on things do we lads... So let us get down to business eh? Bradley bring us one o' they bags frum th' corner there an' put un on the table."

Bradley did as he was bid and Rob undid the drawstring to reveal a cascade of gold and silver coins. As they gasped and felt at the coins he said.

"There' be six o' these bags, one for each o' you. They's got eighty goldies in each one an' thaz jus fer now. If'n your good an' keeps yore 'ead's down an' yore gobs shut there'll be another forty guineas each to come at Michaelmas but if'n you don't, well jes' remember poor old Charley Burns an' my Redemptor friends... Y'unnerstan'? Now off ye pop an' await my call.. Leave slow, one at a toime. An' Bradley, you stay 'ere. I've got summat fer you to do fer me. G'night, Lads."

He stood by the door to see that nobody stopped off at the bar before leaving then he sat down with Bradley, poured a couple of tots and asked the clerk how he had enjoyed his first job and how would he feel about coming onto the payroll. Bradley was enthusiastic as ever and said that if Rob gave him a chance he would prove to be a great asset to him.

"You recall what I said about the Redemptors dontcha? Well you think on... Cos if'n you decide to throw in yore lot wi' me there's no way back. Are ye sure yore ready fer that?"

Bradley nodded and assured Rob that he had no doubts about it. He said he was ready for a change from Warminster.

"Ah now, that might be the rub, 'cos your most important asset to me is your position at the barracks where you can find out things for me."

Bradley looked a bit downcast but accepted the fact.

"Yes, suppose you're right. I'll do what I'm ordered."

Rob eyed him coolly for minute and then pushed a smaller bag to him.

"Well, in that case, you are now in my employ so to seal the deal here is another twenty sovs fer you, but be sure you know the conditions and don' ever fergit 'bout the Redemptors."

Bradley was elated at his new status and the extra money and gushingly assured Rob that he would be loyal and that he'd like to know a bit more about these Redemptors. Rob topped up their glasses and nodded.

"Fust I yeerd of 'em was from Brooksie after that there Burns business when we wuz at the Pelican Inn at Cold 'Arbour. He'd 'ad a few an' told me all about 'em. Apparently these yeer Redemptors wuz militant Protestants wot 'ad come over yeer with them persecuted Huguenot refugees from France about 'undred year ago. At first they waz jus' preachers but tithes and tradin' made 'em very rich an' powerful and a force to be reckoned back when justice in the Catholic courts wuz difficult to obtain. They had travelled with

174

their people into exile but still operated with complete ruthlessness in the face of religious persecution or intolerance, as many a cheating merchant had found out to his cost and off times his health!"

"They bin about a long toime then?" Bradley asked. "An' are they jus' from around 'ere then or is there other places they .er...do their job?"

Rob blew the air from his cheeks and rolled his eyes. "Why don' you jus' bloody listen Bradley an' stop butting' in? Oh course they ain't jus' around 'ere. They got chapters up north an' around Leicester an' in Cambridge where them Puritans do come from... Tha' bloody satisfy you?"

Bradley decided that if he was going to get to know any more he'd better kept his mouth shut and waited for Rob to continue.

"They'd a funny lot, y'know."... Rob was beginning to slur his words and had to concentrate on what he was saying. "They'm very private, loike. Got a way o' recognizin' each other wi' signs an' code words like the Masons. Fust one wot I met wuz a miller from up Marshfield way. Ol' Brooksie vouched fer me. Seemed good folk but I wouldn't cross 'em."

He started coughing and spluttering rum across the table and finally said.

"Now you know all 'bout em Bradley, so beware! G'wan then an' shut the door after you. I'll be in touch soon. G'night, lad."

As he scuffed away up the street Bradley was still not entirely satisfied with the sketchy, bad tempered explanation about the

175

Redemptors and he had every right to be because Rob's information fell far short of the reality

Their roots lay in the far south western area of mediaeval France where opposition to the Catholic Church was endemic. There had always been a history of protest here and the teachings of Luther and other teachers soon took hold and the varying new Protestant sects in France became known collectively as the Huguenots. An uneasy truce was achieved by the Edict of Nantes in 1598 which permitted a degree of religious freedom but when this edict was revoked in 1685 the persecution returned leading to a mass exodus of refugees to northern Protestant countries. Many people fled to the Low Countries and Switzerland but for the vast majority England, where a new tolerant Protestant dynasty reigned, was the Promised Land.

With them travelled The Lord's Soldiers of Redemption who quickly learned that there was little persecution to be fought and that their services were no longer in demand. Like many well meaning secret societies past and present as the need for its existence faded and its members lost the power and influence they had become accustomed to, they turned to a world where there expertise could still be of value.

Protection and extortion became their principal sources of income to which they quickly added crop burning, robbery and in extreme cases, murder. They also extracted tribute from other malefactors operating the area under their control. Their main victims were the small farmers and shop keepers and it soon became apparent that the local miller had a ready ear for the village gossip so they bought up mills and put their own people in charge. Thus the Marshfield windmill on the high ridge to the north of Bath became the Redemptors headquarters for the South West of England.

Life at Rob's compound on the river returned to normal again. After about three days he had started bringing the barrels back across the river in ones and twos to make everything appear normal. Mr Allen's stone cargos continued to be carried daily to Bristol and Avonmouth but nothing further was heard about the robbery for two months or more. Bradley continued his watching brief at Warminster Barracks and apart from a cryptic message from the Horse Guards in London nothing out of the ordinary had occurred.

On a visit to Marshfield to pay his dues and reaffirm his respect to the local Redemptor Elder, Rob dropped in on an old farmer friend he knew on the Tog Ridge and took a long rental on a big stone barn. He explained that he needed storage space for cordage and equipment away from the river where burglary and pilferage was rife and that he intended to import tar and turpentine direct from Scandinavia.

He arrived a few days later with a wagon load of barrels that were safely rolled into his store. Over a period of a month Rob was a regular visitor busily emptying them of the precious money bags.

177

First thing he did was to tally up the haul and separate the Maria Theresa dollars which he divided between three of the barrels. Most of the bags of guineas and gold bars he buried in a pit dug out of the earthen floor of the barn until he got round to packing them.

He took some of the best barrels to a reliable cooper in Wick who refurbished them with new copper bands and replaced any rotted staves, caulking the seams. He also put an inner lid a quarter of the way down from the top making a separate sealed compartment in each one. Rob paid him the money he asked and hinted that the job was for the Redemptors, thus assuring his silence. On his next trip to Bristol he bought five barrels of turpentine and a large tun of tar from a dockside chandler and took them out to his Tog Hill barn.

Over the following two weeks Rob put an equal number of silver and gold filled bags in each of his refurbished barrels, replaced and sealed the false inner lid and topped up the barrel with the turpentine. Sealing the lids securely he painted each one with a generous coat of tar. When they were completely dry he stencilled an address in Portugal on the lid and sides and took them to a shipping agent in Bristol to be shipped out on the next ship calling at Lisbon. The agent dryly checked his books and announced that he had a vessel outward bound for Cadiz calling at Vigo and Lisbon leaving Avonmouth two weeks hence. Rob said that was acceptable and also booked passage for his sister Rachel on the same voyage. Being the youngest child she had always been her father's favourite and he had spent much time with her. One result was that by the age of twelve she could speak fluent Portuguese and she was to oversee the delivery of his merchandise to their Uncle Arturo at Cascais. The sealed orders she carried in her hidden money belt would tell him what to do.

By sheer coincidence Miriam Trandon had booked passage on the very same ship to her sojourn in the Lusitanian sun

----

17

MIRIAM PLANS A TRIP

The thing Lady Trandon complained about most was the constant draught. These Queen Anne brick built houses were fine in the summertime but fired bricks did not keep out the cold and damp even when the courses were layered. The windows did not seal properly either. She would grumble about them continually to anyone who would listen saying that Mr Wood's stone houses were so much better because they had rubble between the inner and outer walls. They were properly insulated to make them cool in summer and cosy in the winter. In truth she would have sold Trandon house tomorrow if she had half a chance but these Queen Anne houses were not considered a-la-mode. These days everybody from Brighton to Edinburgh wanted to live like the Prince Regent.

Although in truth that was not the only reason she would like to sell.

She was still spouting off about it when Alexander returned weary from his weekly meeting at the Command Headquarters at Warminster. The last thing he wanted was an ear-bashing from his

Aunt Miriam but she had strategically posted Agnes at the front door to make sure that he called in at her suite of rooms. Due to the fact that, even though Miriam could hobble around quite well with her sticks, she found that her wheel chair relieved the nagging pain of her long term arthritis in her joints and preferred to use that. As a result she had made her private apartment on the ground floor at the front and there was no way of avoiding it but he stalled Agnes by saying he needed the privy and would be along directly. On his way back he downed a quick restorative brandy from the hall table.

"I am thinking seriously of moving abroad for a while." She announced imperiously as Alexander entered the room. He could sense the tension in the air. "Doctor Jennings says that if I am to find any respite from my aches and pains I should abide in warmer climes and since we are still at war with that beastly ogre Napoleon, France or Italy are out of the question at the moment, so it looks like I shall be visiting Portugal."

Alexander gasped but before he had a chance to give his opinion she blindly blundered on.

"… And Mr Willerby my advocate also thinks it would be a capital idea. As he points out, it is no longer necessary for me to be here. You take care of most of the duties of running the estate don't you?"

Oh, thought Alexander, at last I am being asked for my opinion of something. But he was wrong and the tirade continued unabated. She had been waiting for his homecoming all afternoon and she had no intention of letting this opportunity of giving him a good wigging pass. Sooner or later he was going to say something or other she disliked or attempt to contradict her and she had both barrels loaded, ready to blast him. He hesitated.

"Well, Aunt Miriam I do take an interest in what is happening but surely the every day running of the estate is still in the hands of Mr Barnes, your steward. I understand that he has had that responsibility for donkey's years now and even if I do think it lacks a little open accountability, it is not my place to change things."

Barnes had first come to the estate some ten years earlier and although Alexander thought that the farm should have shown a healthier profit, Aunt Miriam had no complaint about his work so he was not seriously concerned. However her next few words brought him up short as he realized the implication of what was being said.

"Humph!" she snorted. "I am not suggesting any kind of change. I support Mr Barnes totally. So much so, that I have given him my Power of Attorney in all matters of running the home farm estate."

Alexander was dumbfounded at this disclosure. So many of his suspicions now seemed to have substance and he decided to check the man out. For the moment though he meekly accepted his Aunt's veiled reprimand and asked her why she was considering going abroad.

"It is Doctor Jennings' suggestion. He has patients with property in Lisbon and Cascias who swear by the climate. Perhaps I might take a small tour there... My good friend Commander Tetley tells me that there is good passage in the summer and that the Navy has swept the seas clean of the French. He says that I could also visit Bilboa or Santander if I so wish."

Alexander smiled inwardly at her scant knowledge of geography but said nothing more. Having spent time on-station off the Iberian Peninsular he had vivid memories of those wild Biscay storms. No one in his right mind would undergo that from choice, even in the height of summer... And as for those Northern Spanish ports, they were just rat holes filled with Basque pirates, cut throats and army deserters.

"Yes." She mumbled to herself. "The more I think about it the more I like the prospect of time in the sun away from this dreary English winter."

Then, completely forgetting why she had wanted to talk to Alexander she rang her little bell for Agnes and ordered her afternoon tea.

He seized the opportunity and quickly took his leave before she could get her addled brain back on track. She may have forgotten what she had said but Alexander certainly had not. Thinking it would be better if he was not around while she went through her latest fantasy and decided to check out what she had said about the steward.

On arriving at the neglected looking Home Farm buildings Alexander was greeted by a slatternly buxom woman feeding chickens in the cluttered muddy front yard and said that he had business with Mr Ezekiel Barnes and inquired if he was home. She

183

looked him over suspiciously with her shifty eyes and said that her man was not home at the moment but would be back in a day or two. "Wuz there anythin' she could do?"… Again came the hard stare and she said "Any road, oo d'j say you waz?"

Alexander played her at the same game. "Oh, just tell him that a neighbour called by. Good Day to you Mistress."

As he walked back down the hill he sensed that there was something seriously amiss. The woman's belligerent attitude and her cautious answers made him wonder just what was she hiding and made him determined to find what it was. Bearing in mind what his crazy Aunt Miriam had said about her giving Barnes power of attorney, he decided to start at the bank and accordingly he sent a note to Mr Stuckey's establishment to arrange a meeting.

--- -----------------------------

After her raving outburst at Bath and in high dudgeon at her nephew's bland response to her plan Miriam had sent right away for Doctor Jennings and told him to book a passage for her to Lisbon forthwith. She had decided to stay with an old admirer of hers, a retired diplomat who was living out his dotage in a fog of sherry wine and rich food in his Tagus riverside villa. He received her imperious letter informing him of his impending good fortune with a characteristic response. He immediately left for an extended stay in Malta!

Totally unfazed by the lack of response to her plans Miriam continued with her preparations for the trip by sending a letter to the

184

British Consul in Lisbon via a friend in the Foreign Office, informing them of her impending visit and requested that they reserve suitable accommodation for her and a to find a major domo to recruit staff whom she would inspect on her arrival. She also informed the Consul General that her retinue would include her two dogs, her maid and a couple of general servants. Alexander wondered if the ship's Captain had been informed of these extra bodies when he agreed to take her.

She also demanded that Alexander escort her to Bristol and suggested that Jessica might like to come along too. They could get to the port early and perhaps enjoy a couple of days shopping before she embarked. Alexander would find them a smart hotel, she was sure!

To Alexander the whole thing seemed to be spinning out of control!

The big day came round quicker than anybody had expected with a flurry of packing portmanteaux and selecting clothes for all the social functions that her ladyship was expecting to be feted at. The delusions of grandeur grew worse every day until it began to appear like a Royal Tour of the World with Lisbon being blessed first with her gracious presence.

Poor Agnes was at her wit's end with all the frantic preparations to be made. On top of which she had to cope with Miriam's constant changes of mood and a welter of ever-changing instructions. She had only been abroad once before; and then only to

Calais. The thought of going hundreds of miles away on a ship scared her to death... And Janet did not make the situation any better with her lurid descriptions of her own experiences on the trip from India!

However, somehow everything was done by the time they were due to leave. Miriam smiled vacantly as the coachman and a burly groom brought her custom built coach round to the front of the house. It had special double doors on one side and two sturdy oak ramps were stored underneath which hooked onto the door sills so that her chair could be rolled inside, the forward facing seats having been adapted to leave room for it. The groom and the coachman looked askance at the slope but manfully pushed her ladyship up into the capacious coach.

The girls climbed aboard and got settled in, Agnes next to her mistress with Jessica and Janet sitting opposite them. There was a banging of boxes and portmanteaux on the roof, Miriam's sea baggage having been sent by cart a few days previously. Alexander mounted his favourite bay, the groom took his seat on the driver's box and off they went with Mad Miriam waving dementedly at every passing traveller. Jessica thought the whole theatrical performance was ridiculous but contented her self with a wry smile and exchanged glances with Janet.

The procession moved off ponderously down the drive with Alexander riding ahead with four troopers from Ensleigh to guard the passage over the humpbacked New Bridge and along this lonely stretch of the Bristol Road which had gained the reputation for highwaymen looking for good pickings from their lairs up in Newton St Lo. Only recently two of these desperados had the nerve to hold up a mail coach here. Fortunately it was empty, the load of mail bags having just been handed over to the Saltford postmaster so nobody got hurt but they really frightened the driver and guard.

The escort accompanied the lumbering coach as far as the Crown Inn near the riverside village of Saltford where Alexander sent the troopers back to Bath. Miriam immediately took advantage of the stop to use her commode-wheelchair, a performance which required everyone but Agnes to vacate the coach and the coachman and the groom to turn their backs. All being done, she then insisted on stopping at the next inn for refreshment, which she did on several occasions. There were further delays as they hit the low lying land around 'Smokey Canesham' where the usual riverain fogs slowed them down further. Unfortunately the west wind that cleared the mists also brought rain and further delays.
All in all, the relatively short journey to Bristol took over seven hours!

At Brislington Alexander had ridden ahead to the hotel to prepare them for the arrival of the Queen of Sheba: Miriam did not disappoint them. She waved imperiously and grilled the manager about his hostelry and issued her demands. She was annoyed that it was now too late to visit the shops and insisted on the whole party being served dinner in her suite. The manager's eyes rolled skyward and he struggled hard to maintain his temper as Marion raved on and on, reminding him of exactly who she was. She blatantly lied about the nature of her trip hinting that she was on some a secret political mission to the Portuguese Queen. Jessica blushed with embarrassment while Agnes and Janet stifled their giggles with scarves.

The following morning, right after breakfast, Lady Trandon led her party to the quayside shops and traders and on into town with the burly groom, his face red with effort and embarrassment pushing her chair and the girls following behind like a gaggle of geese. They stopped for lunch at a hotel on the Broad-Quay before meandering back with the maids festooned with boxes and packages gazing in the shop windows and at the peddler's stalls in the old market. Alexander did not accompany them, pleading duty and went to visit a fellow Marine Major at the Navy Yard, where he got well oiled and stayed the night.

That evening Miriam, still irritated at Alexander's escape, again insisted on dinner in her suite, this time to the music of a string quartet. The Manager was counting the hours to her departure and the following day took pleasure in padding out her bill outrageously. When he presented it Miriam imperiously refused to even glance at it and threw it over to Agnes to settle. The hotel staff assembled at the portico to see her off and she waved them a graceful goodbye; most of them were only there because they wanted to be certain that she had gone! The manager then locked himself his office and got drunk on a bottle of Navy Rum!

At the dockside there were further delays as the coachman drove onto the wrong quay and had a tortuous time turning the cumbersome vehicle round, earning him some of the most colourful curses the girls had ever heard as he banged into barrels and sacking covered cargo and the iron shod wheels crushed the curb stones. Eventually he found the correct berth and trundled noisily along the cobbles toward the ship. As they stopped, they saw Alexander coming from the opposite direction, his horse picking its way through the confusion. Jessica noted that he looked a little drunk and his hovering smile indicated that he had had a good time with his comrades. Miriam, of course laid into him as soon as she set eyes on him but he mollified her with a hidden bunch of violets and a lavish box of chocolates. He slid off the saddle and helped Jessica from the carriage while the driver and groom dropped the ramp to roll out the old lady. He asked her about the journey and Jessica lied that it had been very pleasant.

He then turned to look up at the ship and his heart skipped a beat and the sky whirled around him... There was a thunder in his ears that he hadn't heard since the battles in India and his mouth dropped open at what he saw. There, twenty feet above him, her raven hair ruffling in the harbour breeze was his Goddess... The very one he had searched high and low for. What was she doing here? He was still staring dumbfounded at the apparition when the Captain came and stood at her side, watching with a mixture of amazement and horror as the men pushed Miriam's wheelchair up the ramp and onto the deck. The agent had not warned him about this! It was bad enough shipping three females but not with one of them in a bloody wheelchair as well!

Jessica had noticed Alexander's shocked reaction to the girl and was behind him as they too made their way aboard to see Miriam settled in and to meet the Captain. Alexander shook hands with him and exchanged naval pleasantries and the Captain turned to introduce the girl. "Lady Trandon, may I present Senhorita Rachel Dacarius returning to Lisbon. I hope you enjoy the voyage."

The best Miriam could manage was a dismissive sniff and said moodily. "This is my nephew Major Coulston. He will not be travelling."

The Captain, somewhat put out with this brusque response, bowed curtly. "Ah, Major Coulston... Allow me to introduce Senhorita Dacarius."

Alexander looked into her face and seeing the look of panic in her eyes, said quietly. "A pleasure indeed Ma'am, but have we not met before?"

Jessica had noticed what had passed between them and mischievously grabbed his arm and moved closer.

"Have you, Darling?" She said with a slightly condescending smile. "I don't remember you telling me about it? Where did you two meet before then?"

Alexander did not know what to say and was shocked at

Jessica's move. Rachel was even more shocked at the developing situation and feigning surprise he said. "Oh, did I not, my Dear? ... I think it was at the last military revue at Warminster." Turning back to Rachel he said. "Ah, yes, you were with Captain Jones if I remember correctly. How lovely to see you again... May I present my fiancée Miss Singleton?"

This time it was Jessica's turn to be shocked but a look of grateful relief passed over Rachel's face and she gave him a small smile.

18

THE DISCOVERY

The elegant dining room of the Officers Mess at Warminster Barracks was bathed in bright spring sunshine, the tall windows reflecting the colourful display of regimental colours and silver trophies on the back wall. At a long polished conference table sat a group of anxious looking officers.

A smaller table had been put across one end to form a T and at the centre of it sat General Sir Aaron Griffiths, Commander in Chief of the Western Division. To his right sat The Commanding officer of the Warminster Depot and a senior Colonel from the Adjutant General's Office in Whitehall: To his left were, The Chief Provost Major (West) and a senior Civil Servant from the Treasury. Seated behind them sat their Aides de Camp and at a side desk, three military clerks to record the proceedings.... One of whom was Bradley Thomas!

The other officers summoned to the meeting were ranged on down the long table, either sipping cold lemonade or making notes on the papers in front of them. It was a riot of colourful uniforms the scarlet of the Generals and the forest green of the Wiltshire Regiment blending with Alexander dressed in his official royal blue jacket of the Commissariat Dept. with a Major's crown on his epaulet and a crossed swords and anchor badge on the right breast demonstrating that he was still officially in the Marine infantry. Next to him wearing the pale blue Dolman jacket and fur pelisse of the Hanoverian Dragoons sat the scar faced Oberst-Major Kurt Mahler.

One of the aides rapped the table for attention and introduced Colonel Burkit-Adams, from the Adjutant General's Office. The assembly jumped to their feet but the Colonel gestured at them to be seated.

"Good morning, Gentlemen I have some shocking intelligence to impart to you. All of you here will recall the meticulously organised and guarded convoy that past through this depot over six weeks ago, yes?"

There were knowing nods all round the table.

"Well, I am pleased to tell you that some twenty days later it arrived safely in Dublin. It had been long awaited by both the Army and the Civil Power as their financial credibility was stretched to the absolute limit. Due in some part to the piratical raids of the French privateers who recently had captured several of our supply vessels sent to that a-cursed country Ireland. However this relief turned sour when it was found that padlocked bullion chests had been sent with the wrong set of keys."

193

There was an audible gasp from the white faced officers.

"A search was made at the Treasury but the missing keys could not be found. A further impasse then arose as it appeared that the chests were Crown Property and could not be broached without express permission from the Treasury, further delaying distribution of the much needed funds."

The Colonel stopped to refresh himself and his aide poured him a glass of water from the crystal carafe on the desk as he paused to let the news sink in. The audience looked at each other with stone faces wondering just what was coming next. Clearing his throat with a slight cough he consulted the official paper again.

" … And, Gentlemen that is not all…Not by a long chalk. So before you start muttering about any Treasury carelessness, I must warn you that this depot is not without some degree of culpability."

There was a shocked intake of breath round the room and an older Major stood up voicing his surprise, saying that 'Sir, I can assure you that every possible security contingency had been taken on such a serious matter and...'

Before he could continue the Colonel held up his hand saying.

"I appreciate your outburst Major but pray wait until I have told you the full story of this incident... You may change your mind, sir."

The Major sheepishly resumed his seat. The Colonel resumed his report.

"In due course the Treasury minister, Lord Trafford was

informed of the situation and to alleviate the impending fiscal crisis in Ireland gave permission for the chests to be forced. At this point, to help you realize the seriousness of this situation, His Lordship took the very radical step of giving me permission to enlighten you as to the value of the cargo."

Again he paused for effect and looked at their expectant faces. After a long moment he cleared his throat and looked down the long table as he prepared to stun them. "At this point Gentlemen we become involved in matters of extreme sensitivity and before continuing I must draw your attention to one of the documents before you binding you to complete secrecy on any and all forthcoming information. Read it carefully and if you agree to the terms and conditions therein, sign it and return it to my Aide de Camp, Major Willis. If however, any of you feel that they cannot abide by such terms I must ask them to leave."

He looked solemnly down at the assembly as nobody rose and the Aide collected the signed documents. At this point he signalled to the guards. "Good. Guards, clear the chamber of all servants and clerks and secure the doors."

There was a rustling of papers and clinking of glasses as the clerks and servants were rapidly ushered out and the doors closed and guarded by two armed riflemen.

Allowing a moment for the officers to settle down Burkit-Adams continued. "These chests contained not only the usual biennial topping up of the Treasury reserves but also back pay for the occupying forces plus payment for the German battalions too. The total value was in the region of sixty thousand guineas."

There was an audible gasp from the room and the Colonel started pacing up and down.

"But Gentlemen, that is not all! Not by a long chalk. It seems that somebody, who shall remain unnamed for the moment, decided that to avoid any similar fiscal crisis in the future he would authorise the inclusion of bullion in the shape of 10 gold ingots for the Dublin Mint." Still pacing he turned to face the now open mouthed officers with a sardonic smile across his face. "And now they had mislaid the keys!...... Is that not wonderful, Gentlemen?"

At this there were guffaws and ribald remarks about pen pushers and dolts from the assembled company but they faded away on seeing the hard look on the Colonel's face as he continued.

"But here's the rub and the mystery too. When the chests were eventually broached they revealed that their precious contents were only bags of stones! Yes Gentlemen, STONES! ... No money. No golden guineas or bars of bullion, just bags of bloody stones! About the only saving grace was that part of the consignment was in Austrian thalers. Not much consolation, is it, eh?

"STONES!" The room exploded with shouts and cries of disbelief. Also, it must said, a frantic examination of individual actions to avoid any blame. Careers could hinge on any unexplained behaviour.

The Colonel rapped the table and looked coldly around the room.

"I have no doubt that a leak of some sort will reach the Irish press and so to forestall any conjecture, a statement has been released to The London Times to the effect that the bulk of the cargo was in Austrian thalers to pay the German contingent of the army which we hope will mute the usual outbursts of indignation. At present suspicion falls on either French agents or Irish rebel factions. A thorough investigation by the Lord Provost's department is presently underway in London and the Thames Valley. Obviously, Gentlemen, there will be similar diligent enquiries made in Bristol and the West Country and I expect your full cooperation with the Provost's Officers in their investigation. As Chief Investigator (West) His Lordship has appointed Major Alexander Coulston. His Procurement Office duties will be taken over by Captain Roberts of the Wiltshire's. All of these matters must remain confidential. Your names are listed here with others I have spoken to. Thank You."

He nodded to his Aide-de Camp who collected the papers and followed him out of the room. For a moment there was silence then came a fevered buzzing of excited theories of collusion and corruption with everyone stressing their non-involvement and trying to distance themselves from the debacle. However, this was not the response felt by Bradley Thomas who was sitting in his cubby hole with his ear pressed to the wall. He had been shocked by the huge amount involved and the prospect if they were ever caught was terrifying! As the panic slowly subsided anger took its place. Rob must have known about it all but he had led them to believe that it

197

was just a few thousand or so. On top of which, it had been he who had told Rob about the shipment in the first place! Oh yes, it was high time he had a word with Mr Rob Dacarius!

Bradley staggered from his hideout into the main office, his mind numbed by the value of the load revealed by the colonel. Other clerks were still busy packing their inks and papers and he too started collecting his things. He was so distracted he hardly noticed the clerk on his left who was also packing up his equipment or the fact that among the quills he had used was a small green feather.

19

JEB'S SUSPICIONS

In the two years that Jeb had been working for Cyrus he had matured considerably and on the verge of his nineteenth birthday he was a powerful young man with boundless energy and pleasant disposition. He was happy and well settled at the stables proving daily that he really did know a great deal about horseflesh and showed great promise as future stable manager.

Returning from a visit to Bristol with Cyrus they had seen a tow horse being woefully mistreated by its owner. The spring flood was in full bore on the Avon and the beast was struggling desperately against the fast moving current trying to tow a cumbersome river barge upstream. It was an impossible task and Cyrus intervened calling the boat man a callous brute but was rewarded with a mouthful of abuse for his trouble and continued to ply his whip to the poor horse's back. Jeb dismounted and shoving the driver aside comforted the beast and wiped the sweat and foam from its mouth. The evil looking water gipsy lifted his whip and snarled at the boy.

"Wotcha fink y'm a-doing touchin' my nag, you snotty nose fart? Gerroff directly or you'll be feelin' some o' wot she's jest 'ad!" Jeb pushed him again, waiting for a response as the man raised his arm.

"Come on then, try it and you'll get a duckin'. I'm not afraid o' the likes o' you, you bullying old goat. Put that switch down an' give the mare a bloody rest. Can't you see that she's worn out, you cruel bastard?"

The driver stepped closer to strike Jeb with the rawhide lash but the boy stepped neatly inside and punched him heavily in the mouth sending him staggering back off the crumbling bank into the water.

"Help me... I can't swim!" He wailed hanging on desperately to the high bank. "I'll 'ave the Beadle on thee. Mark my words, now 'elp me up!"

Cyrus had also dismounted and stood above the man to warn him.

"Now, harken to me, rogue. I have your barge number and if I hear one more threat out of you I will report you to the Water Master and you'll lose your docket to work on the Avon, so shut your mouth. And if I hear from any of my people about more of your cruelty I'll come looking for you. And I won't be alone either, you understand?"

The bargee spat water from his mouth and nodded grimly and Jeb gave him his arm and dragged him up the stony bank to stand dripping before Cyrus.

"Now knave, get thee a length o' strong towline and we will

200

hitch up our two mounts along with that tired old mare o' yours and pull thee above the weir yonder into calmer waters where the river is wide… Now go!"

The water gypsy nodded sulkily but managed a muttered "Thankee, sir."

Cyrus looked warningly at him. "But if I ever hear of your bestial antics again I shall be onto ye, d'y hear? So be warned for I have men watching the river every day, I will haul you before the magistrate and your bargee days will be over! Now get that harness fixed up."

The man scurried to do as he was told and soon they were above the weir and into calmer waters on the wide stretch of river at Bitton. A mile further on at Swineford, Cyrus and Jeb unhitched their horses and turned away from the towpath and passing through the cosy little village of North Stoke they returned to the stables at Lansdowne.

Cyrus had been strangely silent since leaving the river occasionally tapping his fingers on his saddle as though he was making calculations of some sort. As they turned into the yard gate he turned to Jeb and said.

"Well, Jeb, dost think ye could handle it?"

Jeb was jerked roughly out of his reverie and said defensively

` "Andle wot?"

"Chain Horses, that's what. Could you manage them?"

Jeb looked confused. "Don't see why not, they'z only 'ossies ain't they and I bin round 'em all me life, ploughin' an' towin' an' such. Why you finkin' 'bout chain 'ossies?

Cyrus handed his reins to a stable lad and gestured to the office.

"Come inside. I've been thinking about that poor old mare on the river back there and I think I've come up with an idea that I think you'll like."

They scraped the towpath mud off their boots on the grating and Cyrus ordered cider and bread and cheese from one of the lads as they settled at the rough deal table that served Cyrus as a desk.

"I have been thinking about this for some time now but I was usually distracted away from it by pressing everyday duties. Now however, with your help I can see it coming to fruition. I first saw chain horses being used in Austria when I was in my twenties. They depended greatly on river traffic there but apart from the mighty Danube all their rivers were fast and the fickle winds could not be relied on to battle upstream. I think that such a service would pay dividends here in our fine city, not only on the river but also on the steep hills."

Jeb was forcibly reminded of what Old Sam had told him about 'Bath being hell for Horses' and concurred that it would be a good idea.

By late afternoon they had a plan of action to work to which could be quickly implemented. Jeb was authorised by Cyrus to scour the area for good strong horses, preferably English shires or Suffolk Punches or even Pecherons or Belgian Greys if they were available. In the meantime Cyrus would rent stable space in some central location that could serve both the hills and the river. The whole project came together swiftly and when Cyrus took advertising space in the new Bath Chronicle business came flocking in. Strangely enough Jeb's new headquarters were in Shires Yard just across the cobbles from his old boss.

Marcus Harris had finally got Tarleton's daughter pregnant and her father was reluctantly forced to agree to the wedding and the partnership that came as part of the dowry. Tarleton himself was not wild about the arrangement but now had enough money to retire and leave the day to day running to Marcus. It was not the best of moves because Harris was a drunken rake and within two years was forced to lease off part of the yard to pay his creditors. The first thing Jeb did when he moved in was to give Old Sam a job as Head Stableman.

Every morning teams of draught horses could be seen plodding from their stables to land at the bottom of the steep hills of Lansdowne, Bathwick and Widcome while at times of flood others would assist on the rivers. Jeb spent most of his long day riding between these locations keeping things running smoothly.

It was on one of these occasions that he began to notice the rather strange behaviour of one of the big stone carrying trows plying the Avon. One of these broad-beamed, flat bottomed riverboats seemed to be engaged in ferrying men and materials across the river to work on the landing stage outside the militia depot. Several large barrels were already on it and the men were lazily spreading crushed stones along the bank. Jeb watched them for a while and quickly realized that they were not tradesmen of any sort nor even regular workmen with any idea of construction work. He began to wonder just what they were doing there. He had never noticed any deterioration of the riverbank in that area. In fact, up to six months ago the landing stage had been in daily use and was always kept up to scratch. True, these days the boats from Ferry Lane were docking a little further upstream but that was just a matter of avoiding that strong cross-current before the bend in the river. He decided to tell Cyrus all about it on his return to Lansdowne.

Alexander's new duties had made quite a few changes in his life too. Whitehall had insisted on moving the procurement department away from the Warminster depot to a newly built complex of buildings in the hamlet of Ensleigh a couple of miles north of Bath on the edge of the Lansdowne plateau halfway between Cyrus' livery stables and the gunpowder mills at Wooley. Alexander set up his offices here, partly for security reasons but also to allow Captain Roberts acclimatise himself to the complexities of the creaking supply system. It was also close to Cyrus' place and he often dropped in to share a glass of rum on his way home to Trandon House. He was here the night Jeb arrived back with news of the curious doings on the river.

20

PORTUGAL

Even though a fragile peace treaty had been signed between England and France at Amiens the previous year, the two successful revolutions in America and France had provided new hope and impetus to the Irish Separatists under the leadership of Wolfe Tone and Henry Grattan who were now forever disrupting trade and sabotaging English shipping.

In the light of this, wise old Captain Smollet decided to avoid as much of the English Channel as he could. Bitter experience had proved that the St. Malo privateers and the Breton freebooters chose only to respect those international treaties that were to their own advantage so instead, he cast off from Bristol and headed west to Cork on the south coast of Ireland away from the main shipping routes.

Although this part of the country had been pacified and was now well garrisoned with English troops since the abortive attempts by the French to land forces at Bantry Bay in 1796 and '97;

(frustrated mainly, it must be said by the weather) it was still not secure. The most serious invasion happened in 1798 when the French General Humbert landed with a small force on the Mayo coast and defeated the sadly under strength local militia chasing them all the way back to town, a debacle that was celebrated by Irish balladeers as the Castlebar Races! However the victory was short lived with the arrival of regular British troops who rounded up the rebels and the raw French conscripts. There had also been a landing on the Welsh coast near Pembroke where the invaders were forced to surrender by the gentry of the local militia, the impressively named and splendidly uniformed Castlemartin Yeomanry but the security situation was still a long way from being stabilised.

Smollet stayed in Cork just two days, long enough to stock up on fresh water and provisions and off-load some Scandinavian timber. He did not even allow his passengers to go ashore and catching the morning tide made sail due south to Vigo in northern Portugal and then on to Lisbon. All in all it had been a pleasant journey and apart from a small squall in the Bay of Biscay the weather had held and the sea had been relatively calm.

There were only six passengers aboard, Miriam and her maid, Rachel, two Bristol merchants and a Portuguese governess returning from Cheltenham. They all took their meals together in Captain Smollet's saloon and the general atmosphere was friendly and informal. Miriam, of course tried to dominate the company but nobody was impressed with her ludicrous stories and her posturing, regarding her as a somewhat quaint and eccentric old lady. (Which she was.)

In due course after a brief stop at Vigo the ship arrived off the Cabo de Rocca, skirted past Cascais and Esrtoril and into the welcoming mouth of the Tagus to tie up at the port of Amadora near Lisbon. They had arrived safely at their destination and the Captain invited them to his saloon to celebrate their good fortune in a glass of Vino Verde and a dish of fresh charcoal grilled Portuguese sardines

Rachel used her time on board to ingratiate herself with Miriam with the express purpose of getting to know more about Alexander and his family background... She was pleasantly surprised to find that he was Miriam's only living relative and sole heir to the whole Trandon estate but she was a little concerned to discover that he had recently been put in charge of the inquiry into the loss of the Army's payroll. That was an even more important reason to keep close to Miriam which would enable her to keep track of the investigation! Agnes, Miriam's long suffering maid did not take kindly to this upstart's familiarity with her mistress and made her feelings plain even though it did take the pressure off her somewhat.

Being fluent in Portugeuse and familiar with the peculiar Lisbon patois she was invaluable in finding suitable accommodation and staff for Lady Trandon and soon had her comfortably ensconced at a villa in the fashionable surroundings of Cascais.

She also took time to meet up with Uncle Arturo and

supervise the secure storage of the barrels in his caves. He appeared to be very welcoming, saying that he was overjoyed to see her again after all these years (she did not remember ever actually meeting him before) and asking with gushing sincerity about her brother's health and his business. It all sounded innocent enough but she felt a little uneasy with his evasive answers to the most innocent of her inquiries and she was left with the distinct impression that he was up to something and was not to be trusted.

… And as things turned out, her assessment of the situation proved to be quite correct!

Some three weeks later Alexander was surprised to receive a letter from his Aunt. With a wry expression he picked it up from the hall table and slipped it in his pocket to read at his office later. His day turned out to be a succession of boring meetings at various locations in Bath to sort out staff for the investigation team and to check their credentials so it was late afternoon before he remembered the letter and opened it with some trepidation, hoping that she had not cut her tour short and was coming home early.

He need not have worried as it turned out to be more or less what he had expected from Miriam, a missive outlining in rosy terms the dazzling success of her progress through Lisbon high society and boring details of balls and receptions at which she was feted as a golden example of English Aristocracy. She also hinted that she would be returning in September as she was a little disappointed that many of her old acquaintances who now dwelt in Lisbon had had to leave to attend to pressing business away from the city or whose health required them to move to cooler mountain regions. One had even fled to Egypt at the news of her impending arrival. What kind of society people were they? Such appalling bad manners had never happened in her younger days!"

Alex had heard all these ramblings many times before knowing that it was rare indeed for her to have anything good to say about anyone but he paid rapt attention to what came next. She told him about her villa and how helpful that Portuguese girl had been. So helpful in fact that she was seriously considering engaging her as a companion when they returned to England. After all, she tactlessly dictated, Agnes was getting older and was slowing down so it could be a good thing all round. (Poor Agnes, who also doubled as her secretary, was actually writing the letter for her!)

The rambling epistle continued for six more pages in Agnes' flowing copperplate hand outlining more of her ladyship's adventures and of the important people who were going out of their way to meet her. Alexander could read between the lines that quite contrary to her imagined triumph, most people were doing their utmost to avoid her and her overbearing ways. He was about to toss it aside when a tightly folded piece of blue paper fell out of the edge of the packet. It was addressed to him directly. With a furrowed brow and some trepidation he broke the wax with his thumb nail and smoothed out the paper. It was from Rachel and once again his heart jumped as it had on that fateful day at Bristol docks… In a fever of anticipation he read.

Dear Sir,

It was quite a shock to meet with you again at Bristol.
Do you not find it most peculiar that fate should throw us two most unlikely people together so often? I must admit that thoughts of you have occupied my mind from time to time. Your dear Aunt Miriam has much discussed you and I feel that now I know you somewhat better than I did afore and that has enabled me to better understand your actions, unlike yourself who knows me only from what he has seen in passing or presumed. This is a situation that I suggest we rectify on my return to England. It will I hope, enable you, sir, to understand a little more of me and my past attitude towards you.

I trust that you do not think me forward but recent events have decided me to take this action. Let us just say that we Lusitanians have never been able to bear a mystery and like Vasco da Gama and the Princesses of Braganza, we feel a compulsion to find out more of what is of interest to us .I understand from Lady Trandon that we hope to return to English shores in early September, God willing. I look forward warmly to our meeting again and finding a fresh understanding.

Respectfully Yours,
Rachel Da Carius.

Alexander was stunned... For a quarter of an hour he sat in silence staring out of the window not seeing a thing, wondering just how it would feel to meet her again His mind was racing in a fever of anticipation. Why had she written? What did she mean by a new understanding? He found himself quivering with excitement while a thousand questions whirled around his brain.

Foremost was the fervent hope that September would come quickly bringing her safely back to him.

21

THE REDEMPTORS

In the cold light of a late October afternoon Rob was splashing his way across the muddy, low lying Dolmeads flood plain back to his home in Widcome after a long and frustrating day at his compound. Apart from having trouble fixing the rudder on one of his trows he also had to prepare a tender for a new contract with Mr Allen's factor for carrying stone for the construction of the new dock at Avonmouth. Normally Rachel would have been on hand to take care of such paper work but she was in Portugal attending to the business with his untrustworthy Uncle Arturo.

He was gruffly mumbling to himself as he walked trying to work out a way of getting it all done in time when he heard a noise coming from the river bank. He stood still for a moment to listen but realising it was only the guard dogs at his compound barking at a stray cat or something. There was not much likelihood of any intruders with that pack of big vicious mastiffs and wolfhounds on the loose. He also remembered that there would be no one at home either, as his woman Nan had gone to Saltford market with her friend Mary so he decided instead to stop off for a pint at the Ram's Head.

He kicked the mud off his boots and pushed through the studded oak door into the dim low beamed tavern. As his eyes adjusted to the light he looked around noticing the three or four customers and headed across the saw dusted floor to the bar.

"Evenin' Rob." Chimed Solomon the landlord. "Pint is it?"

"Oh aye, evenin' Sol. Bit quite tonight aint it?"

Solomon pulled the cider and said that it was early but there should be a few in later and went through to tap another barrel. Rob took a pull and was just about to light his pipe when a voice at his side said.

"'Ello, Rob." It slurred. "I reckoned you'd be droppin' by."

Rob was shocked to find that it was Bradley Thomas. He was reeking of booze, so Rob humoured him.

"Oh tis you Bradley: Where did you come from then?"

Bradley was somewhat nonplussed at the question. He had expected Rob to offer him a drink but obviously that was not on the cards.

"I wuz in the back an' I yeared you come in. I bin a-waitin' for you as a matter o' fact. It seems that you an' me got summat to sort out. I fink we ought to sit down somewhere quiet, don' you?"

It was obvious that he had been drinking all afternoon building up his Dutch courage for some kind of confrontation and Rob had a good idea of just what it might be as he indicated a small table in the far corner near the hearth. After they were seated Rob put away his pipe and asked. "Well now, Bradley lad, jes' what've you gorron yore

213

mind, eh? Wazz yore problem, eh?"

Bradley looked at him drunkenly and blurted out.

"My problem, ye say? I'd say it were more your problem than mine! I'm not the one wot's tryin' to cheat his mates outa their fair shares izzit?"

Rob's suspicions were confirmed... He had sensed that something of this nature would come up but he had not expected it to come from Bradley. His eyes hardened and he stared hard at the clerk.

"Wotcha bubblin'on about Bradley? If you'm talking about our recent little venture, well, you got what you agreed to... And a portion more if'n I'm not mistook." He added pointedly. "You seem to forget that it's me as took all the risk an' put it together, so jus'what are you gettin' at?"

Bradley hawked and spat a glob into the smouldering fire, slammed his pot onto the scarred table and hissed. "The money, thaz wot! The bloody money! An' I gorra bit o'news for you on that front. See, wot you don' know is that last week there wuz a big enquiry at the barracks. I know that cos I wuz clerkin' there. All these big wigs frum Lunnon come up there. Seems as how they've found out 'bout our little caper an' there's a big enquiry bein' set up wi' my boss, Major Coulston in charge of the West Country part of it. Wotcha fink about that, then, Rob?"

Rob feigned disinterest and simply said that they all knew that sooner or later there'd be some kind of investigation. This was not the response that Bradley had been expecting and his face expressed pure malice as he snarled. "Oh, aye Rob... We all expected summat an' all... but nothin' like wot come next! Y'see, they 'ad Treasury Officers there an' the boss of the Lord Provost's office as well. Colonel Birkit Adams wuz 'is name and when he told the meetin' about jus' 'ow much went missin' I nearly jumped outa me boots. Frum wot he said, it sounds like it were the best part o' eighty thousand pound or summat loik an' we got fobbed off wi' a measly 'undred an' fifty a piece... Now, that's not right, izzit Rob.?" On the strength o' that information I don' fink as we got our fair shares.

Rob looked at him coolly rubbing his stubbly chin.

"Oh, you don't eh, Bradley? An' jes'wot you a-goin' to, do about it then? … If'n you shoot your gob off to the others you'll soon be knocked off top spot wi' me for a start. An' if you go to the Beadle you'll either go to the gibbet at Brizzle a-longa me, for you can be sure I'll involve you to the limit, or you'll spend the rest of yore miserable life rotting away on a Jamaica plantation. So you think carefully Bradley. The choice is yourn."

Brad's eyes grew red and his jaws clenched as Rob's words sank in. Finally he said craftily. "But that ain't all the options I got, izzit? I fink that you're forgettin' someone, ain'cha?"

Rob shrugged his shoulders. "Oh, an' oo might that be? You got the Cap'n o' The Watch in yore pocket then?"

A sickly smile crossed Bradley's bloated face and he smirked

"Well, Rob, ow 'bout them good friends o' yorn then, you know, them there Redemptors? They don't like being crossed up do

215

um? It wouldn't take 'em long to chain you to a stump in Severnake Forest an' leave you to the wolves, would it?" He nodded his head solemnly and slurped his cider.

Rob's face hardened again and he was just about to reply when there was a loud baa-ing of sheep and barking of dogs in the pub yard. The back door was flung open and four weather beaten shepherds came bustling in, loudly arguing about the auction they had been to in Weston. They were followed almost immediately by Jeb who fancied a pint while he was waiting for two of his chain horses to be shoed at the nearby smithy. He said a hasty good evening to Rob and nodded to his companion who he thought he knew. He couldn't quite place the man so he dismissed it as unimportant and joined the arguing sheep men.

Under the cover of this rumpus Rob said carefully. "Well, Bradley I don't know how all this is goin' to turn out but now, you and me know where we stand, don' us? But let me tell ye jus' one thing afore ye go. You'd better think real careful afore you make your move, 'cos if you make the wrong move now, you won' live long enough to see any money at all. Ye can be certain sure of that! Now, you know where I am if you wants to talk further, so I'll wish you good night. "

Without another word he rose, tossed a handful of coins on the bar and made for the door leaving Bradley with a confused mind and a rictus grin across his face.

Hearing the raised voices Jeb turned to see Rob disappearing through the door and stared hard at Bradley suddenly remembering where he had seen him before. He was sure that it was one of the men working on the landing stage behind the militia depot on the river just before the robbery.

At the back door now the shepherds were whistling and shouting as they tried to round up their flock and get out onto the road for the trip up to the pastures at Monkton Coomb. One of them however, seemed to be more interested in what was happening in the smoky barroom and held back a little. Jeb noticed that he had a small green feather in his cap...

Bradley had been right when he said that the convoy carters would soon get to know about the load and it wasn't long before the news of the deception was being whispered around the West Country markets, inns and taverns. Even the prestigious Bath Chronicle picked up and published the story in as much detail as could be gleaned from the rumours and there was much speculation about the amounts involved. From official sources there was nothing forthcoming as ranks were tightly closed. Any leakage of sensitive information could seriously affect careers and future prospects. As it was, the news of Alexander's surprise appointment as Chief Investigating Officer had raised a few eyebrows. Also the fact that the inquiry had been taken out of the hands of the Lord Provost's Department indicated to some that internal collusion was suspected.

Jessica was very impressed at Alexander's elevation in status and was gushing in her admiration when he returned from Warminster to set up his offices in Bath. Ever since the incident at Bristol and in the absence of the hawk-eyed Agnes they had been closer and were often seen dining at Roscoe's Hotel or at the Pump Rooms when Mr Haydn gave a recital. She was even with him one afternoon up at Cyrus' equestrian centre when Jeb arrived with news of the suspicious events on the river.

At his depot near the Monks Mill, Rob sat aboard one of his trows drinking rum and considering his next move. Once the anger of meeting up with the drunken Bradley had passed Rob realized that he would have to move quickly to defuse the situation. Actually eliminating the clerk was simply a matter of keeping him sweet until a suitable opportunity arose. Then a few guineas in the right palm would remove him permanently. However his mention of the Redemptors changed things drastically.

No actual sums lost in the robbery had been mentioned yet and this alone would alert the ever-watchful eyes and ears at Marshfield Mill. It was obvious that he would have to get there as soon as possible to defuse the situation. He did not have much choice. About the only thing in his favour was his in-depth

218

knowledge of the sinister secret society and his long time association with it. He was well aware that any threat of exposure would be ruthlessly put down; but if the danger could be identified as coming from another source then things would be smoothed over; and Bradley Thomas fitted the bill perfectly!

Early the next morning he saddled his mare and rode to Batheaston, then turning north, he took the back roads through North End and St. Margaret's crossing the stream at Ayford Bridge and heading for the lonely Fuddlebrook Hill to avoid the busier main road to Stroud. He had a precious cargo to deliver.

The windy ridge that led from Tog Hill to Marshfield was reputed to be the coldest spot in South Gloucester and it certainly lived up to its reputation that morning. It was nearly eleven o' clock when he passed the terrace of old alms houses on the main Bristol to Chippenham road and clopped down the frosted cobbles of Marshfield's main street and on to the big windmill on the eastern edge of the town, beyond the Guildhall and market square.

Miller Russell was in the yard supervising three men stacking sacks of grain into an open shed when Rob rode into the yard. The miller looked up and said bluntly. "Oh 'tis you Rob... I wuz wonderin' jes' ow long t'would be afore you might drop by. Let's go inside, eh?" He gestured to a nearby cottage.

Rob dismounted and tethered his horse on the lee side of the building and started to follow the miller inside when a hard faced woman carrying a canvas satchel came bustling out. She gave him a shallow curtsy and with a blank stare strode purposefully past to the creaking mill.

"No need to worry 'bout her Rob." Grunted the miller "'Tis only my niece who does some book work for me. You go along in and sit down,' I'll be thar directly. Then we'll see if I can guess jes' why yore 'ere."

Rob took a stool and sat at the heavy old kitchen table Russell used as a desk while the miller filled two leather mugs with rough cider and shoved one across. He took a swig and after wiping his mouth on his greatcoat sleeve said.

"I wuz up this way an' thought I'd come an' give you a bit o' news."

"Oh, ye mean summat as we don' know about already, do, ee?" Rob looked cautiously around.

"Well, I've no doubt that you've 'eard the rumours but I know a bit more than that… By the way, are we alone 'ere?"

"Oh, aye, we're alone alright." Chortled his host. "Jes' you an' me and I suspect that you want to talk about money, right?" He smiled craftily at Rob and continued. "But afore you do, lemme tell you a bit of news. Bit o' bad news, actually about an old comrade o' yorn… Might save you tellin' me a few fibs eh?"

Rob leaned back and taking out his pipe he looked questioningly at the miller who gestured to the smouldering fire to get a light.

"Now Rob," He continued. "You remember Big Silas Morton don' ye? He was one o' Captain Brooks' men. Bit like yourself back then, eh? Well t'other night he wuz a long way frum 'ome down in the Mendips. Bit o' bizzness down in West Harptree I believe, firing a hayrick as I yeard. Anyway, as it 'appens, one of our people in Midsomer Norton wuz tipped off that Big Silas was causin' a bit of stir in the Star Inn so 'e went across to see jes' wot wuz goin'on. Apparently Silas had come a-rollin in wi' two doxies frum Radstock. Spending like a fool he wuz, an' blowin' off his mouth about this big tickle he'd bin involved with, an' that there wuz more a-coming his way soon. He was bragging to the wenches an' whoever would listen 'bout the good ole days wi' Brooksie. Even yore name were mentioned a time or two along wi' some other cove by the name o' Jake summat. He seemed to be carryin' quite a few 'goldies' and some Austrian dollars too. Our man saw 'im tryin' to buy a drink wi' one. "

The miller scraped back his stool and went over to top the mugs up from a small barrel in the corner. Over his shoulder he said.

"He spent the night wi' the girls and left early the next morning to head back to the Severnake Forest but somehow musta lost his way.. They found 'is body in the Wellow Brook near Shoscombe Vale about three days ago an' all 'is money gone. Musta upset somebody or got to talkin' careless, eh? … Izzat wot you come to tell me about?"

Rob froze … He'd known that it was urgent he contacted the Redemptors but no idea just how urgent. He was not sorry Silas was dead. Even old Brooksie was always wary of him due to his drinking and his loose mouth. Rob never trusted the man and it had only been

221

on Bradley's insistence that he had taken him on, but what now? How much did the Redemptors know? This was the thing he had dreaded most. The thought burned through his mind that if he got through this dangerous situation he would kill Bradley with his bare hands!

"... Eh... Wot?" With a start he realized that Russell was speaking.

"Ah said that all this musta come as a big surprise to you Rob"

"Oh, aye, wonder jes' wot Big Silas 'ad been up to? Tho' I don' remember no Jake ever workin' for Brooksie."

The Miller looked at him seriously and rejoined "Well, one o' my colleagues wuz talkin' 'bout that t'other night. He said that you night be able to throw some light on the matter. As you know, the brotherhood don' take kindly to people a-workin' away frum their own manor or keepin' us in the dark. It upsets the delicate balance of things, y'see. But I told 'im that you waz probably busy gerrin' yore new business off ground. 'Ow's it goin' then? I yeard as you wuz doin' some exportin' too... Portugal ain't it?"

Rob felt a surge of relief as he recognised an opportunity to ease the situation and seized the moment. "Well, Mr Russell, as usual you seem well informed and tis true that I did provide certain services for a gentleman from Warminster. For which, I must admit he paid a generous fee just at a time when I needed it to launch my turpentine exportin' venture."

Russell eyed him craftily and prompted him.

"An' may I ask, 'as that got to do with yore visit 'ere today?" Rob responded by saying that he had to fetch something from his horse that would explain his visit. The miller nodded his approval but as Rob left the room Russell checked the loaded pistol lying in the drawer next to him.

Rob was back in a minute carrying something wrapped up in muddy sacking and dumped the heavy object on the old table.

"An' jes' wot might that be, a present for me?" Russell asked, his hand edging to the half open drawer.

"Well, ye might say that." Replied Rob and opened up the burlap to reveal a bright ingot of pure gold the size of a small brick. Russell's eyes bulged.

"How in Hades did you come by that?" He gasped.

Rob sat back and watched as the miller stroked the ingot and held it to his cheek weighing it in his hand.

"It came to me by courtesy of the party who engaged me to do that bit of river work I mentioned. He gave me three of um. You 'ave one; the second went to the Jew Isaac Mendoza in Brizzle as security for him financing my Scandinavian venture. T'other I keep for any emergencies that might surface."

The Miller nodded sagely. "As ye say, ye nivver know jes' wot might come around do'ee? By the way, who wuz this gen'uman then? I forgot 'is name for the moment."

Rob looked bland and flatly said. "That's not surprisin' Mr.

223

Russell, as I can't recall tellin' ye! Truth be known, I nivver learned that meself. My orders came by a second party an' the settlement too, a sort of agent yew might say. A young cove from Warminster 'e wuz.. Name o' Bradley summat as it 'appens. All I know is, he worked at the barracks there. "Fust I knew 'bout it wuz when 'e turned up at the yard."

"Bradley, eh? …Well, not that it's of any importance anyway but no doubt us'll get to the bottom of it soon."

The miller picked up his present and thanked Rob for calling and hoped it wouldn't be long before they did business again.

As Rob's horse clattered out of the mill yard farm Russell stood at the door and gestured to a figure watching from the mill gantry to come to the office. It was the woman he had told Rob was his niece. She bustled in without ceremony and sat behind Russell's desk, folded her arms and demanded belligerently.

"Well, Miller, what did yon rogue 'ave to say for his self?" Russell told her that it was nothing of note and that Rob was just paying his dues and reporting things from the river.

"Just about time too." She sniffed. "Cos Brother Ambrose was on the brink o' havin' 'im brought in. As he said, we bin earin' all sorts o' rumours goin' round 'bout certain river men. We can't let these smart jakes take liberties can we or they'll all be soon at it? You'd better send a note to our man out Severnake way to find out more about this 'ere Jake too. It looks like time we 'ad a talk to 'im an' all." Changing tack she added. "Tell that lazy knave Dickon to saddle the bay mare and have everything I need ready in an hour's time. I want to be in Axbridge by this evening and intend to question the Constable there. I would like to know more about some o' these French émigrés settlin' at Bridgewater. They've got their own boat there apparently an' we don' want 'em shippin' in any dangerous Papists do us? Send your report direct to me at the Green Briar Inn at Sidcot"

Surprisingly Russell waited respectfully until she had finished and then quietly assured her that her orders would be carried out directly.

Even Rob himself would have been surprised to find a woman with such authority but within the Puritan ranks women were as influential as the men and always had been. Russell's so called 'niece' was in fact Marie Dubord came from one of the original Huguonot families and the Redemptor's Western Region Controller. Russell waited at the mill yard gate until he saw her leave the village. He had made no mention of the gold bar, deciding that he just might need it in the near future… and if by chance Rob got topped, well, who would know about it anyway?

As Rob walked round the back of the building he saw Dickon checking one of the hind hooves of the bay mare. As he bent to tap the shoe Rob noticed a strange bright green feather stuck in the back of his belt.

22

ALEXANDER INHERITS

Up at the Ensleigh Provost compound Alexander was sitting in his office gazing blankly out of the window at the dazzling white crushed stone of the parade ground where a group of builders were putting the finishing touches to a new stable block. He was quite surprised to note, how, what had started as a simple turnpike office was rapidly turning into a small barracks complex to guard the northern approaches of Bath when a dispatch rider clattered into the courtyard below. A clump of boots on the stairs told him that the message was for him and he stood by his desk as the dusty, sweating rider was escorted into the room by the uniformed sentry.

"Dispatch from GHQ Warminster, Sah!" He bellowed, presenting his receipt chit and placed the crown embossed saddle bag on the desk. Alexander signed the chit and gestured for the trooper to wait outside before breaking the seal on the communication. It read

From.   Major G.C. Roberts. Adjutant to General Coker
        Commanding Officer S.W. HQ. Warminster.
        28th September 1803

To.   Major Alexander Coulston. R.M.I
        Lord Provost Dep't.(West) Bath.

Enclosed is an extract from the coastguard at St Mawes received yesterday 27th. inst. from the Royal Navy cutter Edward from the fleet standing off Ushant which may be of concern to you personally.....

Further news is that, responding to distress signals from the merchant ship Avon Lass three days out of Lisbon to Cork and Avonmouth, Bristol, we regret to inform you that Lady Trandon, one of the passengers aboard, passed away due to a stroke in the Bay of Biscay on the 25th inst.

The Fleet's Surgeon went aboard to investigate and finding early signs of cholera on the body ordered burial at sea.
The ceremony carried out the same evening, Captain Smollet officiating.
Request you inform all next of kin.

Captain George Travers, RN,

A note attached expressed sympathy with his loss and informed him that the lady's effects and property were in the charge of her travelling companions Miss Agnes Porter and Senhorita Rachel Dacarius and that, God willing, the Avon Lass will dock at Bristol 30th inst.

The communication shocked Alexander to the core and for a moment he was stunned, unable to speak or move. Then his military training took over and he called the dispatch rider in and told him to bed down his horse with the stable officer and get something to eat in the cookhouse.. It would be too late now to return but he could pick up his return dispatch at the Guard Room at seven the next morning. As the rider saluted and clattered back down the stairs he began to ruminate on the implications of the tragedy.

Foremost, there was the title to consider and as Miriam's only living relative, (her brother George having finally met his maker a year ago in an Indian brothel,) he would, of course, have to inform the Heraldic College in London and have his inheritance confirmed by them but in actual fact he was the new Lord Trandon, 6th Baron Staverton... He smiled to himself... It had a nice ring to it! Yes, very nice indeed... His happy reverie was brought to a sharp halt however by realisation that his aunt's unexpected demise had brought with it many obligations and responsibilities. On top of the social side of things there was the vast, scattered estate to manage. He had already heard whispers of strange deals and slack accounting by Miriam's steward who abused her blind trust. One of his first tasks would be to

228

demand a full reckoning and question the man in depth about his suspicious dealings. In the meantime however there was a whole heap of things to be done here at Ensleigh so pushing the concerns of Trandon House to the back of his mind he called in the Orderly Clerk and dictated a note to the barracks thanking them for the information and requesting compassionate leave to attend to his new found responsibilities. At the top of his own private list was the meeting up again with his beautiful Senhorita!

The news of his ennoblement was quickly the talk of the town but for Bradley Thomas, newly promoted to Chief Clerk of the Provost Liaison unit at Warminster Barracks, the news had serious implications too. He would have to move fast if he was to get his hands on the money he considered his due and decided to seek a meeting with The Redemptors as soon as possible.

Ten days later in the low beamed room that served as the office at the stables in Lansdowne, Cyrus and Jeb were enjoying a liquid lunch when Alexander arrived to show them the brand new suit of clothes he had just collected to celebrate his new elevated status. Clearing a space on the table he deposited two large flat boxes on it. As they watched on impatiently, from one he brought out a beautiful dark maroon velvet frock coat and a canary yellow embroidered waistcoat and from the second, a pair of pure white buckskin breeches, white silk stockings, a pair of black patent leather pumps and some hand tooled tan riding boots.

Studiously pretending not to be interested Cyrus cast an eye at the name on the box lid and casually said "What have you got there then? That lot must have cost a pretty packet, I dare say… Massari ain' it"

"Well, come on then, milord; let's see what you look like with 'em on." Jeb chortled, banging his mug on the table.

Slipping on the jacket Alexander preened like a dance hall macaroni saying "Well, how d'ye like the cut o' Lord Trandon's jib now, eh?" Both Jeb and Cyrus nodded in unison and agreed that he really did look a credit to his new title and passed him over a tankard of rum toddy.

Milan, the capital of Lombardy, was famous throughout Europe for three things. Its bankers, its singers and surprisingly, its tailors; and the Massari family were prominent in all three of these. The eldest, Ceasari, was a leading banker, Piero was a major booking agent for the opera and Otello, the youngest one was a tailor. His shop in Bath was on Lower Church Street almost opposite Ralph Allen's house and was patronised by the most discerning dandies and men- about- town. His reputation as tailor and stylist had been first established in Milan and as a young man he moved to Venice and later to London. He set up shop in Mayfair where he rapidly became disenchanted by the extended-credit seeking politicians and city gents. These customers, while spending fortunes on horses, carriages and high living often kept their tailors waiting years for settlement.

It was about then that he heard about the prodigal spending habits of the adventurers and gamblers in Bath and it didn't take Otello long to realise where his future lay. Like many other European traders before him he hurried there to get his trotters into the overflowing money trough. Painfully aware of his London experience, he set high standards from the start and would not undertake any orders unless the client came recommended and placed a substantial cash deposit. In a mere four years he had built up a very healthy customer base and enhanced his already considerable reputation and in the process established an industrious Italian community in his workshops behind the crumbling old Gascoyne Tower on the Upper Borough Walls.

The fashion show over, Cyrus put down his tankard and looked hard at his friend banged his pipe against the edge of the table and after blowing it clear he said. "Ye know, Alexander there could be a problem with your new found title."

"Oh aye, do you mean all the fuss that comes with that bunch of charlatans that calls itself "The College of Heralds?"

"Nay, tis not that," Riposted his friend "I was just thinking... It is not fitting that Lord Trandon, as you have now become, can continue with the humble rank of Major, as high sounding as it maybe. Protocol insists that you should hold the rank of at least Colonel; and that I fear, will be a very expensive promotion to purchase, for there is no other way and it is always a seller's market. It's either that or to resign your commission altogether. The options are clear."

"Well." Alexander mused. "I don't fancy resigning my commission. I have put in too much work on this robbery to leave it now, so it looks like I'll have to take the expensive route I suppose."

In response to this sad statement Jeb said. "Well, I don't know anythin' 'bout commissions an' such but seller's market or not, I've allus found that there's a bargain to be 'ad somewhere if'n you look close enough."

"Yes." Cyrus concurred. "Why don't we get the latest Army List and see just what's on offer. A friend of mine bought himself a colonelcy in a Scottish Fencibles regiment which had not seen action since the '45 and then it was only garrison duty in Perth. Got it cheap, he did and then just deputised some yeomanry farmer to the position. I know he never saw Perth. In fact I doubt if he ever left Exeter!"

Changing the subject, Jeb brought up the expected arrival at Bristol of the boat from Portugal.

"Well, I bin thinking that iffen yew wuz goin' alone you could jes' ride down there but to bring back two women you'd 'ave to go by carriage, tho' there is another way."

Alexander turned to look at him. "Oh aye, Jeb and what might that be, then?"

"Well 'ow about goin' there by boat, ye know straight down the river? Y'see, I 'appen to know that the Dago jade is the sister of Rob Dacarius who has them stone trows workin' 'tween Bath 'n

Brizzle regular an' he's sure to be pickin' 'er up, innee? Cyrus and Alexander nodded in agreement and Jeb continued. "So I'll tellee wot, I've gotta go down to Bathwick to pick a couple o' nags up this afternoon so I'll call on 'im an' sort it out."

***

At first Rob was pleased to see Jeb whom he knew from the pub and to hear that his sister was coming home from Lisbon... The situation there with his Uncle Arturo was causing him much concern and he would welcome Rachel's first hand report but he was not too pleased to be carrying the man who had been given the job of catching the payroll thieves. He was in an awkward position... If he refused such a reasonable request it would look suspicious and he had enough trouble brewing already with Bradley and the Redemptors so he reluctantly agreed to the request.

The problem regarding Alexander's rank was soon settled. From the Army List a vacancy was discovered in the 1st Lampeter Dragoons, an obscure yeomanry regiment that had been raised to guard against the repeat of the French invasion attempt in West Wales. The depot was in the market town of Tregaron and as the vacancy had been open since the old colonel's death three years ago, a certain Major Harris had taken over. Alexander saw no reason why the man should not continue to do so and bought the colonelcy for a song. After this brief hiccup Alexander felt that he could settle again to his job.

23

RACHELS RETURN

Alexander announced the sad news of his Aunt Miriam's passing to the assembled staff at Trandon hall and assured them all that things would carry on as normal, adding that if anyone felt that they did not wish to stay in his employ that he would release them from their obligations and give them a good reference.

As bad luck could have it (at least from his perspective), Jessica was also present and came and stood close at his side, holding his elbow in a gesture of solidarity. The gesture did not go unnoticed and was the subject of some hot gossip in the kitchen later on. Harrison the butler scolded them and said fie on such tittle-tattle and to get on with their tasks, even if secretly he was himself intrigued to know just what was going on between her and the new Lord Trandon.

Someone asked if there would be a memorial service and before Alexander could answer, Jessica took charge saying that she would see to all the details and that because Alexander should not have to bear the grief all alone, she would accompany him to Bristol to pick up his aunt's effects and escort Agnes back to Bath.

It was about the last thing in the world that Alexander wanted... He had been looking forward to a passionate reunion with Senhorita Rachel and perhaps a day or two together at a discreet hotel but what chance of that was there now with Jessica pushing her beak in? He tried to dissuade her saying that he was going by river in a commercial boat but she dismissed his objections and with sad smile at the assembly said it was the least she could do. Alexander ground his teeth and thanked her for such thoughtfulness... (Secretly he could have strangled her!)

After the staffs were dismissed back to their duties, Harrison scuttled furtively out of the back door and made his way up through the woods to Home Farm to tell his friend and fellow conspirator the important news. There were changes coming and they must make plans.

And so it came about that early in the morning of the departure Cyrus arrived at the ferry landing below South Parade in a finely appointed barouche bearing Alexander with Jessica snuggling close to him and ever-present Janet looking sour faced. Jeb had also decided to come along on the trip as he had to collect two chain horses from the special smithy at Salford where they were being fitted with cleated winter shoes. As he pointed out to Rob, there was also the advantage that with the autumn rains beginning up river, the

235

flow was brisk and the two nags could make the return journey easier.

Jeb was quiet and looking thoughtful when the others had arrived. He didn't explain what was troubling him but having got to the South Parade half an hour earlier he had been gazing over the parapet at the river when he saw a furtively figure leaving the boat yard… It was the same person that he had seen arguing with Rob in the tavern... The one he thought he had seen loading barrels on the day of the fire…but he was not sure about it.

Noticing that his passengers had arrived, Rob and his two crewmen fished out the sunken cable with a grapple and warped the trow across to the ferry landing. Rob immediately recognised the Major and pulled his hat down to hide his face but Alexander who had had only a fleeting view of him in the inn yard at Warminster a few years back, did not recall him at all. The only thing he remembered vividly about that day was the beautiful raven haired girl in the crowd.

Still with a sour face Janet stepped aboard and then helped her mistress over the gunnels and with much muttering and tut-tutting the ladies finally were seated in the stern and Alexander found a small keg to sit on by the rail while Jeb made his way for'ard to help the crew clear the landing and hoist the chunky square sail. At Boatman Inn the mast had to be un-stepped and dipped to clear the hooped bridge to Locksbridge Island but it was a regular manoeuvre which did not delay them too much and soon they were at the

Saltford Lock where Jeb went ashore to pick up Dolly and her son Jason from the smithy. Not wanting to spend more time than he had to in Alexander's company, Rob said that he and the crew would be waiting in the Jolly Sailor till Jeb got back.

Half an hour later Jeb was back with the horses which were well used to getting aboard barges so with the aid of the planks and a loading ramp they were soon settled with their nose bags at the prow.

The trow proceeded peacefully down stream, the only small problem appearing in the fast current beyond Hannam Court and the mud banks of the Conham Bend and its weir but again this a regular hazard to the crew who handled it smoothly and by mid-afternoon they had arrived at Bristol docks. This was familiar territory to Rob and before entering the commercial quay he hove to and went ashore to inform the harbour master of his cargo and intended purpose. Since the advent of the Napoleonic wars this security control was strictly enforced as a precaution against sabotage or illicit smuggling by French or Irish agents. The official was happy to see him again and directed him to the berth occupied by the Avon Lass in the inner basin. No sooner had the trow nosed into the basin than the ship loomed up on the starboard side and Alexander saw his treasure waving enthusiastically to him. Jessica looked on tight lipped and moved closer to Alexander's side

The military sentry stood by the gangplank and presented arms as he saw the officer approaching. Alexander returned the salute and the First Mate invited them aboard. Alexander halted on deck and saluted the quarter deck as the ship was flying the flag of the Fleet Surgeon who had just finished his inspection and signed the quarantine documents to say that the vessel was clear of any sign of plague. Captain Smollet came out of his cabin to greet them followed by Agnes and the beautiful Rachel.

Again Alexander's heart jumped and this time there was real warmth in her smile. Jessica glanced quickly away to avoid greeting the glowing Miss Dacarius and gestured Janet and two crewmen from the trow to see to the ladies' trunks. Not that Rachel would have noticed her anyway as she only had eyes for Alexander.

Flowery introductions were made with bows and handshakes while Alexander and Rachel looked longingly at each other but reluctantly joined in the charade. Jessica caught their mood and dragged out the formalities as painfully as possible by asking Captain Smollet spurious questions about his voyage and Lady Trandon's demise. Alexander looked at her harshly, puzzled by this strange behaviour. Agnes however unwittingly burst her balloon by announcing that her mistress had insisted that Rachel should reside at Trandon House as long as she wished as a reward for her help and companionship in Portugal. The news had Jessica spitting feathers!

Finally the long welcoming performance was completed and the party descended the gangplank and boarded the trow for the return journey to Bath, which with the aid of Jeb's chain horses would be completed by early evening at the latest.

After craftily, sending Janet off to help Agnes supervise the loading

238

of the trunks, Jessica invited Rachel to sit beside her at the stern to tell her of all the happenings in Portugal affectively putting the damper on any hopes that Alexander may have had of having an intimate conversation with his long awaited beauty. Alexander stood by the rail chaffing at the bit and rehearsing just what he was going to say to Jessica when they got back home.

As he stood there cogitating, a crewman wearing a head cloth came up to him, saluted and handed him a package which had been left behind by the Portugese lady. Alexander nodded a vague thank you and absentmindedly put it in his pocket. As he clopped down the gangplank behind the others he idly wondered why the man had a bright green feather stuck in his head cloth.

The fact was that Agnes's innocent announcement had really thrown Jessica. The last thing she wanted was to be sharing the house (and who knows what else?) with some gypsy fortune hunter. She had plans for Alexander's future and the prospect of a title added another reason for wanting to derail any ideas he may have had about getting closer to this Portuguese peasant.

Rachel too was flustered but her woman's intuition was well attuned to the ways of the world and it didn't take her long to see through this new found bonhomie on Jessica's part but she continued to play the gauche country maid. What followed was what she had expected as Jessica went into a long diatribe the upshot of which was that Rachel would be accepted in the house just as both Janet and Agnes had been: As part of the domestic staff! Such a development did not fit in at all with Rachel's plans and she had no intention of being a skivvy for anyone... Least of all this bossy bitch!

Realising that there was nothing she could do at the moment Rachel excused herself and went to talk to her brother in the cabin. Apart from a warm greeting and a welcoming kiss she had but a brief moment to tell him of their Uncle Arturo's suspicious behaviour.

"So what's the old tomcat been up to eh, Rachel? 'as 'e done worr I axed 'im to do?" Rachel wrinkled her nose (a Portugeuse gesture of disapproval) and said that as far as she knew the barrels were still in the caves at Montijo but that he seemed mighty glad to discover she was leaving and that she thought that the sooner Rob himself could go out and inspect his cargo the better. She also added that he should not go alone because in her view, Uncle Arturo was not that reliable when it came to family loyalty! Rob did not enlighten her as to his plans but was now even more certain that it was time to get moving.

Deciding to change the subject he asked his sister just what was she playing at, making up to this bloody Marine? Had she forgotten what he had done to Brooksie? And on top of that did she realise he was the officer tasked to catch the robbers? Was she going mad or what?

She calmed him down by pointing out the advantages of living under the same roof. For one thing she could keep abreast of developments and warn him of any impending danger. He reluctantly accepted her reasoning and with a snort returned to the wheel as they were approaching the tricky bend at Hannam.

By the time they got back to Bath it was growing dusk and Rob pretended to be too busy readying the trow for an early start next morning that he just grunted as his passengers profusely thanked him and departed. When Alexander gave him a couple of crowns as a gratuity he simply pocketed them, nodded and turned away.

Once his passengers had left to pick up their carriage and horses as arranged at Laura Place, Rob sent one his men to escort Rachel to Widcombe Village and sat by candlelight in the wheel house sampling a new bottle of rum. While he was sorting out the latest Avon navigation charts he could feel the growing tension…There was a sense of danger in the air as though some kind of noose was tightening around his neck: … And this performance he had just witnessed on the boat had made him even jumpier. What was it all about? His little sister flashing longing cow eyes at the man who had killed her lover and who herself had once sworn vengeance on?. That had been the last straw!

It irked him too that this very officer was now in charge of the investigation of the crime but he did see one small window of opportunity…. Perhaps with all the complications of the death of his aunt and the new responsibilities of his inheritance, it might be some time before the Major could get any in-depth investigation rolling. Accordingly Rob decided to bring forward the plan he had been considering.

For the first time in their lives it seemed that he and Rachel had a differing set of priorities. Having finally decided on a plan he took a last swig of the rum and went ashore to sleep in the hut in his compound. In the low mist of the following morning, having seen the trow off to Ralph Allen's dock he got started.

His first move was to visit his storeroom at Tog Hill and select the barrels he knew contained bullion, load them onto his cart and transport them himself to the shipper's warehouse in Bristol to be sent to Lisbon on the next freighter. The factor saw nothing unusual in this and happily accepted the cargo and the prepaid tariff saying that the cargo would be in Portugal in a month's time. Later in the week he rode down to Poole and booked passage on a boat to Vigo from where he intended to travel overland to Lisbon....He was just in time!

Two days later Bradley showed up again at the tavern in Widcome and warned him that he would not wait any longer, telling Rob that if he did not get satisfaction by Michaelmas, he would do what he had threatened. Rob, who had already made his first moves pretended that he would agree to Bradley's conditions but pleaded that as it was already late September he would need more time to arrange things but that he would pay Bradley fifty crowns now if he would wait until the first Sunday after All Saints Day when he would pay him his full share. Grudgingly Bradley accepted the condition saying he would come by the yard in a couple of days to collect the cash, adding that if there was any delay he would immediately go straight to the Redemptors. Rob did his best to appear intimidated by the threats and that he was fully aware of his position. As the door slammed behind his tormentor Rob had a little smile on his face. He would be far beyond the reach of the Redemptors in Catholic Portugal when Bradley met a welcoming committee in Marshfield..... If he lived that long,

Watching the whole performance from a corner table had been two noisy card players one of whom now stood up and took there mugs to the bar. While waiting for the refill he twirled a small green feather in his hand.

24

A RE-APPRAISAL

Rob was not the only one to be taken aback by the changes that seemed to be happening. Alexander too was surprised by the transformation of the hitherto shy and retiring Jessica.

In place of the demure and rather plainly dressed prim young lady there appeared a fully blossomed woman about town. The lustrous copper coloured hair, previously confined beneath fussy bonnet was now a crown of glory curled and piled high upon her head in an elegant coiffure and her new clothes were of the latest French émigré style. Her three-quarter length coat was in golden brocade decorated with pearls and semi precious stones, cut with soft shoulders and a gentle flare which perfectly complimented the dress. This was an elegant creation in layers of diaphanous silk and muslin a fabric that only required the faintest hint of perspiration to cling to the body like a second skin. It was cut in the classic Greek style with the waist high under the bust line; a style that was merciless with anything less than perfect breasts, which Jessica carried off to perfection. Her ankles were encased in fine white silk stockings and her shoes were gold pumps with blue kitten heels. She sat close to Alexander and proprietarily held his hand

They were in high ceiling'd room in Queens Square at the opulent offices of the solicitor Mr James Willerby to hear the official reading of Miriam's will in the company of Alexander's own attorney, Agnes and her brother Tom, two of Miriam's elderly cousins and another lawyer representing the interests of her deceased brother's daughter in India and Mr Stuckey, Miriam's banker from Milsom Street: In short all the interested parties.

The sun streamed in through the tall nine foot windows and in the corner a large mahogany case clock ticked sonorously to perfectly compliment the rambling monotonous saw of the elderly Mr Willerby as he waded sluggishly through the whys, where-ins and legalese of the will's preamble. Everybody looked bored and stared around the office vacantly till he finished with ".....And so to the final bequests of Miriam Mary Trandon, the late Countess of Staverton."

At that news a collective sigh of relief hissed round the room, much to the disapproval of the speaker who paused and glanced sourly over his pince-nez at the company before continuing to outline Miriam's last wishes, taking the long way round everything and relishing his captive audience.

Finally the forty minute performance was over and he looked challengingly at the worn down assembly and asked if there were any questions or points he could explain in greater depth: If there had have been nobody there wanted to be subjected to any more of Willerby's snobby ramblings and reached for their hats and coats as soon as the door closed behind him.

Surprisingly Agnes had been particularly well looked after. Alexander and for that matter everybody who had seen Miriam's spiteful side was fully expecting her to be as insensitive to her long serving and loyal companion as she had been in life but the provision made for her was generous indeed. First there was a lifetime annuity granted of £300 per year, a very substantial sum for those days and then the provision of a rent free riverside cottage and a pony and trap in the hamlet of Kelston on the far western edge of the Trandon estate. For one of the few times in her life Agnes was ecstatic and smiled at her weather-worn brother. The prospect of a comfortable retirement together by the river was very pleasing indeed.

The two distant cousins got the Besant family house in Bristol and the market garden at Clifton and her niece in India got Miriam's share of her brother's plantation in India.

As everybody expected, the bulk of the vast Trandon estate went to Alexander along with the title of 6th Earl of Staverton. Old Willerby had taken the opportunity to point out that he was unable to give a true valuation of the bequest because as the statute demands, this could only be done by an appointed assessor.

About the only one who felt a twinge of disappointment was the appointed assessor himself, a short but prosperous looking, ruddy

246

faced man who was standing quietly at the back of the room. This was Elias Stuckey, a successful Chippenham draper turned banker who had made a fortune in the mad frenzy of the late building boom of the 1780's, shrewdly consolidating his profits and doing his best to rein in Miriam's spendthrift ways, for which he hoped the lady would have been grateful…but alas there was nothing for him. He caught up with Alexander as he was leaving and requested a meeting at the first opportunity.

The reading over, Alexander with Jessica firmly holding onto his arm clattered down the stairs and out into the bright crisp sunshine to meet Jeb and Janet who were waiting in Queen's Square with the sparkling barouche. Once aboard Janet passed her mistress a Russian sable lined cloak and as Jessica pulled the travelling rug over her knees she cast a critical eye around the square and turned to Alexander and chirruped.

"Well Milord, I think today calls for a celebration, don't you? Let's have champagne at Corbett's Hotel on South Parade. It's much more exclusive than the boring old Pump Rooms."
Corbett's was also the most expensive watering hole in the city!

With a rather sickly grin Alexander signalled his agreement and they headed down Milsom Street, past the lounging groups of mashers, rakes and macaronis who stared whistled and waved their canes at this stunning new beauty in town. Watching the open coach from an upper window was a tall powerfully built man with a brutal scarred face wearing the pale blue dolman jacket of the 3rd

Hanoverian Dragoons who was bowled over by this gorgeous unknown newcomer. Oberst Major Mahler twirled his blond moustaches and decided that he would make it his business to conquer this paragon of beauty by eliminating her escort. For a moment he let his eye wander to her companion and he froze. A terrible look of pure hatred crossed his face. Because Alexander was wearing mourning black he had not recognised him at first but now he was more determined than ever to take this woman who clung so close to him.

Mahler's hatred stemmed from the fact that in his capacity of Chief Investigator, Alexander had insisted on interviewing everybody involved in the transportation of the bullion and that he had had the temerity to demand an explanation of the duties of Mahler's regiment who were the principle escort. The proud German interpreted this as a personal slight on his honour and was seething with anger, seeking redress for the insult. Now it appeared that there was another reason to obtain satisfaction. Ah yes … A luscious prize indeed.

A few days later Alexander called in the bank and was greeted by the genial Elias who, truth be known, was rather regretting his outburst at the solicitors. Nevertheless he led the new lord up to his personal parlour on the first floor where privacy was assured.

"May I tempt you to a glass of Madeira, Major? Or should I say Milord?

"Ah now Mr.Stuckey, let's have none o' that!" laughed his guest. "Just call me Alexander as you always have done. I don't think that I will ever loose my rough marine's ways and adopt the correct aristocratic demeanour. Too long at the sharp end of life I suppose."

Stuckey nodded his understanding remembering the days before his fiscal success when the gentry would look down on his country manners... But his hard cash had soon changed all that. He gestured for Alexander to take a seat and moved behind his huge desk where he ruffled through a file of papers and selected some sheets. .

"I imagine you are wondering why I asked you to drop by but I feel that it is now incumbent on me as your late aunt's banker, to give you a true picture of the financial position of the Trandon Estate and perhaps air some of my misgivings. You see, over the last few years I have become and increasingly concerned and I consider that Lady Trandon's blind trust in her steward is perhaps, shall we say, misplaced."

Alexander said that he too had been taken aback by his aunt's bald statement that she had given her power of attorney to Barnes and that he had in fact been trying to get hold of the man to explain certain discrepancies in the accounts.

"Well, at least it is good that you also have become aware of some of his dubious practices and that it is time to act. As my old father would say… 'When you are stuck in a hole the first thing to do is stop digging'…. and as it happens, there is something that can now be done. You see, the mandate giving Mr Barnes the power ceases with your aunt's death and requires your signature to renew it… But I most earnestly suggest that you do not do this. I have no doubt Old Willerby would trot out some delaying legal precedent so that he can squeeze the last groat out of you but the power rests with you and your banker. Here are the papers curtailing the privileges of Yeoman Barnes, all that is required now is your signature and a request for a full audit of the estate."

Alexander was dumfounded and reacted angrily. "I knew that the blackguard was up to something! In fact I tried to raise the subject with Aunt Miriam on several occasions but she would not hear a bad word against the man… I would be grateful if you would spend a little time digging deeper into this matter as soon as possible. Consider it as a commission for which the bank will be reimbursed. In fact I think it is time for a full valuation of the Trandon estate as a whole"

"What a capital idea!" Stuckey exclaimed. "Now you are beginning to behave like a proper aristocrat and I have just the people to handle it. I suggest Fletcher and Lambert, surveyors and land valuers. They come to me highly recommended by Sir William Pulteney himself who was very pleased with their assessment of his Bathwick estate. They will re-mark your boundaries, measure your

holdings and give you an accurate valuation within six weeks. I happen to be having lunch with Chris Lambert at the Saracen's Head on Friday and will be glad to issue your instructions if you wish."
Alexander said he approved of the idea and to lighten the mood Stuckey filled the glasses again and said.

"You might also be pleased to learn that your connection with the sea is not yet at an end either. You see one of the items that Old Willerby lumped together in the bulk of the estate was a ship... Or at least a part of a ship"

"A ship, ye say?" Alexander put down his glass.

"That's right." continued the banker. "Lady Trandon inherited a substantial share in a trading venture. They are modestly successful Anglo-Dutch Company based in London with a squadron of three-masted Dutch fluyts. Currently they are making two or three voyages a year plying twix Rochester and points east of the Cape of Good Hope trading cloth, ironware, hides, guns and powder... Homeward bound the cargo is mainly spices, silk and batik cloth, teak furniture and fancy brass wear. All good commercial items with a ready market in Europe... What d'ye thing about that then Milord?"

"How did he come by that?.. From what I've heard Old Teddy never even went to the coast?" Alexander asked

"Oh, as is often the case here in this mad city, it was taken as collateral for a gambling debt and when the debtor died his share in the trading company passed to his lordship and through him to Lady

251

Trandon. God willing, one of their ships is due to dock at Southampton next month. I thought as ex-seafaring Johnny you might like to go and inspect her."

Alexander sipped his wine and said. "I might do just that. Does this venture make money then?"

"Aye, it does fairly well. We get the accounts twice yearly and seems healthy enough to me. P'raps as well it does.
The banker looked blankly at Alexander who, frowning, asked. "What dost thou mean, by that, Mr Stuckey?

"Well," Said Elias slowly "I think that it was fortunate that Lady Trandon never mentioned it to that knave Barnes or he would've got his claws in that too! I know this because my bank has been informed of several notes held against the estate by the oddest parties... If I did not know better I would say that he was in cahoots with some one inside Trandon House who had access to Her Ladyship's private correspondence." At this Alexander frowned but the banker was quick to reassure him, saying "Oh no, don't fret that your inheritance is threatened... But I would be much remiss in my duties not to inform you that there it is a considerable sum of the estate's money still unaccounted for."

With that, the banker put the signed documents in his desk drawer and gave his solemn assurance that he would have the promised full report in two weeks time. Alexander was still seething when he returned to his office!

25

JESSICA INHERITS

It had all started when Alexander had returned home unexpectedly to collect some papers and discovered Jessica in full cry: She was standing on the stairs berating the assembled staff in the main hall below her. Her voice was imperious as she informed them that she was in charge now and that things would certainly have to change and that they could soon be replaced if they did not meet her exacting standards. The old ways would have to go!

As he came through the front door she suddenly stopped her rant causing the servants to turn to find out why. At the sight of his livid face and raging eyes they scuttled away as fast as they could back to their jobs. Alex beckoned and Jessica followed him into his room with down cast eyes closing the door behind her.

Turning to her he shouted. "And just what the Hell do you think you are doing Madame? How dare you presume to be mistress of Trandon House? Which, I may remind you, is my house now.....
And may I also remind you that you are simply a paying guest here."

Alexander was raging up and down the dining room while Jessica stood white faced with anger and humiliation by the window. He heard the door creak and turned to see Janet staring in fright and on the brink of tears at Alexander's outburst.

"And you wench." He shouted. "What are you doing here? You shall kindly refrain from following us about like a lost sheep. I wish to speak to your mistress of private matters and not to provide you with below stairs tittle-tattle. Get gone from my sight… Now!"

To add emphasis to his orders he violently kicked Jessica's straw bonnet which she had dropped with the shock of his onslaught. With a squeak and a whimper Janet scuttled off slamming the door behind her.

Jessica just looked mockingly at him and clapped her hands. "Oh, bravo, sir! What an impressive demonstration of your masculine power. I would wager that ladies from here to Cheltenham will be shaking in their shoes!"
Jessica's sarcasm was cutting and for a moment he faltered.

"Do not trifle with me Madame!" He raged. "You know damn well what I am saying. Do not take on airs and graces in my house, or outside it for that matter. And do not presume any relationship with me that I have not asked for! By all means Madame, have your little pantomime games but do not attempt to pass an opinion on the company I keep. Has it never dawned on you that I have made my preferences clear?"

She rolled her eyes skyward. "Oh, really sir? How I pity you and blush with scorn and embarrassment at your antics with that Lusitanian Gypsy. Presumption ye say! Pray tell me then, why did you introduce me to that doxy as your fiancée when we were seeing your Aunt off to Portugal, eh? I can assure you most strongly sir, that there was no presumption on my part then!"

She could hear Janet's sobs from behind the door and turned to face him coldly and said haughtily "It seems that your jumped up title has not taught you any decorum or changed your boorish shipboard ways. Lord Trandon indeed! Let me tell you sir, you have a long way to go before you warrant that accolade! You shall hear more of this humiliation, I trow....Pagh!"

Without a further word Jessica picked up her ruined bonnet and with a mocking glance walked out of the room leaving Alexander purple with rage.

In that strange hiatus of suspended time between the nostalgic Christmas festivities and the exciting challenge of the coming New Year, Alexander was sitting in his Ensleigh office bored and moodily staring out of the ice rimmed windows at the white expanse of the hoar frosted Lansdowne plateau and fitfully sifting through a pile of mail that his clerk had left on his desk. For the most part it appeared to be the usual stuff, copies of memos and standard inter-departmental correspondence from Warminster mainly monthly reports, requisition requests and duty rosters etc.

Deciding that it could all wait until the creaking military machinery began to turn again in January; Alexander sighed disgustedly, swept it all aside and took a bottle of dark Jamaican rum and a crystal tumbler from his desk drawer. Pouring himself a hearty measure, he rolled back his blue leather captain's chair and faced the small fire in the grate, eased off his canvas topped high boots to warm his toes and settled back to enjoy his tipple.

He was just beginning to drift off into some day dream of his past adventures in the Caribbean when his eye caught the corner of a letter sticking out from the middle of the pile. It seemed to bear a Royal Navy crest and he reached across to pull it out. True enough, it was from the Lords of the Admiralty in London and was addressed directly to him.

'Well' He thought. 'This is most singular!' and hastened to break the seal.

Enclosed was a copy of the standard naval report detailing recent events on one of the Indian stations and a private note to him regarding a certain paragraph on page seven and asking him to take whatever action he saw fit regarding it. He turned to the page which turned out to be news of recent postings and the arrival or departure of various personnel... A big red star marked one corner where Alexander was shocked to read of the sudden death of Admiral Singleton at one of the hilltop bungalows where he had gone to partly take a cure for his gout but mainly to get away from the oppressive summer heat of the dusty plains. There was also a note asking him if he would be so good as to inform the admiral's daughter who he understood resided in Bath, of this tragic unexpected occurrence?'

Alexander's first response was to snort derisively... He was still smarting from their last battle when she presumed to haul him over the coals about his relationship with Rachel. or 'That soot-headed Romany hag' as she so genteelly put it, and felt a spiteful delight in the fact that he had actually been ordered to be the bringer of the bad news.

After a moment, however he mellowed when the full seriousness of the event hit home and felt strangely uneasy. Would she move out from Trandon House? How would that feel? Since his Aunt's demise he had become accustomed to her presence in the house and he grudgingly admitted that she certainly ran the house very efficiently.... Yes, things would certainly be more difficult for him if she did leave... Although, he reasoned she would not have the confidence to strike out on her own. She had become too accustomed to parading around town on his arm so it was most unlikely although Aunt Miriam had once warned him to keep her close or he would lose her. Admiral Singleton would certainly have left her the wherewithal to make such a move!

The first thing he did on returning to Trandon House was to inquire from the footman if Miss Singleton was home and if she was, to tell her that Lord Trandon would like a word. He poured himself a brandy from the crystal decanter on the hall table but he had to wait a further ten minutes before she came languidly down stairs and acknowledged him with a brief nod of her head and a curt "Yes?"

Alexander, remembering the icy atmosphere of their last conversation made his news as brief as he could, simply telling her that he had received an Admiralty signal which contained some most distressing personal news about her father.

She took the document and perused the outlined paragraph without registering any emotion and then handed it back to him saying very stiffly. "I thank your Lordship for this communication. Although I cannot say that the information is totally unexpected but one is never ready for such events, is one? Is there anything else your Lordship?" She asked sarcastically. "No? … Well, may I bid you good evening. "

As she turned to go Alexander said woodenly. "Er, there is of course the matter of an inheritance. If you should require any help in legally processing it please call on me I should be only too happy to help. Remember that I have recently gone through much the same experience."

With a thin smile she said "Why, thank you again, sir. Such a windfall is indeed particularly fortuitous at this time as I have recently decided to take a lease on Sir Francis Myatt's splendid house at 62 Great Pulteney Street which I am given to understand was only built in '98 by Mr Thomas Baldwin. His Lordship has been appointed British Consul in Rio de Janeiro and required a tenant of quality. It will be ready for me in about a month's time. In the

258

meantime, from Tuesday week I shall be staying at Pratt's Hotel."

She finished with a casual wave of her hand and asked him to excuse her as he had a great deal of packing to attend to.

Alexander was dumbstruck. She was actually moving out. He had considered the prospect but never seriously… and now she was off!

"I would certainly deem it a favour." She continued. "If you could make some inquiry on my behalf for a reliable carrier as I do not intend to burden your warm hospitality for very much longer." And with that brief hint of sarcasm she turned and climbed to the first landing where Janet was furtively peeking from behind a pillar leaving him open mouthed.

Over the banister she delivered her Parthian shot. " So now sir, as far as I am concerned you can go ahead and make your Gypsy whore mistress of Trandon House and wallow in the mire together undisturbed. You do know, of course, that she was one of the camp doxies who serviced the highway robber Captain Brooks… God alone knows what she caught from him! Goodbye to you, sir!"

Alexander was still reeling from the encounter with Jessica the next morning. He sipped his morning coffee and cognac and tried to sort it out in his mind. It was really not like her. 'Why was she so vitriolic about things? He could understand her sadness at the news of her father's death but as she said she had been half expecting it and one would have thought that she would be a little pleased at her inheritance. Why had she exploded at him? He remembered how elated he had felt when fortune smiled on him. After a moment's consideration the only explanation he could find was that, unlike him, she was accustomed to a pampered life of privilege and the legacy had been expected.(It did not cross his mind that his own recent tirade might have had something to do with her of her aloofness.)

He asked the footman who was pouring the coffee, why wasn't it Mr Harrison attending him as normal. The man replied nervously that saying that Mr Harrison had had an urgent message that his sister was ill and gone to visit her in Bristol. 'That's strange.' He mused 'I don't remember him ever mentioning having a sister.' Aunt Miriam told him that she had engaged Harrison on the solid recommendation of Sir Arthur Edgerton from Brighton, umm, most peculiar. Thinking nothing more of it Alexander shrugged and dismissed the servant.

Feeling a little better now, he reached for the morning mail on his desk. On top of the small pile was an official looking envelope bearing Banker Whitley's seal which one of the bank's couriers had brought barely an hour ago. He took another sip of his coffee before breaking the wax seal with his thumb and flattened out the paper on the table.

As he read it his improving mood came to an abrupt end. His suspicions had been well founded, there was indeed trouble ahead!

To Sir Alexander Coulston, Lord Trandon.

From Elias Stuckey Esq. Banker and financier

25 George Street, Bath.

Feb 16th 1804

My Dear Alexander

I do not feel comfortable addressing you so intimately but as you prefer it, I will obey...

A few days ago I received a report from Fletcher and Lambert informing me that they are well on with the boundary marking and the measuring chains are out but there was some intelligence that concerned me greatly and I hasten to inform you. It seems that when the surveyor's men called at Home Farm to acquaint your steward of their business, they found it deserted. Yeoman Barnes was nowhere to be seen. The house had been stripped bare as had the tool sheds, stables and barns. The only livestock to be found were a few scraggy hens and a starving dog on a chain and the only vehicle left was a rickety cart with broken spokes. In short Barnes and his kin have absconded!

The surveyors made enquiry of the Kelston Hall tenants and were told that Barnes had family on the Somerset Levels. So if he has gone to ground there is little hope of bringing him to justice, for it is a misty, dismal place full of close knit, primitive folk who don't take kindly to incomers. Many a stranger asking questions there has disappeared without trace in the marshes like the Blind Yeo River

261

that never reaches the sea!... Acting on this disclosure I put the bank's agents on the case and they have confirmed that Barnes has been selling livestock, equipment and produce to a certain Ellis Starkey, who has big holdings south of the Polden Hills down on the Somerset Levels so it seems that the Kelston Hall people were right. Apparently the deception had been going on for a number of years and had only come to light on the death of Lady Trandon hence his abrupt and secret departure.

I am informed that Starkey's country seat is at Westonzoyland but apart from that little is known about him apart from his dubious reputation as a volatile rake and bad gambler but local tittle-tattle has it that he has taken on a new Major Domo there. However, as Barnes is nowhere to be found nothing could be proved against Starkey who, when asked about the transactions, replied that he had bought the goods in good faith and paid fair prices. The chances of any redress are slim but I advise you to avoid any dealings with this Mr. Starkey in the future; but there is a little good news too.

Mr Norris, the agent at Poole informs me that the fluyt 'Marta Kraus' will dock there in three days time with cargo to auction and as you own forty per centum you may like to go down and inspect it.

Your Obedient Servant and friend
Elias Stuckey.

As the bad news sank in Alexander realised that there was little he could do about it at that moment due to the necessity of putting the final touches to the investigation and preparing for the forthcoming trial but he would certainly not just let it rest at that. At least things could not get any worse now Barnes had gone although the disappearance of Miriam's butler still puzzled him a little. Maybe Elias' suspicions could be correct.

In fact, about the only good thing was the fact that he would not now have to take Jessica to Poole where she could get her hands on his cargo of fine Chinese silks!

26

THE MENDIP MURDERS

The Chief Investigator's establishment at Ensleigh now consisted of a head clerk and four office staff to handle the paperwork with a Field Investigation Team of one Captain, two Lieutenants, a sergeant, two corporals and a platoon of Wiltshire Yeomanry from Warminster, seconded to the Lord Provost's department, each of these troopers serving each as dispatch rider or escorts in turn. To maintain the chain of command Alexander's adjutant had been promoted and given the substantive title of Chief Investigator, which in the light of his elevation to the peerage would no doubt become permanent. He retained his personal clerk, Bradley Thomas at Warminster to receive and pass on information as it came in.

Although Bradley was still useful to Rob in some capacity he suspected that he was not being straight with him and was constantly on guard watching for any suspicious move. Added to this concern was the knowledge that if Rob was caught he would not hesitate to involve him to the hilt. Bradley also realised that he was no longer at the centre of the action and he was getting jumpy. Today's dispatch added to his panic

Apparently another body had been found in the Mendips. This time in one of the Wookey Hole caves in the Cheddar Gorge. It had been found by four boys who reported it to the Axbridge constable who identified it as a Jackson Vellon, known locally as Cornish Jake a convicted smuggler, another one of Captain Brooks' highway robbers. The news really frightened Bradley. What was happening? That made three of the old gang killed, Charley Cavey, Big Silas and now Cornish Jake... Someone was targeting them... But who could it be? Was it Rob or another one of the old gang? And then it hit him! ..... Who did Rob say chained Charley to a stump in the Servernake forest? Ah yes! The evil Redemptors! ... It could only be them... How much did they know about the robbery? And more to the point, who was going to be the next victim? He decided to bring forward his plan of action unaware that Rob had forestalled him and was already on his way abroad.

The Axbridge constable's report had been very sketchy and considering the close proximity of killings and the revelation that all three men were from the same area, Alexander decided to look deeper into them. He decided to send Captain Harry Fenwick and Lieutenant George Beswick undercover to investigate the three recent murders in the Mendip Hills He also told them about what had happened at Trandon Home Farm and to keep an ear open for any news of the elusive thief Zeke Barnes or Harrison.

They looked very convincing as a road surveyor and his assistant seeking building land when they stopped for the first night at the Farmers Arms at West Harptree and took the opportunity to have a word with the landlord and some of the locals. They gathered some bits of gossip, mostly trivia but it did seem apparent that people of the area had been warned off about talking to strangers. The following morning they were at the upper end of the Cheddar Gorge and gingerly led their horses down the twisting path towards the entrance. They had already talked to one of the farmers whose hayricks had been torched and got the names of four or five likely suspects, two of whom along with one of the murdered men had been on the list from the Axbridge beadle. The trail led to the Star Tavern in Midsomer Norton where they decided to spend a couple of days there trying to find out more. Plying their host and a couple of locals with drinks they slipped in the confidential information that they were surveying new bypasses on the Exeter Road which would cut out some of the difficult terrain, marshland and such. They also pointed out that businesses on this new route would also prosper from the passing trade. At this the landlord bought a round of drinks (an almost unheard of thing!) and set about telling the two surveyors about his tavern's good reputation and excellent service.

"Do you ever get any trouble though?" Harry asked casually. The landlord said that it was very rare indeed but he did let slip that there had been an incident a month or two back with a couple of tinkers but he had called in the help of certain friends who sorted it.

At this a few of the regulars looked askance and made excuses and moved away from the bar. A couple even abandoned their drinks and went out of the pub. By this time the landlord had had a few drinks too many and in his efforts to enhance his pub's reputation confidentially told them that he was under the protection of a certain religious order that kept a stern watch on things. He tapped the side of his nose to indicate the extreme secrecy of this information, saying quietly. "I can't tellee no more than that, 'cept to say that they as caused it won't be doing' any more, not never! D'y unnnerstan?"

The drinks flowed freely, with their money lubricating the conversation until at one point Harry asked quite casually if anyone knew the whereabouts of a certain Ezekiel Barnes as there was a reward poster out for him in Bath. The poster gave a description of him and offered a reward of twenty guineas for information. At this the drinkers ooh'd and aah'd saying that they could use that kind of money but shook their heads ruefully. One man however, said that he remembered meeting a strange family on the road to the Levels a few weeks back who said they'd come from Bath. The man was with a woman and a boy and girl. They had two big wagons, one with a tall hooped canvas tilt and another loaded with farm equipment driven by him and the boy while the women were shepherding a small herd of mixed live stock behind them. He said he recalled the incident clearly as the man had tried to sell him a piglet. Harry took the man's name and said that they would report his information to the Bath

267

Guildhall so he would get his reward when the culprit was caught.

On their way back to Bath the two Provost Officers called at Wellow and Radstock, where a few well placed gold coins soon brought forth the two tavern girls who were in the Crown that fatal night. Three days later they were back at Ensleigh and had more pieces of the jigsaw in place and some information for their boss.

27

BRADLEY'S BETRAYAL

Muffled up in a long caped greatcoat which had seen better days and a thick woollen scarf and hat Bradley Thomas slipped through the postern gate of the barracks and into the chilly October evening. It had been a long, worrying and tedious day. Ensign Roberts the raw young officer who was now the liaison officer for the Lord Provost Department had run him ragged all day. The man had no experience at all of office routine but stiffly rejected any attempt to be guided by Bradley. Oh No... He was not going to take advice from some civilian; even if the person had been doing the job for almost three years and had been recently promoted to Grade One clerk!.. Ensign Roberts had his own way and would brook no other. The result was that things took twice as long to do and on the days Bradley had to go over to Ensleigh to report to Alexander, nothing got done at all.

He was still muttering to himself with his head down in the wind when he was accosted by a woman wearing a dark hooded cloak. There was nothing unusual about this as the area around any military establishment was often the hunting ground of girls of easy virtue looking for lonely soldiers and he was just about to brush her off when she spoke.

"Hello there, Young Bradley, I thought yew waz jes' 'bout to ignore me"

Bradley stopped in his tracks as he recognised the dulcet tones.

"Wot in Hell's name you doin' 'ere Melody Watson, you trollop? You shouldn't be around here! You know well wot Rob told yew. Wotcha want anyway?"

He looked round in panic to see if anybody from the barracks had seen them and seeing a nearby alley way dragged her inside.

"'Hold on there my brave lad, you'm don' fink as I'd come yeer alone do'ee? Jes' turn around an meet my brothers Alfie an' Jack. They usually don' let me out of their sight, 'specially when there's them rough soldier boys around."

Bradley whirled round to see two big bulky farm boys looking steadily at him

"Wotcha 'afta bring them for? We're old friends aint we?"

Melody eyed him coolly. "Well, I duuno 'bout that... You wasn't 'zackly pleased to see me, wuz yew? But don' yew worry none Bradley, Good as gold they are. They won't 'urt yew none...Waal, not less'n I tell 'em to!" She added menacingly. "Tell yew wot, why don' we find a nice little tavern an 'ave a chat eh?"

The party then adjourned to a small hostelry at the other end of

Warminster High Street where Melody and Bradley settled down at a table and the brothers stood at the bar in the vault where they could keep an eye on things.

Now thoroughly scared, Bradley tried to pour oil on the troubled water and asked quietly what she'd like to drink and ordered for them all before inquiring further into the reasons for this meeting. After the slovenly waiter had brought the drinks, Melody tossed off her fur-trimmed hood and slipped the cloak to her shoulders and like many men before him Bradley was mesmerised by her beauty and the magnificence of her figure. Finally he managed to gulp.

"Well now, old friend, jes' wot is the problem? How can I 'elp yew?

Melody looked over the rim of her leather cup and said quietly. "You'll recall that little bit o' bizzines we did with Mr Rob of course and will no doubt be thinking; its got summat to do wi' that eh?... Waal, you'm right. It concerns a little matter of the eighty goldies that I wuz told would be forthcoming when all was done and dusted. An' frum wot I bin yeerin' lately I fink that pay day is well overdue... An' as yew wuz the one wot got me to do it, I am seeking satisfaction frum yew! So 'ow about it?"

Glancing over nervously to where the brothers were silently staring at them Bradley told her that everything was on track and that there had been a little delay in getting the, err, merchandise, safely in a secure place but that he was going to visit Rob in a weeks time to collect the due moneys for all concerned. She seemed mollified at the

271

confident reassurances but said that there was a bit of news that he had failed to mention. Bradley asked her casually what that might be.

Melody glanced over at her brothers and turned back to look deep in Bradley's eyes. "Yew recall Big Silas and Toby Vivian don'tcha. Waal, it seems they wuz out West Harptree way some weeks back doin' a little hayrick job fer a farmer frum Bishop Sutton and by some mishap they wuz both found dead in the Wellow Brook a couple o' days later. On top of that Tommy Kirkman got picked up by the Axbridge beadle and old Cornish Jake wuz found dead in Cheddar Gorge! So wot d'ye fink's goin' on Bradley? Soon there won't be any of the old crew as needs payin' out will there? And if yew, Rob or anybody else thinks I'm jest goin' to wait around till I get knocked on the 'ead, you've got 'nuther think comin!" She paused for a minute to let her words sink in before continuing. "So bear this in mind Bradley... I'll take yew at yore word an' I'll wait till my birthday on November the twelfth. But if nothing is forthcomin' before then, I will take steps that yew wont like, unnerstand? If'n yew wanna gerrin touch wi' me meantimes, jes' try the tavern at Dilton Marsh."

With that stark warning she signalled her kin and swept out of the door leaving Bradley tenser than ever. He was well aware of her prowess with her daddy's rifle and the reputation her brothers had for mindless violence. Good God! Not even Brooksie would employ them. He sat with his head in his hands trembling.

Of all the problems facing him this was the last thing he had expected!

In a daze he stumbled back to his dreary room behind the barracks

He would not forget the hard stare that one of the brothers gave as they left or the scruffy waiter with that strange green feather in his apron strings who gave him a sheepish grin as they left.

"Wot you want 'ere? Wot you 'angin' around for?" Bradley was shocked. He turned around to see a thick set man about forty with a pair of mastiffs on a double leather leash staring belligerently at him. "Oi axed yew jus' whaddyuh want, eh? You bin coming round 'ere fer the last three days. So, wot you lookin' for, eh?"

"Er nuthin'." Bradley stammered. "I wuz jes' 'opin' to see an old friend of mine called Rob Dacarius. You seen 'im anywhere? I got meetin' with 'im 'ere."

They were on the riverbank outside Rob's compound but somehow to Bradley's eye it didn't look the same? Where were the barges and why weren't any of the crews around?

"Rob, ye say? Well, ye won't find 'im 'ere anymore. This yard belongs to Mr Allen now. If yew'r a-lookin' to collect a debt or summat, well you'm too late. He's long time gone. From what I heard he'd got a contract on the Grand Union Canal haulin' coal, so

Mr Allen bought 'im out. 'Bout three week back it were. I'm lookin' after the place till the builders get started."

Bradley gasped and his head swirled. "But 'E jes' can't swan off like that! I've got business with him."

The security guard slackened the dog's leashes menacingly and rasped. "I don' care wot bizzines you got wi' this 'ere Rob. 'Tis my job t'keep Mr Allen's property secure, so you'd best be on your way afore I let the dogs loose."

He stomped off without further word and slammed the gate. For a moment Bradley stood there open mouthed, stunned by the news and the realisation that Rob had scored over him again. He spat viciously into the river and shouted loudly over the gate.

"Well, iffen you do see 'im, you can tell Mr Bloody Dacarius that I am off to Marshfield to pass the news on to his friends up there... An' I'm sure they'll find a way of getting' in touch with 'im... Jus' you see if they don't!"

With a face like thunder he stormed off past the Monks Mill and back across Pulteney Bridge into the city.

The hack that Bradley had hired was wheezing like an old kettle by the time he rode into the mill yard in Marshfield and asked to meet the boss on a matter of business. Miller Russell had seen him approaching from the gallery of the mill and walked over to greet him cautiously.

"Yore wastin' yore time an' mine if you'm come 'ere a-lookin' fer a job, son. We ain't 'irin today. Wot's it you want?"

Bradley introduced himself saying that he had come on a matter of mutual interest concerning Mr. Dacarius of Widcome.

Russell eyed him suspiciously and signalled his foreman to come over. "Ah, so you're a friend o' Rob's are you? And what may I ask is your name and profession, son? ...Rob might have mentioned you."

Bradley drew himself to his full height and said who he was and that he was a partner in a business venture with Rob.

"I seem to have heard yore name, tho 'twas not from Rob. Why don't you come into the office out of the cold? One of the stable lads will take care of your nag."

He led the way inside and the foreman came too and stood by the door. "You'll 'ave to excuse Walter, Mr Thomas but he will make sure we are not disturbed. I'm sure that what you've got to tell me is a private matter."

He eased himself into his chair and indicated his guest to take a seat. While Bradley was getting himself settled Russell slid open his desk drawer and checked that the pistol he kept there was close to hand.

Bradley poured out his story giving the miller chapter and verse of the robbery. In his desperation to get revenge on Rob and to enlist the help of the Redemptors he told the miller much more than he had intended.

Russell and the foreman exchanged meaningful glances at significant revelations but said nothing to the informant. When Bradley had finally got it all out the miller stood up from the table, stretched and nodded to the foreman who mumbled something about a cart being due and scuttled away. Waiting until the door was closed and the sound of the foreman's boots had faded, Russell looked across the table

"Well, Bradley, my lad." He said. "That's certainly an interestin' tale. wot you tol' me. This yeer Rob seems to have treated you cruelly to betray you so after you trusted 'im. Tis no wonder you're seethin', I would be meself!" Bradley was about to start again with another tirade when Russell held his hand up. "Tellee wot tho'. Why don' you go 'cross to the Crown and get yoursel' a pint. You'm can't miss un, big place on the main street. I'll join you direckly once I've checked in this cart load." With a false smile he clapped Bradley on the shoulder and gave him a handful of coins." You jes' go across an'gerrem in... We'll talk more about what we can do, All right?... Well, off you go now."

It would have been difficult for his own mother to have recognised Harry Fenwick as he lolled drunkenly against the tap room bar of the old Crown Hotel in Marshfield's main street. The once tall, straight backed young officer in his immaculate uniform

276

had become a dirty, drunken, slumped-shouldered tavern waster. His bleary face sported a four-day stubble and his calico waistcoat was stained by split drink and old food. This was his third night in the barroom and he put the word about that he was an unemployed groom from Swindon who had been on his way to Bristol to find a job on the docks. The lanky landlord watched him a moment and then beckoned him over.

"Ere you," He said. "Y'say you're lookin' fer a job? Well George, my reg'lar pot man 'as broke 'is leg thatchin'. Fell off a bloody roof 'e did, so that leaves Oi a-lookin' for another. You interested?"

The scabby drifter's eyes lit up and he growled roughly "Oh aye! Oi could do that bloody job standin' on me yead! Wotcha payin' an' when can I start?"

The tapster gasped as the boozer's foetid breath hit him.

"Tellee wot, I'll givee a trial tomorrow. Be 'ere sober sharp at noon an' 'ave a bloody wash an' shave. Can't 'ave you lookin' like you got the pox. It'd be enough to turn the customers off their ale, right? By the way, wot's yore name?"

"Perkin, like me father. Perkin Sharp but everybody calls me Perks"

"Oh aye. An' you gorra place to stay then?"

"Er, well, now that you mention it, I bin lookin' but …."

The Innkeeper nodded. "Oh I see... I can well unnerstan' that no bugger's goin' to tek you in lookin' loik that and stinkin' like a

277

midden. But I'll tellee wot. This place wuz the village lock up at one time and we got three cells down in the cellar. You can doss down in one o' them… Least that way I'll bloody well know where you are!"

"Oh, right Boss!" Chortled Harry. "That'll do fine for me. Soon as I finish me cider, I'll go an' get me bundle".

The move paid off for him the very next day when during the busy midday rush hour his quarry edged furtively into the tap room and ordered a pint of scrumpy. He immediately recognised Bradley from a visit to the barracks at Warminster when he had called at Alexander's office and for a brief moment feared that his cover might be blown. However a quick glance in one of the polished metal servers told him that his disguise was fine and the generous smear of horse manure he had applied to his breeches added an extra convincing pungency. Harry quickly put his head down and moved into the scullery where he dumped his slop swilling tray of mugs and pots into the deep stone sink half full of lukewarm greasy water, nodding at the blousy, kitchen maid.

"Oh gerrout o' yeer, you stinkin' tramp.. You could do wi' a bloody good scrubbing." She yelled. "An' I'm jes' the one to give it to yer 'an all!" She added with a gap-toothed leer at a waiter who was standing near the window puffing on the butt of a discarded cigar. Harry scuttled back to the barroom where he found that Bradley now had company. It was the stocky Miller Russell so boldly he moved a little closer and began to collect pots from the bar and he heard the miller's greeting.

"Ah, you found the place all right then? Good, well let's get a table an' 'ave a little talk, eh? That 'un by the fire ower there'll do us fine."

As the busy lunchtime passed noisily Harry caught odd bits of the hushed conversation between the two plotters... Enough to know that there had been some break up with one of Bradley's associates, who appeared to be either Spanish or Portugese as he was referred to as 'A garliky smellin' Dago.' and that he was a river boat man of some kind. He heard the scrape of stool legs and quickly turned to see the miller shaking hands with his guest

"Right Bradley me lad, off ye go now... An' remember that we Brothers are lookin' after ye now jes like we bin lookin' after our people 'undred years or more, so your cares are over now. All you gotta do is just bring us any documents you might have regardin' this matter, or owt else as I can show my colleagues an' we'll see to yon Rob for ye!"

Bradley bit his lip and nodded grimly. "It's good to know that Mr Russell, you've really put my mind at ease. I know now that you'll see me right an' show that rogue an' that poxy sister of his that he can't rob a person of his due share. Soon as I hear any news I'll be back to let you know. Good night, Mr. Russell."

Harry watched him go and saw the miller turn to his foreman who was standing in the corner and flash a secret smile as he raised his glass. The foreman quietly slipped outside to watch Bradley's old hack plodding out of the village.

Just after two thirty the following morning another male figure quietly eased open the latch on the back door and tiptoed into the pub yard. Glancing cautiously around him he listened in silence for a moment before moving swiftly through the gate into the lane. By eight thirty Harry was enjoying a hearty breakfast with his Commanding Officer at Trandon house, his mission completed.

There was only one thing he could not work out though... Who was that strange waiter he'd seen in the pub's kitchen who seemed to be listening in and why was he wearing a green feather in his pocket?

28

ROB IN PORTUGAL

After a rough passage Rob's ship arrived at Vigo in northern Portugal five days later than expected. The delay had been mainly due to the ineptitude of the Flemish Captain and his inability to get on with anybody, particularly, the sailing master. The two had been at loggerheads most of the journey with the Captain giving the vaguest of orders and the Master doing his best to ignore them. As an example of this ludicrous situation, although they had arrived in the roads of Vigo just after two pm, it was early evening before they were warped to their berth which almost incited the crew to mutiny and caused severe discomfort and insecurity among the six passengers who, like Rob quickly left the ship at this first landfall.

Rob stood on the dockside in the pouring rain trying to get his land legs and thanking his Maker that he had arrived safely and wondering what to do with the four barrels that he had brought with him. Looking up from the glistening cobbles he saw the welcoming light of a lantern over a tavern door and cautiously wove his unsteady way towards it. Kicking open the warped planks he lurched dripping wet inside the smoky den… It looked exactly what it was, a cheap dockside tavern that one could find at any seaport in the world. A bright fire of pine roots flared in the chimney and the usual crew of seamen, tarts and dockland drifters were scattered on stools some playing cards, fondling the women or crowding the rough bar.

" … Tardes Sehnor..."

Alexander cut the barman short and gestured to a bottle of rum throwing a gold coin onto the bar. The barman stared at it and just shook his head while holding firm to his bottle.

A whining voice at his elbow said. "Your Eenglish gold is of no use in 'ere Senhor. Maybe in Lisboa where there are eengish sailors ... but not 'ere."

Rob turned to see a short, thick set, dark haired man with hooded sad eyes and a neatly trimmed van Dyke beard who tossed some coins to the barman took the bottle and pocketed Rob's coin.

"Permit me, sir to introduce myself. I am Diego Caraban, retired sailing master, now the main supplier of necessities to our brave seamen. In short, I am a ship's chandler and provider. My warehouse is just along the dock. I am at your service."

Rob shook the outstretched hand and introduced himself as a business man seeking to establish himself somewhere away from the wartime restrictions of England and beyond French interference, hence his visit to Portugal. --- It was a good cover story and Rob had gone over it a thousand times in his mind imagining every possible scenario until it was perfect. His Portugese companion appeared to accept this and suggested that they take 'their' bottle to table to talk further: Perhaps he could be helping Sehnor Dacarius to establish himself in the country. Who knows what may develop?

Rob put on a serious expression and asked. "Regarding the nearby warehouse you mentioned, Sehnor. It is possible that I may need such a facility, do you have any storage space available at the moment?"

Caraban stroked his little beard and nodded, saying that he could possibly arrange some secure space although of course he would have to know what was the nature of the merchandise and for how long before he could quote a rental price. Rob told him a fanciful tale about his busy Scandinavian import business and that the first consignment would initially take the form of several large barrels of Norwegian pine resin, turpentine and kraft-baum a compacted kindling of resin saturated split pine which would catch fire from a spark even if it was wet (It was a product very much in demand by ship's cooks and winter travellers.) and that if this foray into the Iberian Peninsula was successful, he intended to expand the imports from Scandinavia and eventually to transfer all his affairs out of England.

When Rob had finished talking Caraban eyed him coolly and taking a pull from his cup said. "This proposition could be of some interest to me... Why don't you come by tomorrow and look over my establishment? Perhaps we can come to some arrangement to our mutual advantage. I can also change some of your gold into escudos if you wish. "

The two traders toasted each other and ordered a meal and more drinks, all on the chandlers' account, of which Rob realized he would be obliged to pay his share, and spent pleasant evening swapping stories. Caraban explained that he took over the warehouse from his father when he decided to retire to his comfortable house in the Canary Islands. Somehow the old man had managed to get a contract to supply chandlery to the Royal Navy who kept a more or less permanent station in Portugese waters. This led in turn to a contract to provide goods and services to the British Embassy in Lisbon and his father had insisted that his son left the sea and managed this depot in Vigo. That had been back in '99 but now the old man was dead and Diego became head of the family and inherited everything. The more he heard the more Rob could see that there were great opportunities with contacts like these and warmly encouraged this new friend to tell him more. As the evening proceeded Caraban had a word with the landlord of the tavern and arranged a room for him telling the man to charge that also to his account. Rob thanked him profusely but refused his further generous offer of a 'puta' for him. He had enough experience to know the risks of seamen's doxies!

The following morning he watched his barrels being unloaded and trundled down to Caraban's warehouse and snugly settled in. It was time to call his snaky Uncle Arturo to a reckoning!

Rob was not the only one seeking a reckoning for a few hundred miles away to the north another similar scenario was taking place.

Since his brush with Melody Watson and her brothers, Bradley had been careful to avoid the taverns and coaching inns of Warminster and took every opportunity to visit Bath. His new promotion had been confirmed and one of his perks was that he had the use of a horse from the cavalry remount paddock for official business and it was a privilege that he used to the full, telling the Sergeant Farrier that due to the confidential nature of his reports they had to be delivered to Lord Trandon in person. So it was with some surprise and shock that while he was enjoying a warming rum toddy in the vaults of a rough pub in Grove Street, he saw the two Watson boys coming through the door.

"Evenin' Bradley." Said Jack, the bigger one "We've been 'opin' to catch a glimpse of you for a week or two now. Our Melody is in a right state. She was expectin' you to call in at the Ram's Head."

"Oh aye," said the other brother. "So we said we'd have a look around for you. A friend from down in Widcome told us you wuz spendin' time 'ere in Bath.. So we kept an eye out for you an' now 'ere we are, all together eh!" He added, nodding to Bradley's mug. "So If you're buyin' we'll be glad to join you in a pint."

Bradley started to bluster and stammered out a complicated explanation that he had new duties which kept him out of

Warminster for a week or two but it didn't wash and they just stared at him blankly until the beer arrived. "You can tell your Melody that there's been a bit of a delay on the payout and I've…"

Jack slammed his mug down and shouted. "Oh, shuttit Bradley! As soon as we finished this yeer ale y'can tell 'er yerself. C'mon now drink up, we're off!"

Bradley blinked at Jack's sudden change of tone and a few heads at the bar turned to watch the scene. Next thing he knew he was being dragged and thumped along the river path to a cart hidden under the last arch of Pulteney Bridge. Without ceremony Alfie gave him a heavy punch to the kidneys and as he lay gasping across the cart they tied his hands to the tailgate and gagged him with a filthy rag.

"Now then." Alfie said quietly. "You're gonna pay fer all the worry you've given our baby sister, you crafty lyin' toad."

Without a further word they began to kick and beat his legs with their heavy blackthorn sticks until he collapsed after which they threw him on the cart and after trussing him up securely headed to the house in Widcome village where Melody was waiting for his explanation.

Racked with pain and feeling more dead than alive he was dragged into the flag floored kitchen where Melody sat warming her knees before a bright log fire. Turning to her brothers she asked if he had said anything. They both shook their heads and glared at the whimpering dishevelled figure saying that they thought it best for her to hear his tale herself. Seeing that his only salvation was to tell all

286

he knew, Bradley gave her the full story of Rob's treachery and that he was working somewhere up on the Grand Union canal. Of how he had promised everybody involved large sums of money but somehow they were being picked off one by one, before they could collect. He also told her about his visit to Marshfield and finally said that the real villain was Alexander who was determined to investigate the robbery... If somebody could get rid of him the sensitive case was likely to be dropped, or at least postponed and all would be well. Melody listened attentively to what he had to say and then told her brothers to lock him in the cellar and get him out of Bath in the morning. She knew now what had to be done.... But unknown to her it was too late...Bradley had already overplayed his hand at Marshfield.

29

FORTUNE SMILES ON RACHEL

One summer afternoon a boat pulled into the landing stage at Trandon House and a burly crewman stepped ashore. Rachel and a friend were taking tea on the front lawn and eyed the newcomer with some suspicion as he boldly approached them. He touched his cap and wished them a good afternoon and said that he had a note for a Senhorita Dacarius. Rachel was surprised that anyone knew that she was there but said that she was the lady he was seeking. The man hesitated and said that his instructions were that the letter was to be given to the Senhorita only and that he would require proof of her identity.

Rachel started to protest and point out that her friend here could most certainly vouch for her but the man shook his head and brought out a crumpled piece of paper from his waistcoat. He stared at it a moment and then asked bluntly where she was born and where was her brother? She bristled at such impertinence but then realised that the man was not going to hand over the letter until he had the right answers. Sniffing indignantly she told him that she had been born in Weymouth and that her brother was presently in Portugal on family business. At this the man brought out a sealed package and handed it to her without a word. She rummaged in her purse for a few coins but when she looked up the crewman was back aboard his boat and casting off.

Excitedly she broke the seal on the package and unfolded the letter. There were just four lines of text and an address in Bristol, stranger still, it was written in Portuguese. It read that a certain party had news for her from her brother and if she would present herself alone at the address below and ask for Messer Mendoza she would hear something to her advantage. Her companion, an old friend from Widcome was curious about the cryptic note but Rachel was not forthcoming and just brushed it off saying that it was about arrangements for the delivery of some imported furniture. Her friend pretended to accept this weak excuse and said she must be leaving as she too had urgent matters to attend to. Inwardly squirming with embarrassment Rachel rang the little hand bell and told the maid to tell Albert to bring round the post chaise and take Mrs Roberts back to Widcome. And on that, rather cool note they parted.

The following midday Rachel arrived at Bristol Docks on the mail coach and disembarking asked directions to the address she had been given. It turned out to be in a quiet street of tall houses near the market. In a high old stone wall she found a scarred oak, iron studded door with a black number painted on it. She pulled the iron bell rod and as a panel opened, a gaunt, lined female face appeared and inquired her business there. Rachel presented the letter which the woman perused casually, obviously un-fazed by the foreign text and told her to wait. A minute later bolts scraped and clanged and the big door slid smoothly open.

Inside was much different from the tatty slum-like exterior, with polished floorboards and expensive deep maroon and dark blue Persian rugs scattered along the central hall which was lit by a skylight panel showing a series of doors on one side opposite which was a long narrow dresser bearing framed Hebrew texts and a multi-branched candelabra.

She turned to look at the woman who had let her in but there was nobody to be seen. Another door opened silently on her right and a tall, thin figure gestured for her to enter. The man was obviously Jewish with dark deep set eyes and a large hooked nose, and looked to be in his sixties. He smelled of fresh rose water and was wearing hooked toed, backless oriental slippers, a round yarmulke skull cap and the long dark grey sleeved cloak they call a gabardine.

"Good day to you, my Dear." He smiled. "You really do look like your brother Rob. May I velcome you to my humble abode. Vill you take some tea? Ah, please forgive me; I am remiss in not introducing myself: I am Isador Mendoza."

His gentle voice and worldly charm were completely at odds with his appearance and Rachel was fascinated by him and said she would

290

love tea. He clapped his hands in the Eastern manner and the woman who had let her in appeared. He spoke rapidly to her in a strange guttural language and she shuffled out silently. Waiting until the door latch clicked, he continued.

"I hev some good news for you but first let me explain something. You see, your brudder Rob an' me, ve are business partners. We stand together on several ventures und I am his banker on matters of international finance, hence my letter to you. As zis matter is of a most confidential nature I zink that it vould be prudent to pursue our discussions in Portugese, shall we?"

Without hesitation he switched fluently to the other language. "Rob's last letter intimated that his stay in Portugal may be an extended one due to the development of certain commercial opportunities. That being the case, he has instructed me to open an account for you with one of my associates in Bath. There will be an initial deposit of five hundred guineas available on call in your name. Further deposits will be made from time to time. I am honoured to be the bearer of such glad tidings and hope this news will relieve you of any pressure."

Quite suddenly the door was flung open and the servant woman entered carrying a tray of rattling cups and plates of cakes. She glowered at Mendoza muttering something and shuffled moodily out banging the door behind her. As Rachel was in a state of shock she hardly noticed the incident and sat dumbfounded. Five hundred guineas! Could it really be true?

All her nagging concern melted into fresh air: Now she could confidently hold her head up in any company and not feel that she was totally dependent on Alexander.

"Oh, thank you very much, Messer Mendoza." She cried breathlessly. "I am truly astounded. I hardly know what to say, although I must admit to a great curiosity about Rob's welfare... Is he alright?"

"Ah, I know that your brother is fine, my dear... Do not concern your pretty head. I hear monthly reports and receive his mail from the sea captains as regularly as if he was still in Bath." He replied benignly and patted her hand.

Emboldened by his warmth and charm she asked why he had come to England when he had lived in such a pleasant place as Portugal. The weather was much better than here and the people seemed friendly too.

Again his face took on that sad expression and he smiled gently and said "Ah yes, my child perhaps to you it does, for you are a Christian and not of a persecuted race as I am. The Catholic Church regards us Israelites as sinners and blames us for every catastrophe that afflicts them. True they will let us stay but under strict conditions and tax us heavily, proscribing what we may and may not do. The Church is powerful and rich for zey claim a tithe on everything. Even from our great mariners like Vasco da Gama and Magellan. No, the church can never be seen to be wrong. If a trading voyage is successful they proclaim that it was God's mercy that brought the sailors back safely ... And of course if some ship flounders or a jungle disease takes lives, the church says that the crews must have been sinners and the Lord punished them...Tell me, what can we do?"

He shrugged then paused as if to silently pray slowly shaking his head.

"Some of my faith did stay behind but to escape the Jesuits but had to deny their faith and be baptised as Christians. The Spaniards and the Portuguese call such people Murranos but I vaz determined not to become one of them and came to this land of toleration... with its rain and cold!"

He smiled at his own little joke and looked at her calmly before switching back to English

"And now I must be returning to my counting house to attend to this transfer of funds. My sister Miriam vill sees you out."

With that he rose, kissed her hand and led the way out into the passage where his iron faced, suspicious sister was waiting by the front door, anxious to see the shvartza shiksa off the premises.

Thirty miles away to the west, in the flagstone floored kitchen of a dank old farmhouse within sight of Glastonbury Tor another meeting, albeit not such a pleasant one, was taking place where the elusive Zeke Barns was being abused by his former business partner .

"….And who is this bastard upstart that has turned you off then? Ellis Starkey was boiling with anger and stared belligerently at the quaking, speechless Zeke Barnes. "…We were doing very well until he came along. Why didn't you just keep your bloody head down and jolly him along? You do know you've cost me a lot of money and we've lost a good cheap source of merchandise, don't you?"

Barnes finally found his voice and started to object to this tirade saying that it was not his fault that the old lady had died but Starkey just ignored him and raged on about his losses as a winter hailstorm rattled the ancient windows.

He had arrived about an hour ago in a raging temper shouting that he had been betrayed, having received a message from the Axbridge Beadle containing some sinister news. Apparently one of his agents reported that two men staying at the Star Inn in Midsomer Norton were buying the locals drinks and making suspicious inquires. They professed to be surveyors but their horse's brands marked them out as the Provost's men. At one point they had asked about Zeke Barnes talking about a reward and some yokel said that he had met him on the road to the Levels.

By this time Starkey had the bit between his teeth and kicked viciously at a stool and swept the table clear of the lunch time debris sending tin plates and jugs flying. "For the best part o' six years we had a damned good thing going!" He screamed. "Harrison said this

294

would happen. The old dame trusted you and we were all getting a nice taste out of it until this jumped up Marine wrecks it all!... Well, don't just stand there like a bloody scarecrow, talk to me you dolt. What are we going to do about it?"

Glaring at the trembling man he slammed his hand on the table and stamped around the kitchen in a wild frustrated rage.

Suddenly he stopped and shouted "Right, that's enough! I can see that it's useless expecting you to do anything so I'll have to handle it myself as usual, even if I have to kill this jumped up new Lord!: Just you keep your head down and your eyes and ears open and don't even try to contact me, and don't even think about visiting Bath for a long time. They've got a bloody fine likeness of you on a poster outside the Guildhall offering a reward for sight of you. I'll let you know what to do when the time comes, right?"

Barnes dumbly nodded his head and his tormentor stormed out of the room slamming the door violently behind him.

30

JESSICA'S REVENGE.

TARAAR! The Big Day had finally arrived! …It was October 12th 1805 and for weeks now the Bath and Bristol newspapers had been trumpeting the latest sensation and giving regular updates on the progress. Now, at last it was ready! All Bath was a-buzz!

It was the opening night of the New Theatre Royal and every seat was taken. The play chosen was Shakespeare's Richard the Third, supported by a musical farce called The Poor Soldiers. It promised to be a wonderful night for all…. and so was; with the exception of a few unfortunate patrons!

As the evening closed in, the area around Beauford Square and Saw Close became a fairy land, a glittering scene with lanterns and even fireworks. The militia band resplendent in their scarlet tunics, led the procession of gleaming carriages, still arriving from every stately home and grand hotel for miles around. Cabs and sedan chairs too with their perfumed and exotically costumed passengers, added to the bustling confusion as the air rang with the profanities and curses of the drivers and chairmen. Urchins ran around the coaches shouting and holding their ragged caps for any loose change and generally getting in the way while at the corner of Kingsmead Square a group of more sinister beggars and drifters kept their shifty eyes on the crowd looking for likely victims to rob.

Eventually the theatre doorman and two of the ushers went to sort things out by channelling the Sedan chairmen to the side entrance in Saw Close and then bullying the rough and rowdy denizens of the pit (The Hoi Polloi. as they were known) to the lower entrance in St Johns Court. The carriages were then directed to flow in one direction, arriving in Saw Close from Westgate Street, dropping their passengers at the approach to Beauford Square and then departing via the Upper Borough Walls towards Pulteney Bridge or further up the dark street to Queen's Square.

In the foyer Jessica surveyed the bustling throng as she waited while her escort Major Mahler gave their coachman his instructions for picking them up later. At twenty three she was in full bloom and looking absolutely magnificent. She wore a shimmering dark green satin dress in the latest fashion, and her glossy Titian hair piled high in a complicated coiffure. Her already perfect complexion was enhanced by subtle use of the finest cosmetics and the flawless skin of her sensational cleavage stopped many a conversation dead.

She had always had good taste and the sophisticated elegance she had learned at Mrs Blundell's Academy had added an indefinable air of quality. She was a rich young woman now and had spent her money wisely: Her clothes were from an émigré Parisian couturier, her household staff from Italy and her new mansion in Pulteney Street was the talk of the town. She wallowed in the attention of the smart theatre goers and gracefully nodded her acknowledgement of their approval, occasionally bussing the cheek or touching hands with particular acquaintances. Her smug preening however was rudely interrupted by the harsh voice of the usher as he banged his staff on the tilled floor to announce a new arrival.

"Lord Alexander Trandon and Senhorita Rachel Dacarius"
All heads swivelled away from Jessica to greet the newcomers at the entrance and her heart jumped when she saw the couple. Alexander was wearing his blue military tunic complete with an array of medals, shoulder chains and the white and red lanyards of the Lord Provost's Department His skin tight blue overall trousers carried a broad red stripe above his gleaming black boots and silver spurs. Then she slid her gaze to his companion and her heart sank... Instead of the highly stylised, up to the minute Georgian modes, Rachel had adopted a more simplified costume which highlighted her earthy natural beauty, setting the men gasping and the women glaring in mute shock. Instead of being piled high or in a classical chignon, her radiant blue-black hair fell in a glistening cascade over her snow white shoulders almost to her waist, the line only broken by a wisp of a delicate Kashmiri shawl while her make up, in this age of paint, powder and patches, was unusually refined and understated. It was obviously the creation of an inspired cosmetician, the delicately

298

applied kohl eye shadow lifting the unique mauve tints of her large eyes and her long curling lashes, a rich orange red lipstick accentuating the un-rouged translucent quality of her skin. Her pale blue evening gown was just as eye catching. Although it had the seductive décolletage of the times, instead of the bodice ending below the bust line and billowing gracefully to the ground in the Athenian fashion it extended to the natural waistline fitting like a second skin and accentuating the flare of her smooth hips. She did truly look like some exotic Goddess leaving Jessica seething with wild frustration and jealousy, her moment of glory stolen by this peasant slut!

The bell rang for the audience to take their seats and the crowd began to move into the auditorium amongst them Alexander with Rachel on his arm. As they passed the silently raging Jessica, Alexander turned and bowed sardonically saying formally.

"Ah, Miss Singleton, how delightful you look tonight. We offer you our sincere condolences for your sad loss, but I must say that you wear your inheritance well and I hear that your fine new mansion on Great Pulteney Street is the talk of the town... We must visit you soon, as I am given to understand that one can meet some very attractive and accommodating people there".

Jessica gasped in disbelief...What had he said? WE? What, him and that gypsy tart? Never! Reaching for her last reserves of self control she replied tightly. "Ah, Major Coulston, how nice to see you again... and in such, er, shall we say elevated company." Alexander was about to remind her of his promotion to <u>Colonel</u> when Rachel's pressure on his arm made him realise Jessica's game and he held his tongue. However before he could make any reply, with a wry smile Jessica disingenuously gestured to the passing throng saying. "Who knows, perhaps we will meet again…and."

Without a further word Alexander turned and walked away leaving her livid with anger but before she could respond Kurt Mahler arrived breathless.

"Ah, Dollink, Sorry to be delayed… It vaz zat verdammlich coachman who could not understand his orders…It is all settled now … I told him….."

Cutting across him she hissed. "Oh shut up you pompous oaf! Where have you been? Where were you when I needed you, you clown?"

Completely taken aback by her verbal attack Mahler stuttered. "I do not understand... Vot is wrong? Has someone insulted you? Have you been attacked?"

For an instant Jessica was about to dismiss the incident when an evil thought crossed her mind and she turned her head away.

"But vot happened Liebchen?" He persisted. "Please tell me."

She turned back to him biting her lip and forcing crocodile tears. "Oh Kurt… It is true. I have been vilely insulted. That coarse Major Coulston, who was once my friend, suggested that I was allowing my new house to be used as a place of ill repute. It is absolutely intolerable! I will not have it said that I am some kind of Madame!"

Mahler's eyes bulged and his face took on a crimson colour as he growled. "Vat? Mein Gott! I shall kill the swine. For much too long now I have suffered his secret insults and the flaunting of his new title and his promotion. He has gone too far this time! This is the moment I have been waiting for!"

Carried away by the tension of the occasion Jessica poured out an embroidered story of how Alexander had insinuated that she was a procuress and that her new house was a brothel. She fanned her face and neck briskly to emphasise her anger and Mahler stormed off to find the rogue who had so mortally insulted his lady and make him pay for his insolence.

Alexander and Rachel had just settled into their seats when a liveried usher whispered that a gentleman would like a word with him in the foyer, adding that it appeared to be a matter of some urgency. With a gasp of impatience Alexander excused himself and hurried to the foyer only to be confronted by a red faced raging German cavalry officer who accused him loudly of insulting the lady he was escorting. Alexander was completely taken aback and said that he held the lady in question in the highest regard and that they were old friends. Surely there must be a mistake? Perhaps she had misconstrued his meaning? But the big German would have none of it. He insisted that his lady had been abused and her honour scandalised by Alexander's remarks and that could mean only one redress... A duel!

Alexander was momentarily taken off guard but quickly realised that Mahler considered that he had the advantage and was determined to force the issue so he accepted and said that he would arrange for his seconds to make the necessary arrangements. Tradition allowed the challenged party the right to choose the weapons and Alexander said that this too would be settled by his seconds. Mahler nodded his acceptance clicked his heels and turned away without a further word.

Jessica had been watching the heated exchange from behind a pillar and gasped when she realised the enormity of what she had done: Whichever way the meeting went she would be the loser; but worst of all, what if her beloved were killed?.. But then again, people would ask who her beloved was? But deep in her heart Jessica knew that she had loved Alexander from the first moment he had crossed her path. Oh! What should she do now?

As for Alexander, once he overcame the shock of the challenge, he became concerned about the choice of weapons and relayed his worries to Cyrus and Jeb as they sat in the comfortable best lounge of the Star Inn on the Paragon. In the main bar the regular gang of wealthy wasters were discussing the varying talents of their companions at the previous night's post-Assembly Rooms debauchery, while in the tap room the artisans and farm lads were loudly enjoying the skittle alley.

"I mean" Stated Alexander, moodily gulping down his brandy. "That German bastard has already butchered three men in duels, two of 'em with pistols and an Ensign from the Wiltshire's with a sabre. He cut the poor fellow to ribbons before finishing him off: Even the Duke of Brunswick took offence at it and threatened to send him back Hanover if any scandal like that embarrassed the King again. There might have been a few Georges ruling us but there is always an undercurrent about them being Fritzes but right now we have enough on our hands with the Frogs!"

Cyrus considered this for a moment and was about to speak when Jeb butted in saying.

"Well, I wunt say as Oi would know more 'bout these things than two dyed-in-the-wool gentl'mn like you, but as Oi see it, the choice o' weapons do rest wi' you, so why don'ee pick summat yuh feel good with?"

Alexander and Cyrus looked at each other in surprise but agreed that Jeb had a point.

"Well," Persisted Jeb. "Worra mean is, wot did'ja use to use in yore days at sea. Y'know foightin' off them Frenchies if'n it weren't a pistol or a sword?"

Alexander considered for a moment and said. "Well I found a boarding pike did the job very well. It's handy enough to use on a crowded deck and long enough to keep trouble at bay."

"Well then, thaz yore answer, ain't un?" Snorted Jeb. "Remember, Alexander, tis yore choice!"

Of course, in the army, the naval boarding pike with its spike and axe head was not used but the nearest thing to it in service was the spontoon or half pike, a seven foot sturdy ash shaft with a small crossbar and topped by a long sharp double sided steel point and the heel sporting a sinister pointed brass spike. They all agreed that it would do the job very well!

Mahler was shocked when he heard of Alexander's choice of weapons from his seconds and flatly refused to fight with 'Peasants Weapons' but reluctantly agreed after the two Hanoverian officers pointed out that the barracks was already buzzing with news of the challenge and that he would be accused of cowardice if he refused. Anyway, as they reasoned, there was plenty of time for him to familiarise himself with the weapon as at this time duelling was officially banned in the army so a time would have to be arranged to select a suitably secret venue that would and fit with their individual duty rosters.

In the end, a date three weeks hence was agreed and the venue was to be a hidden clearing near the old burying ground in the woods at Smallcombe

----

The day came round quickly and in spite of it being late April a hard morning frost still clung to the stubbly grass in the valley and no early morning birdsong came from the tangled undergrowth of the dense Smallcombe woods: This was to be the day of reckoning, the one that the jealous Jessica had once demanded so forcefully but was now regretting.

Although this unique contest was strictly illegal details of it had been well circulated in this gambling mad city and much money had been secretly wagered on its outcome, therefore both parties had arrived by different routes to avoid any curious spectators. Mahler and his seconds came from Jessica's house on Great Pulteney Street via Bathwick hill, crossing the picturesque as yet unfinished canal and turning right to cross the meadows to the burial ground in the narrow valley, beyond, while Alexander's party had crossed the Avon at Southmead and come up Widcome Hill. The surgeon and his assistants were already at the wood as were the two official stewards and the Duel-Marshal standing talking in low tones near the carriages and at the arrival of the antagonists they moved silently to their places.

As the choice of weapons was so unorthodox the killing ground had been marked out by orange flags beyond which was considered out of bounds and any violence there was deemed to be no longer covered by the accepted duelling protocol and subject to common law. At opposite sides of this space stood the contestants and their seconds while at the centre stuck in the hard ground were four military spontoons, their cruel points sparkling in the frosty sunshine. These were not the ceremonial slender varnished poles with an ornamental polished brass crossbar so often seen on parades festooned with ribbons and pennants. These were the real thing, with battle scarred four inch diameter shafts topped with the deadly steel blades with razor sharp edges and wicked points. The stern marshal examined them for a moment then checking his hunter called the contestants to the centre.

Handing their heavy caped cloaks to their seconds Alexander and Mahler marched in their shirt sleeves smartly towards him without exchanging a word and the official, after a brief coughing fit brought on by the cold morning air, asked them both formally if they had perused all avenues to reconcile their differences before coming to this situation. Receiving only stone faced stares and nodding heads he shrugged resignedly and told them to select their weapons and take their places.

Alexander, as the challenged party was first and without a second glance laid his hand on the nearest spontoon and returned to his side while Mahler carefully reviewed the remaining three and chose carefully before returning to his station. In the silent minute that followed a distant church bell chimed six and with neither party having any objections and all formalities having been observed, the marshal waved his scarlet handkerchief and declared the duel begun.

From the outset it was obvious that Mahler had used the intervening three weeks practicing avidly with this new weapon. He had engaged a retired Sergeant at Arms to coach him in the use of the half pike. He quickly learned that there was much more to handling it than he thought and learned its deadly menace. With the half pike spontoon there were no minor wounds. Its sturdy ash shaft would drive the razor sharp blade with its hardened triangular tip through the toughest boiled leather buff coat of a cavalry man like butter and with the bronze spiked butt securely grounded would deter any charging horse or infantryman.

From his side of the clearing Alexander watched with grudging respect how smoothly the big German performed the classic evolutions and how he handled the heavy shaft with ease and confidence: Truly, this man was a master of the duel whose skill with sword and pistol had been proved time and time again and regarded this weapon to be just another part of the challenge.

For his own part Alexander felt completely at home with the weapon. His prowess with its naval equivalent had been honed on many boarding parties and saved his life on more than one occasion.

They approached each other warily, Mahler adopting the classic military position of the high port with the shaft diagonally across his body and the point high while Alexander held the shaft low and balanced horizontally in his right hand. As they approached within striking distance Mahler lowered his point and stepped briskly forwards, his weight fully committed to this first thrust. Just out of range Alexander sidestepped and flung up his pike catching the shaft a quarter of the way up with his left hand and sweeping the vicious thrust aside. Undeterred Mahler came at him again and this time Alexander stepped to the right and turned to his left swinging his pike round and hitting his opponent hard on back of the neck with the bronze plated butt of the shaft. The forceful blow would have finished a lesser man but while it sent Mahler to his knees, his bull-like neck absorbed the damage and he rolled away and returned to his defensive position shaking his head. He had obviously been advised by his tutor, that although the advantage with the pike was always defensive, a sudden switch to the attack could often be effective. Consequently he quickly stabbed again and opened a cut on Alexander's left forearm. Alexander reacted immediately with a pass at Mahler's throat missing by a hair's breadth and drew blood from his cheek as his wily target slid below the sweep. They were now face to face inside the effective stabbing range, puffing and panting with the dead weight of their ineffective weapons and pushing and shoving to find an advantage. Sweat was running down their faces but neither could relinquish his hold on the shaft. It was a desperate struggle but Mahler was the bigger man and soon his weight and height began to tell forcing Alexander to disengage, a very dangerous move indeed as now he was back in range of Mahler's broad blade. In separating he suffered another cut, this time in his right thigh and moved quickly away.

The confident switching of position and sudden lateral attacks showed that Mahler had taken the lessons of the Sergeant at Arms seriously and it required some quick thinking on Alexander's part to stay clear of the danger area. It was quite apparent now that Mahler was banking on getting inside the effective stabbing range again where he could wear his opponent down and he advanced boldly.

As Alexander, limping now from the deep cut in his thigh, shuffled a little to his right to block the assault he suddenly remembered a similar incident that happened to him while boarding a Dyak pirate ship in the Malay Straits and moved in again with the pike held high. Exactly as his pirate opponent had done, Mahler lowered his weapon and charged blindly, intent on skewering his wide open opponent but suddenly Alexander was not there. He had dropped to the ground, rolled under the oncoming spearhead and rammed his pike through Mahler's legs not quite tripping him as intended but causing him to stumble The German staggered and as he clumsily turned to find his opponent Alexander stabbed his weapon backwards and upwards ramming the wicked bronze butt point into his upper chest just below the right shoulder. Mahler gasped and dropping his weapon feverishly pulled at the impaling shaft, falling to his knees when Alexander withdrew the spike.

Alexander, still breathing heavily, his arms covered in rivulets of crimson blood quickly reversed his weapon and held the pointed blade at the throat of the prostrate German pricking it lightly but enough to draw blood.

A look of incredulity passed across Mahler's face. In twelve years he had never lost a duel and now here he was, at the mercy of the man he had tried to destroy. How could such a thing happen and in front of such distinguished company too? ... Soon all the Army would know of his humiliation at the hands of a lowly officer of

Marines armed with a spear. He would be finished. He closed his eyes and waited for the death thrust but it did not come yet. Still holding the point steady against Mahler's windpipe, Alexander addressed him "Herr Oberst Mahler. You have fought an honourable battle and now I hold your life in my hands but I shall not take it and bear you no further grudge for your imagined insults spawned in blind jealousy, if you give your parole that you will leave England to serve overseas. I care not where, nor do I care whether you take your mistress or not. That is entirely her affair."

By this time the surgeon and other officials had gathered round and awaited Mahler's reply. He was drifting in and out of consciousness but managed to whisper his agreement before passing out altogether as the assistants rolled him onto a stretcher and hurried him back to the carriages. Alexander too was weak now and sat on the damp earth to have his wounds bound up by the doctor while the Duel-Marshal pompously declared Alexander the winner.

Sitting aloof on his high seat the surgeon's coachman had seen it all many times before and waited moodily until the wounded man was bundled into the carriage and the stretcher folded up on the roof. Without a second glance at the trampled blooded grass, the driver chuck-chuck'd to the bays and they trundled off down the rutted lane to Horseshoe Walk. There were only two things on his mind, the breakfast awaiting him at the Ram and why was the Surgeon's Mate wearing a green feather in his hat?

Meanwhile, back at her luxurious mansion on Great Pulteney Street, Jessica passed a tense morning anxiously awaiting news of the outcome at Smallcombe but no answer came, even though it was less than a couple of miles away. Desperate for news she even dispatched Janet to the shops and peddlers around the North Gate and in Walcott Street Market to ask around but nobody could tell her anything.

It was late the following afternoon that a dispatch rider arrived at the house and handed Janet a letter for her mistress. It was from Major Kurt Mahler bluntly informing her that he had been urgently recalled to special duties in Hanover and he would write further from there. He did not mention the outcome of the duel and she never heard from him again.

Although that is not strictly true, because some years later in the late summer of 1815, a letter was forwarded to her which had arrived at Warminster Barracks, having been found on the body of a cavalry officer in the Kings German Legion killed while leading a charge that broke the French line at the Battle of Waterloo...

It was addressed to Lady Trandon and simply said that she had been the love of his life and he would always love her.

31

ENCOUNTER IN MARSHFIELD

The breakthrough came quite unexpectedly one Tuesday in early May when Harry was back working under cover at the Crown Inn. Around seven in the evening the miller came in with his lanky foreman. They seemed very excited and before they got down to some serious drinking Russell ordered a lunch of cold cuts and all the trimmings, with gin, wine and beer for six to be sent over to the mill at twelve thirty the next day. Russell tapped the side of his nose and intimated to the landlord that it was an important business meeting. Harry was in the back scullery scraping plates when he heard the distinctive rasp of the miller's voice and sidled back into the bar.

At the sight of him the landlord shouted. "Oh! Thar y'are Perkins y'skivin' toad! Gerr'over there an' clear away that bloody table fer Mister Russell an' quick about it, or givee a clip roun' th' ear'ole!"

Harry dropped easily into character and becoming the cringing, obsequious pot man mumbling. "Aye, zur, roite away zur."

and shuffled over to stir the smouldering fire into life and give the scarred wobbly table a perfunctory wipe with his cloth

"Thar ye be, squire." He said with a gap toothed leer and the foreman shoved him out of the way calling him a 'Fockin' stinkin' eejit' and told him to get the drinks. As he returned with the tray of drinks the conversation stopped abruptly but he caught the tail end of it and distinctly heard Bradley's name mentioned and that of a woman, possibly Marie. They waved him away anxiously but they continued to talk in hushed tones. There would be the occasional outburst of denial or some bad tempered wrangling but even that was quickly stifled whenever someone came close. By the time they broke up at around nine Harry had established that there would be several other people at the meeting and that a visit from the Provost Marshal's men was well warranted.

Alexander now had a courier in place to aid communication. It was one of his troopers in the guise of a travelling knife grinder and tinker who had rented a hut from a farmer at the far end of the village from where he could watch the comings and goings along the Chippenham to Bristol road. Later that night Harry passed on the news to him and at eight o'clock the following morning the grinder trundled his cart into the pub yard and informed Harry that by 1.30 the troops would be in position and the raid would go in at 2pm.

The round-up worked like clockwork. Harry and two of the girls loaded up the pub cart with the platters of cold meats and savouries covered with snow white cloths, the bread was in wicker

313

baskets and the wines and spirits in a wooden box. Nestling next to them was a small keg of porter. The foreman met them at the gate and directed them to a large upstairs room where a long table was being set out by a couple of local women. The kitchen girls said that it certainly looked a lot cleaner than the last time they brought food over and they ribbed the foreman about it.

"Oi, Walter, oo ye got comin' today bloody Queen Charlotte?"

But Walter was not in the mood for banter and brusquely told them to mind their own affairs and get on with the job they were being paid to do. While setting up and venting the keg, Harry kept a weather eye open for any untoward problems and got on with arraying the bottles, mugs and glasses neatly on the long sideboard. Soon everything was ready and the diners began to trickle up from downstairs.

They all looked satisfied with whatever they had been discussing. Apart from Bradley, they were mostly locals from the pub but there were two people he had not seen before whom Russell treated very respectfully, toadying to their every need. First, came a tall, middle aged corpulent man who's most notable features were his florid boozer's nose and the thick gold chain he wore across his expensive light blue silk waistcoat with a diamond fob on one end and large gilded hunter on the other. The other unknown party was a smartly dressed bony woman in her forties who surveyed the gathering coldly with narrowed eyes.

Soon the drinks and the banter were flowing and the striking of a nearby case clock made Harry realise that it was time to be moving. Pleading that he had forgotten the corkscrew he scuttled away to the jeers and curses of the locals. As he left the mill he noticed that the square and the main street were empty, there was not a soul to be seen while tethered outside the Crown were a couple of cavalry horses and as he crossed the main street he saw a platoon of militia cavalry waiting in the side street. One of the troopers was about to break cover to stop him but an NCO put his hand on the man's arm and they let him go by. In the pub yard were more horses but when he came through the back door into the barroom there were no customers in sight. Instead standing behind the bar drinking brandy were Alexander and a major of the Wiltshire Yeomanry, while, in a corner, tied to a chair and guarded by four troopers, sat the glum faced landlord. Standing by the fire with a pint of cider in his hand was the travelling tinker.

Outside there was a bark of command and the cavalry squadron clattered into the mill yard followed by a group of green coated riflemen, shouting scuffling and firing warning shots behind the mill wall but soon everything went quiet. Then sixty yards away across the square, a line of loudly arguing prisoners led by Russell came staggering out of the mill yard escorted by the platoon of infantry and hemmed in by the mounted militiamen. Two black prison vans with barred windows were waiting for them at the far side of the square and they were herded roughly aboard, then with

315

one guard standing on the rear step and another sitting on the roof they were hustled away to Bath..

By six o'clock in the evening they had all been ensconced in the Grove Street lock up and the following morning they were taken before a Bath magistrate. He remanded them in custody for trial at Bristol Assizes, the charges being too serious to be dealt with on a local level. All the Marshfield locals were sent to the lock-up on Bridewell Lane in the shadow of the Upper Borough Walls while the strangers, including Bradley were ensconced in special cells built in the cellar of the militia drill hall; ironically, the very place where the adventure had begun.

The news quickly spread and the press were right onto it. The Bath Chronicle reported the affair in depth as did the Wiltshire papers and the North Somerset Press. Directions were received from the Lord Provost's Department that it would be in the public interest to play down the robbery angle and concentrate on the more lurid activities of the Redemptors and their involvement in the Mendip Murders.

As soon as Rachel heard of Bradley's involvement she wrote a letter to her brother and as the contents could be incriminating she took the early morning stage coach to Bristol and delivered it in person to Mendoza for onward delivery to Rob in Lisbon. The Jew said he had a fast boat leaving the following day for Vigo and her letter would be there in four days.

The net was cast far and wide for anyone connected to the

Redemptors but in line with their typical response to any exposure the cult cut all communication with the captives. However what with one of their regional collectors, Marie Dubord and the flamboyant, high living, Axbridge Beadle now being in custody and the growing discontent of the West Country shopkeepers and farmers at the constant violence, intimidation and extortion, they were slow to institute a covering policy. Within a month the whole network was rolled up and their influence destroyed. Daily convoys of suspects and local chiefs were being transported to prison hulks in Bristol harbour.

Bradley's case was different. He was the only one arrested who had been directly involved in the heist. At first he tried to implicate Melody Watson, saying that she had seduced him into the plot using the information she had gleaned from the soldiers in the tavern but she flatly denied having anything to do with it. Grasping at straws, he next claimed that Rob Dacarius had been the organiser and had forced him to help. This dangerous accusation alarmed Rachel and on Mendoza's advice she quickly spread some of her new found wealth generously around Warminster and Widcome to ensure that no one could testify that Rob had done more than hire his boat to Bradley. Jeb was called and said that he had seen them together a number of times in the Bell Inn but the barman corroborated Rachel's explanation of the meetings. With little more to go on than Bradley's unproven allegations and the fact that he was now in Portugal, Rob was dropped from the investigation. A further deposit in Rachel's bank account signalled her brother's gratitude.

The jury then unanimously found Bradley guilty. The penalty was death but it was decided that he would be allowed to escape the mandatory sentence for robbery of the Royal Exchequer by turning King's evidence and telling all he knew. In the event he proved to be a good source and most of the gang were roped in too. In the end his sentence was commuted to transportation to Canada for twelve years.

At their trial the Redemptors all were found guilty. Three of the assassins were hanged and Russell, Walter Crowe his foreman, the Controller Marie Dubord and the flamboyant Axbridge Beadle were flogged, branded, and transported for life to the West Indian plantations. It all proved too much for Marie and somehow she managed to jump overboard from the ship in the Bay of Biscay and was never seen again.

32

ROB RETURNS

Ever since receiving Rachel's letter Rob had been on edge, wondering just what was happening back in England so he was relieved when a courier handed him a second letter that had arrived by ship from Bristol that very morning. Generously tipping the messenger and closing his office door he tore open the sealed package.

It was from Rachel briefly giving him the latest news and enclosing three pages from a special edition of the Bath Chronicle reporting the trial in detail. He blew a relieved breath when he read that Jed Turner and Whitey Crane, the last of Captain Brookes' old gang, had been hanged for murder and that Bradley was on his way to the wilds of Canada, however his biggest anxiety faded when he read that the Redemptors had been exposed and their power broken. He smiled when he read of the big parties and bonfires of the Huguenot communities celebrating their freedom from persecution by the very people who had posed as their protectors. He was also pleased that evil Marie Dubord ('the Beast of Bridgewater') and Jeremiah Allen, the crooked beadle from Axbridge had finally been caught. Rob had always suspected that the Redemptors had a mole in local government but he was surprised to find who it was. The best news of all was that he himself was off the hook, being portrayed as an innocent boat owner who had been duped into helping the robbers. More importantly, that there was no one left to say otherwise!

The affair with Uncle Arturo had also been settled once and for all a few nights later in the caves above Montijo beach in Lisbon harbour, when he had been caught red handed by Rob and Diego stealing gold from the barrels he was supposed to be guarding. At first Arturo protested his innocence but with the surprise arrival of two of his crew he turned nasty and drawing a knife he moved in to attack his accusers. For an instant Rob froze but he had been expecting treachery from Arturo somewhere along the way and had come prepared and without hesitation he drew a loaded pistol from the bag he was carrying and shot Arturo dead. The two crewmen hesitated a moment undecided just what to do but before they could make a move Diego went at them with a machete catching one with a deep gash on the neck as they ran off into the night. Rob and Diego then hitched a mule to one of Arturo's carts and rolled the remaining barrels to a ramp where they loaded them in and trundled down to the cove where their caravel was moored.

By early the following evening they were nosing into Vigo

Harbour where they stored the barrels in Diego's warehouse until Rob could contact Mendoza's representative and deposit the rest of his merchandise with his mysterious banker. Secret passwords were exchanged and the Jewish agent exchanged a certain sum into escudos some of which Rob used to buy a fully legal and notarised partnership in Diego's business. The affair now being complete Rob made arrangements to return to England, taking his new partner with him.

Back in Bath changes were also being made. Officially Alexander's role was completed as most of the questions about the payroll robbery had been answered and the culprits punished. In fact everybody was quite relieved that the affair was closed. At least the trial was over but in spite of a generous reward being offered for information, as yet no money had been found so things could by no means be considered settled.

Bradley's fantastic tale about barrels was laughed out of court by the jury. What barrels? Where were they? The money chests had never been moved from their places in the cellar! The only money that had surfaced were a few Maria Theresa dollars and sovereigns flashed by a couple of dead fire raisers down in the Mendips!

Further questions were pointless. Therefore, to calm the latent fears in certain corridors of power that if the investigation went on too long or delved too deep, important figures may have been implicated and reputations damaged, it was quietly put to bed

The Lord Provost's office said that they were very pleased at Alexander's efficient detection methods and said that they would like him to continue in the role, promoting him to regional controller with a substantial increase in pay and a bigger operating budget. The first thing that Alexander did with his new funding was to take advertising space in the Bath Chronicle offering a £5 reward for information. All his friends and colleagues were pleased with the successful outcome and organised a party at the New Assembly Rooms to celebrate.

Ever since the Mahler affair Jessica had kept a very low profile, most people in town having guessed that she was responsible for the whole debacle. She did however respond to Cyrus' invitation to the party as to do otherwise would have looked churlish. She also realised that to regain her popularity and impress Alexander she would really have to make a mark.

Rachel in the meantime, apart from sharing the pleasures of Alexander's bed, was revelling in her new position as Chatelaine of Trandon House and being seen out and about with him at some of the most fashionable functions and soirees in the city. She saw this celebration as a chance to consolidate her position by arranging the function with great style and aplomb

The venue chosen was the famous Blue Room behind the yellow walled Octagon gambling salon in the New Assembly Halls, which in those days was regularly used for wedding receptions, investitures and other private functions. A small string quartet was engaged to promote a social atmosphere and Herr Gruber was booked to provide one of his superb a cold buffet from his select White Meat shop in Abbey Green.

All Alexander's friends from Bath and some of his fellow officers from the barracks at Warminster had been invited. As the official host Cyrus had brought along the radiant Mrs Edwards as the guest of honour and Jeb, who was now manager of the expanded livery stable and chain horse depot in Shires Yard and a junior partner in Cyrus' company, brought along his brand new wife of three months. It turned out to be none other than the delectable Alice who had been detailed to look after Alexander on his first visit to Mrs Edwards's house. Also, as befitting his now elevated status he had purchased a small but elegant house on the Lansdowne road just above the turnpike gate.

Rachel herself had gone to great pains this time to look the classic Regency Belle, hair piled high, bodice cut low and groomed to perfection but feeling somewhat miffed that her rival had not yet arrived. Perhaps she had lost her nerve as well as her lover she sneered and got on with being the perfect hostess.

When the party was in full swing and the speeches and toasts had all been made there was a sudden change in the music of the string quartet and a strange wailing was heard in the air and the measured cadence of the music changed to a bright bell-like tingling and a throbbing drumbeat. All eyes turned to the stage where three turbaned figures wearing long silk coats had joined the powdered and periwigged players. Two of them sitting on small stools, were picking out a complex melody on the strings of long sitars, nestling the brightly coloured gourds between their brown knees while the third was blowing on a fat bellied pipe and keeping time by clashing small cymbals on his fingers and the rings of bells around his ankles. There was the smell of incense in the air and suddenly a throbbing of drums was heard from the gambling room and the door was flung open to reveal three massive black Nubians wearing baggy pale blue silk oriental trousers and bright orange sashes round their waists. They were beating out a complex rhythm on deep narrow drums slung on broad patterned leather straps across their powerfully muscled shining black torsos, large turbans with peacock feathers nodding on their heads. Behind came four sumptuous dancing girls in diaphanous costumes displaying with every twist and turn the seductive curves of their lithe brown bodies.

The audience stood aghast at the spectacle but there was more to come. Behind the dancers came a small fat Indian man equally bejewelled and sumptuously dressed waving his heavily ringed right hand in acceptance of the adoration while on his left arm was the most breathtaking beauty so far. The players changed the rhythm and style of the music to a Turkish sound and the beauty began a harem dance.

The gorgeous apparition slid away from her escort and moved to the front of the group. She looked more Arab than Indian with her glowing café-au-lait skin and her long shining Titian hair pulled tightly back by a heavy jewelled ivory clasp, falling in a flowing mane down her back. She wore an eye catching small jewel encrusted bolero jacket which barely covered her full high breasts and exposed a bare brown midriff with a large emerald shining in her navel. Her diaphanous harem trousers showed every detail of her perfect rounded belly and there were miniature bells around her slender ankles while on her feet were a pair of fine green leather hook toe'd slippers. Her big green eyes were lined by kohl and the lashes shining while in her right nostril was another emerald from which dangled a fine gold chain to her gold earring. She was breathtaking and her dance mesmerised the gaping assembly with its sinuous twists and turns and her expression of complete abandonment. As the music rose to a climax she whirled like a dervish and collapsed into an elegant cross legged pose with her fingers entwined as though in a supplicant prayer... She was superb and everybody was fascinated and intrigued to know who she was. At that moment she rose, modestly acknowledged the adoration and then looked directly at Alexander and gave him a ravishing smile – And suddenly everyone knew...

It was... JESSICA!

For a moment they stood in stunned silence and then one brave buck began to clap and the salon exploded in rapturous applause and cheers. The dancing girls moved smoothly through the crowd being accosted at every turn by admiring men while the women shyly touched the rock hard muscles of the black drummers and whispered salacious comments to their friends. The Indian musicians played one short final number and rushed off stage to join in the celebrations and get their fair share of attention.

Jessica ran to Alexander's side and kissed him fully on the lips her face flushed with the euphoria of her golden moment and her eyes shining with excitement. Alexander, quite rightly swollen with pride told her that she was absolutely amazing and totally surprising. This was the last thing in the world he would have expected her to do. She blushed like a school girl at his enthusiasm until Janet dashed over like a mother hen to where her mistress was sitting and draped her in a splendid long emerald green silk cloak.

The Head Waiter gestured irritable to the waiters and they bustled in with more drinks, the musicians struck up a lively polka and the party responded with vigour and shrieks of loud laughter. At the door from the Octagon gambling room the Duty Manager carefully tabulated every drink that passed him, for the bill to be settled at the end of the evening and next to him stood a stone-faced Rachel, her eyes aglow with hatred and jealousy.

Jessica caught her expression but simply tossed her head in defiance and held on lovingly to Alexander's arm as she introduced him to her escort the Maharaja of Khohima, a title he had chosen with some care for the truth was somewhat more mundane. Later, as they sat at a table in a quiet corner Jessica told Alexander all about him.

His name in fact was Vikram Parradesum, a playboy who

had inherited a vast tea growing estate in the Assam Hills. On a visit to Trinchomalee he had met Admiral Singleton who introduced him to some friends in the East India Company. The ruthless traders gave him a warm welcome as one of their own and within three months they were in business together. Noting his passion for the high life and his curiosity about the celebrated delights of London and Bath they offered him a contract. In return for giving the East India Company exclusive trading rights, he was offered a generous pension to keep him in the style he had become accustomed to and a rent free grand mansion in London's fashionable Mayfair for as long as he chose to stay.

Vikram took to the high life like a duck to water and even brought his family over, sending his sons to an exclusive public school. Of course certain officials in the Colonial Administration saw to it that every obstacle would be put in his way should he ever wish to return, not that he ever would want to. He was enjoying every minute of the new life and had willingly joined his benefactor's daughter in this charade.

Meanwhile, finally losing patience with the scene of abandon and gaiety Rachel left her position and made her way to the buffet pointedly ignoring Alexander and Jessica's intimate tête-à-tête in the corner. She took an orange syllabub from the table and sipped it distractedly wondering what to do next. It seemed obvious that Jessica's sensational entrance had done the trick and now Alexander was like a puppy at her side... Perhaps it was time for her to make a move.

Just at that moment she heard another commotion out in the yellow gambling salon and saw the ushers trying to stop a group of noisy revellers from getting into the to party. Finally they burst through pushing the ushers aside and she saw group led by two burly men with two very striking women standing at the entrance. She gasped when she recognised the bigger of the two men...

In the sudden hubbub occasioned by this gate crashing incident Jessica looked up and displaying her penchant for nicknames chortled. "What ho, and who are these two Don Diegos? They must have a few gold doubloons to be able to afford the charms of Maria and the Mullato. Top of the fillies they do say... I cannot say that I ever liked Madame Di Sienna but they say she gives good value for money, as her new house at Axford's Buildings testifies! .. And now here comes Caroline Sinclair. It is beginning to look like a whore's convention! Her escort is rather shady too. With that eye patch I'd say we were in dangerous company indeed for that is Ellis Starkey"

Shocked at his first sight of Barnes' accomplice Alexander started to rise but Jessica's hand held him back saying "But tarry a moment, it looks like your Gypsy playmate is trying to get her claws in as well!"

Rachel had suddenly come to her senses and rushed towards the new arrivals realizing that it was her brother Rob... All the way from Portugal! Laughing and crying at the same time she hugged him and gave him a warm kiss while the foreign looking woman on his arm gave her an evil questioning stare and clung closer him.

"Tis alright, Maria." He calmed her. "This is my little sister Rachel welcoming her dear brother back to the fold. Be happy for me."

Rob threw his arms around Rachel and she stood close to him with her hair now tumbling down round her shoulders and for a moment Alexander got a vision that for some reason shocked him and as he watched the noisy arrival of the new guests a feeling of deja-vue overcame him.

At first he was seething with anger at the sight of the robber but there was something else. He didn't know exactly what it was but the feeling so disturbed him that he told Jessica that he was not feeling well and asked her to excuse him. His surprise move confused her and stopped her in her tracks. Her carefully laid plans for the evening (and her future) had been going swimmingly but now something had broken her spell on him. With a fixed smile she merely nodded and fluttered her fan to show her displeasure and dismissed him

Cyrus and Jeb had also witnessed this exchange and like Alexander were taken aback by the change in Rob's appearance. This character here was bulkier and more prosperous looking. Gone were shaven head and the gaunt face and the powerful raw-boned frame of a hard working river man. This apparition had long thick black curly hair, a neck like a young bull and sported a fashionable short beard and flowing moustaches. His partner was similarly attired and they looked like two wealthy Portuguese businessmen... Which in fact they were!

In a daze Alexander turned and pushed his way through the crowd to the entrance where Rachel was ecstatically introducing her brother to the guests. She looked up in surprise at his approach and when he said that he was leaving, she sarcastically spat back that he could spend the night with his new found harem slut for all she cared. Unable to explain his reasons he wished her goodnight and left the salon.

Half way across the yellow gambling room he stopped and looked back at the group around the salon door: Someone else had joined the party. The sinister Ellis Starkey was talking animatedly with Maria who appeared to be giving him instructions. Rob was still looking at him coldly and talking out of the side of his mouth to his business partner while Rachel and Aimee were in a close animated conversation. Rob said something to them and they stopped talking and there was a look of complete hatred on their faces as they stared at Alexander. It shocked him for a moment but he stared back and then turned on his heel. As he disappeared into the crowd Maria turned to the man with the black eye patch and gave him a distinct nod. Without a further word he turned and gestured to a watching footman to join him as he slipped out of a side door on some urgent errand.

S

33

THE ASSASSIN

Some strange disturbance had certainly unsettled Alexander and he decided to spend the night at the inn on Upper Church Street where he went on his first visit to the New Assembly Rooms. He told the doorman to find a link boy to light him through the darkened streets and as they passed around the north side of the Kings Circus, he heard again a church bell chiming. It was one o'clock and like on his first visit he checked the time on his faithful chronometer mumbling that the chimes were still wrong and that the Bishop ought to fix it.

As they stopped the link boy raised his flaming torch high and Alexander caught a glance, as he had on that first night, of a bizarre figure lounging in a doorway. He was oddly dressed but the one thing that caught Alexander's eye was the small bright green feather in the man's lapel. He turned to tell the link boy to hold his torch higher but when he looked again the figure had vanished.

Alexander walked on still pondering on the evening's strange events and as he entered Brock Street, it suddenly came to him where he had first seen Rob. Once again his mind travelled back to the day of his arrival at Poole. He recalled the ship, the soft snow flurries, the stagecoach journey and the traumatic affair with the highwayman..... But more than anything he remembered first seeing Rachel and how he had been fascinated by her beauty and then he recalled the stone-faced man at her side staring hatefully at him and muttering threats and promises to her.. .Then he realised... It was Rob.... He was one of the highwayman's gang!

Still totally unaware of any danger threatening him and still possessed by his awakening, Alexander stood for a moment under the lantern at the door of the tavern considering the reactions of the people he had just left, trying to find a reason for the blank stares and urgent hushed conversations and also realised ... They knew that he knew!

Thirty yards away in the dense shrubbery at the corner of the Royal Crescent a lurking, dark-cloaked, hooded figure lifted a slim hunting rifle and took careful aim at the lone officer but at that very moment a cab came clopping round the corner from Catherine Place heading for Brock Street completely masking the target. Suddenly in the bright moonlight the horse caught a glint from the rifle's brass bound muzzle and tossed its head in fright causing a momentary loss of concentration as the assassin fired. With a loud roar the ball splintered the front pillar of the cab and ricocheted gouging a furrow from the top of Alexander's shoulder, ripping off his left epaulette in its passage and whirling him off his feet. Three inches further to the right and he would have been a dead man. As he struggled groggily to his feet in shocked surprise the tavern door burst open and a crowd piled out into the street, shouting and pointing to the damaged cab and the foaming horse.

Nearby a puffing watchman who had just climbed up from the basement of a house on the Royal Crescent turned and waved goodbye to the buxom cook standing at the doorway thanking her for the mug of hot beef tea that had been very welcome on such a cold night. Wiping his grimy greatcoat cuff across his mouth, he had just stopped to open up his lantern when he heard the sound of a horse's whinny and suddenly from the copse on the corner a shot rang. In the confusion that followed he saw a horse and rider break cover and ride straight at him as if to run him down. Although now an old retired infantryman he still knew how to re-act and stepping to one side he swung his heavy staff hitting the horses muzzle squarely. The mount screamed and reared unseating the rider who was quickly subdued by the crowd from the tavern. One of them pulled back the hood of the groaning figure and a cascade of blonde hair tumbled out.

"I know 'er!." Yelled the watchman." She comes frum near Warminster she does. She's a barmaid at a pub in Dilton Marsh…Thaz the Watson girl. No mistakin' 'er. Once seen never forgot, that's our Melody! "

They dragged the struggling cursing girl to her feet and held her tight. Alexander looked at her with disgust and with his good arm picked up the fallen gun he sniffed the muzzle saying.

"Aye... She's the one alright. It's just been fired. Get a rope from the tavern and tie her to that tree... and get me a towel to staunch this blood."

At that Melody struggled and cursed even more believing that they were about to lynch her until Alexander told her that she was under arrest and would be held in custody until her fate was decided. There were sinister undertones to this incident that reeked of Rob Dacarius' meddling which Alexander wished to expose.

"We should 'ang 'er right 'ere an' now." Shouted the irate cabbie "Nearly killed my mare she did. Wot woulda 'appened then, eh, wi' me left no way of earnin' a crust? String 'er up, I say."

Alexander turned to the shouting driver and told him that his cab was now hired for the night by order of the Lord Provost and to calm his mare and do what he was told. As the man started to object Alexander told him that he would be paid in cash when the night's business was concluded, adding that if he made any further fuss his cab would be requisitioned by the government and he would have to wait some time for his money!

As there was no further complaint he wrote a note to the Commander of the Militia camp across the river requesting him to put six men in the coach and return here, also for him to send a company to cordon off the Assembly Rooms. His next move was to send a boy to collect his horse from the nearby livery table and ride up to Ensleigh to summon Harry and the duty squadron to meet him at the Assembly rooms where he would be overseeing the arrests.

Pandemonium was rife as he arrived there with indignant guests shouting and trying to break through the militia cordon. One of the first people he saw was Jessica who was almost hysterical with her efforts to find out just what had happened to him. Alexander called to her and ordered the militia to let her through.

She burst clear of the mob and clung desperately to him, tears running down her cheeks. He kissed her and soothed her fears and as they embraced a light rain began to fall and Alec realised just what a proud fool he had been. Here was a woman who loved him and who would make his confused and brittle life complete. He loved her now and in his heart he knew he always had. It had been his foolish pride that had kept them apart so long. She looked at him through her misted eyes and she could read his mind. She also knew in her heart that this was where she belonged. With her wild jealousy she had almost lost him once in the duel with Mahler and now this had happened, something completely beyond her control and it had really frightened her. As the thought swept over her she held him closer and swore that they would never part again. She had known from the very first time they met that the hand of destiny was in control but her feisty nature kept her kicking against admitting it… But now all that had passed. She was his, come what may and their foolish games of pride were over forever. She kissed him again and said quiet simply "I could have lost you tonight so please my Darling Alexander take me home and stay with me. I don't want to be alone tonight or ever again."

Holding her firmly to him, he led her to the coach where a distraught Janet was begging the coachman to go and find out what was happening. She grabbed her mistress and hugged her close calling her 'Child' and stroking her hair like a baby.

Just as Alexander was settling them in the coach the Militia Captain came to report that the scene was now secure and a platoon sat the rear of the building had caught a group of fugitives trying to escape including a couple of well known pickpockets, a German trooper in civilian clothes and Maria's special footman in the company of a certain Ellis Starkey.

A few minutes later Harry arrived with the squadron from Ensleigh to take over.

Ten days later in a sparsely furnished room at Grove Street gaol Melody was sitting on a stool in front of a well worn table waiting to be interrogated by Alexander. In one corner a sturdy cold eyed female gaoler stood watching her every move while on the other side of the room two clerks were sitting at a trestle table taking verbatim notes of the interview. One recording Alexander's words and the other Melody's

Like the other suspects, she had been held in solitary

confinement since her arrest and looked pale and drawn, her hair pulled back in a grubby ribbon, wearing a shapeless dark grey prison smock and on her feet a pair of loose wooden clogs. Alexander looked at her sternly while she fidgeted on the stool giving him a nervous smile. After a moment he cleared his throat and said quietly.

"Well Miss Watson, are you ready to explain your actions and tell me just why you tried to kill me, for that is one of the Court's charges against you?"
The accusation seemed to awaken some defensive mechanism in her brain and she smiled more broadly

"Oh, no, zur! I never intended to do you no 'arm." She cooed. "That gun was lying there on the ground so I got down to examine it. I just picked it up an' it went off in me 'and... Twas nuthin' but an accident, I swear. I never seed tha' gun afore."

Alexander dismissed this fabrication as being the child of hope rather than experience and replied "Oh really? Well, let me tell you what we've found out about that gun. It has an interesting provenance." Melody just gaped not knowing what provenance was.

Getting no response Alexander continued "My Sergeant Armourer tells me that the butt plate bears the trade mark of Mr Beresford the gun dealer on Broad Street, who told us that his father had taken it as payment for a wager from a Hanoverian officer in about '92. He said that from the octagonal barrel it appeared to be a much modified '55 calibre Jaeger rifle made by Wenger of Hamelin. He confirmed also that he had supplied it to Lord Bath as a prize at

337

the annual shooting contest at Longleat back in '96."...Melody looked at him blankly as he continued. "...and do you know who won the prize that year? Well, let me tell you, it was a Dilton Marsh farmer by the name of Zachariah Watson, who was I believe, your father... and your musketry instructor too. Am I right Miss Watson?"

Melody knew she was trapped. Everybody in Dilton Marsh knew what a good shot she was so she just nodded and bent her head.

Alexander smiled as though dealing with a child. "And what about those cartridges in the saddle bags, did you find them too?"

"Don't know nuffin 'bout 'no cartridges They musta come wi' the nag."

She suddenly realised that she had said too much and frowned hoping Alexander had not taken it in but he had.

"Well then, where did you get that horse from? Someone must have supplied you with such a fine looking beast. It is certainly no farm hack, in fact looks suspiciously like a cavalry mount to me... We'll soon know the owner when the brand is identified so why don't you tell me?."

Melody looked up sulkily and muttered. "I ain't tellin' you nuffin. Tis really yore fault as I am 'ere anyway. If'n you 'adn't pulled in Bradley Thomas I wouldn't be in this mess today. He woulda got me my due reward from Rob but now you've gone and pulled 'im for nuthin' as well. No wonder they all hate you!"

Calmly Alexander asked exactly who was it that hated him?

Melody suddenly exploded. "They all do!" She fumed. "Rob, Miss Maria, Cap'n Warmley, Rob's sister, Squire Starkey, an' all the Germans... Everybody! Why don't you jes' let us be? ... Aint nobody 'armin' you, is they?"

Her violent outburst stopped Alexander in his tracks. 'Robs sister, Rachel, his sweet Rachel? No, surely not! It was true that blood ties are the strongest of all, he reasoned but even so he couldn't believe what Melody said was true.

Casting aside all personal doubt his face hardened and he told the fuming girl just what she was facing. "I don't think you realise just how serious the charges against you are, do you Melody? They include the attempted murder of a King's officer, conspiracy to rob the Royal Treasury, the theft of a cavalry horse and God knows what else we'll find.... Any one of these charges would earn you twenty years in prison or transportation to the colonies...and a branding as well! So you'd better consider your future Miss ...and come back here when you are ready to co-operate a little."
He turned away from the shocked white face and told the turnkey to take her away.

Amongst the mail waiting for him at his return to Ensiegh Alexander found a brief note from a Weymouth Magistrate saying that the evidence of a man involved in a case that had come before him just might have some bearing on his present investigation.

339

Deciding that some first hand information was required, He sent Harry Fenwick, and three troopers down to the coast to bring the man back to Bath.

Three days later Harry was back with the suspect and joined Alexander in interrogating him. The man's name was Fergal O'Connor, a small time crook who dubiously claimed to be from Warminster. In a shaking voice with many stops and starts he told his story. The charge against him had been the possession and attempted sale of some stolen property which he claimed to have bought in the Crown Inn at Radstock from Charley Cavey and Big Silas Jordan, two of the men murdered after a series of hayrick fires in the nearby Mendips. More importantly he said they had told him that they had been members of Captain Brooks' gang and they had tried to recruit him to do a big robbery with them. The man behind it was Black Robbie, otherwise known as Rob Dacarius.

Alexander had always been uncomfortable with the result of the earlier trial, feeling that something was missing. After meeting Miller Russell and the others involved he sensed that there must have been somebody else controlling the whole thing and had suspected that it just might be Rachel's brother.

It was starting to look like he might have been right after all.

At one point Alexander had asked O'Connor if he knew who the Redemptors were. At this the man went white and started shaking, refusing to say anything more. Alexander reminded him that he was already deeply involved but that he could offer him a way out. The man nodded his head grabbing any chance to escape the dreaded hulks. If he would testify in court he would be released, given new identity and a free passage to Jersey with enough money for a fresh start. Fergal stared at Alexander for along moment and then said he would do it. To prevent any leakage of his future plans or O'Connor changing his mind or even being got at in the Grove Street gaol Alexander decided to hold him in secure accommodation at Ensleigh and gave Harry orders to that effect.

Most of the following week was taken up with the witness being grilled by Harry and Alexander and his statement checked out. Undercover agents were sent out to Warminster, Weymouth and the Mendips to search for other witnesses and evidence. Within a week the men were back with the story confirmed and sworn statements from various other parties. With this information added to the recent testimony of Melody Watson, who at the prospect of branding and transportation willingly filled in all the gaps, Alexander decided he had enough evidence and that it was time to make his move.

Rob was pulled in and lodged at Grove Street Prison on charges of stealing Royal revenues, smuggling and aiding and abetting military unrest. Concerned at possible attempts to either free him or bribe the warder, Alexander arranged to have teams of his men on guard there round the clock.   Other smaller fry who were detained included the obsessed Maria di Sienna, the footman from the casino, the few remaining members of Rob's gang and the German dragoon who had supplied Melody's horse. He had been

341

Major Mahler's servant and wanted to avenge his master's humiliation at Alexander's hands.

In spite of Alexander's suspicions no charge was made against Ellis Starkey who claimed that he was only getting away from some woman by using the back door but at least it gave the new Lord Trandon a chance to evaluate Barnes' partner in crime at first hand. Rob's partner Diego smelling trouble in the air headed to Bristol at the first chance he got and booked a passage on the next boat back to Portugal.

Alexander's sudden move alarmed quite a few important persons in the Treasury and in Whitehall too where there were those who had presumed that the matter had been dealt with by the conviction of Bradley Thomas and the destruction of the Redemptors. They were relieved that the trial had passed without too many shadows being cast on certain parties and even though the attempt to make it a closed military tribunal had failed.

This time however, it was a different kettle of fish. The national press had got wind of it, with the London broadsheets leading the way, foremost of whom was the Universal Daily Register rejoicing in its new title as the Times. The trial was to be at Bristol Assizes in two months time and in public, giving Alexander's lawyers ample time to prepare the case later. The proceedings would be reported on, country wide and who knows? Heads might yet roll

34

ROB'S TRIAL

The attempt on Alexander's life was not all that surprising in the light of Maria's insane jealousy. This was not the first time he had snubbed her and now she thought she would kill two birds with one stone: get rid of her abuser and save a good friend. She told her friend Ellis Starkey who heartily encouraged her in this plan. He really did not care one way or the other about Rob's fate but if it meant getting rid of his own enemy he was all for it. In her innocence, Rachel had told Maria all about her brother's former life and mentioned that one of the other girls with the gang was unusually adept with a rifle and she had won prizes for it. Maria took note of this snippet of information and decided to contact the girl, thinking that such a talent might be useful to her one day.

Maria had actually known Rob some time. When she was merely a child he would often visit the brothel run by her Uncle Silas at Redcliffe but of course, back then he did not even notice little Mary May the scullery maid and in no way connected her to the seductive courtesan now known as Maria di Sienna. They made the connection again when Rob settled in Widcombe when he had been forced to change his profession after the death of Captain Brooks and right now she was very concerned about his sudden arrest. Some time after the first trial ended without him being charged she had been contacted by Mendoza who told her of his impending return and she was there to greet him on his arrival at Poole. She was somewhat discomforted to find that he had brought his business partner with him but that did not stop them spending an idyllic few days sampling the delights of the best hotel in Bournemouth before returning to Bath.

Unfortunately she could not get on with his sister, ironically about the only other person as concerned as herself about his fate. She realised that Rachel was too involved with Alexander to be able to see clearly just what her brother was facing and, she admitted to herself that she was somewhat jealous of the attention that Rachel was getting from the proud officer. In any event, she felt that she and she alone should be his saviour and began feverishly to organise his defence, though she had sneaking doubts about the reliability of the luscious Melody if they ever got her in the dock.

Up at Ensleigh It seemed that somebody had been reading Alexander's mind (or was there perhaps a spy in his camp?) because barely a week later an order had come through saying that it had been decided not to hold the trial at Bristol Assizes. No reason was given, and he would be informed of the venue in due course.

Alexander was incensed at the news and felt shocked to have been dismissed to the sidelines such a cavalier manner when he was supposed to be in charge of the investigation and prosecution. Surely, he thought, considering the enormity of the offence, the stealing of the army payroll and funds destined for the Dublin Treasury, that the trial should be heard at a major venue... In fact he thought that in view of the national interest the Old Bailey in London would be deemed a more suitable venue. However, as he discovered later, it seems that some major reputations were at stake, not least the public confidence in the Younger Pitt's administration. There was also the voracious, radical press with young independent editors bent on exposing governmental bureaucratic sloth and incompetence

In a desperate bid to prevent too much being exposed the Lord Provost's office tried to make it a closed Court Martial but vigorous lobbying by the press and defence lawyers, who pointed out that the accused was in fact a civilian, frustrated the attempt. Unabashed, the Establishment then tried to transfer the trial to Longleat House. This desperate move was in turn countered by the prosecution who pointed out that the eccentric Lord Bath was likely to be called as a witness for the prosecution. That was the last thing that the Lord Provost wanted so the attempt was aborted!

After much discussion and procrastination an acceptable compromise was reached and the venue chosen was the Court House in Bath: At least reasoned the Lord Provost, surely a small, frivolous city like Bath would not merit the same irritating press presence as the last trial in Bristol. It was a decision that also suited Alexander as he could continue to hold his suspects in the nearby Grove Street Prison and in spite of all delay the trial finally opened almost a year after the crime.

Alexander had been meticulous in preparing and collating the evidence but even the Lord Provost himself had been under pressure from certain quarters to trundle out one of the useless old time serving blunderers to represent the Crown in the hope that the case was presented badly. However Alexander was insistent that the Lord Provost's Office produced a young career hungry barrister to present the case.

The young man's name was Henry Corbett. He had spent some time in London at the Inns of Court before following the feeding frenzy of lawyers old and young to Bath where there legal business was booming. There were property deals to oversee, mortgages to arrange, inherences to handle and bankruptcy proceedings to be dealt with. But this was everyday fare and whilst earning him substantial fees, a juicy case involving robbery of the Crown's possessions with a possibility of extortion and multiple murders, all of it covered by a sensation hungry national press, would be a boost to his career and was too good an opportunity to miss.

Accordingly he made it his business to meet up with The Chief Investigator and offer his services. Alexander, for his part, bearing in mind the dry as dust unimaginative prosecution barristers he had come across, was only too happy to take on board such an enthusiastic young driving lawyer and the partnership was formed.

Once more the whole town was a-buzzing with the excitement of the coming trial and landladies were doing grand business. So much so that rooms were at a premium and there had been a report in the Bath Chronicle that one party of wealthy young women had paid a hundred guineas for one month's rental of a suite of four rooms on fashionable South Parade and that the chair-men had doubled their fees for the duration of the trial. In preparation for the expected throng of voyeurs, adventurers, pimps, rent boys sharpened up their game while the ever- competitive courtesans took great pains to look their most sensuous and alluring.

It could never be said that the Lower Town was a fragrant place but now a new aroma was mingling with the river miasmas and the open sewers. It was the sweet smell of money!

The trial was opened by the Mayor of Bath and the first week was taken up with the selection and swearing in the jury, the decisions of procedure and various other formalities including the positioning of the press benches so as to cause the minimum disturbance to the smooth running of the trial. Next the representative teams of lawyers were introduced and the usual pedantic, protracted arguments about court protocol were thrashed out. The Prosecution, rather to chagrin of The Lord Provost and his friends, was to be led by young Henry Corbett.

For the defence Rob, with his new found affluence, could afford to retain the services of the veteran advocate Charles Edward Priestly. This was the same Priestly who had gained his spurs as a prosecutor in the sensational libel case brought against Warren Hastings by Lord Combleton. Incidentally it was one of the few cases he had actually lost but the resulting publicity had made him a golden boy at the Inns of Court.

The following Monday the business started in earnest when the case was outlined by Justice Pearson from the King's Bench citing their serious nature of the offences which included, murder, robbery of the Crown's property, extortion, and attempting to assassinate a King's officer. The charge of conspiring to foment mutiny in the Army in Ireland was dropped, as was that against Major Mahler's servant who had supplied Melody with the charger. He had been swiftly posted back to a punishment battalion in Hanover as the news of the impending arrests leaked out...

The small fry such as the three remaining ex-members of Brook's old gang and various others who would be dealt with first had, already been brought in from the various holding units and were being held in temporary cages in the basement of the building. They were then brought up and charges against them read out by the Clerk of the Court and the judge signalled for the first part of the trial to begin. The heavyweights such as Rob, Maria and Melody would be arraigned later.

Henry Corbett opened by outlining the case for the prosecution. Thanks to Alexander's painstaking investigations and careful checking of the known facts plus the able team of advising solicitors Harry could steer a clear and concise path through the sequence of the crimes and within two weeks all the accused were declared guilty as charged. Sentencing would come later.

The next up was Maria. She made a stately entrance into the hushed courtroom wearing a demure costume of bottle green velvet highlighted by a wispy lavender silk scarf with matching gloves and kitten heeled shoes. Asked for her name and station she told the court proudly that she was 'Donna Maria di Sienna, widow of the late Visconti di Sienna and of independent means, a statement which elicited gasps and more than a few raised eyebrows from many in the public gallery who knew her true calling!

Henry stood up and politely wished her a good day and proceeded to cross examine her, at which her demeanour completely changed to indignant demands as to why she had been brought here and that the charges against her were ridiculous. She didn't even know the girl who had tried to kill this fellow... Why on earth should she want anyone dead? And before she could be asked anything further she burst into loud crocodile tears causing some in the gallery to applaud her as if she were in a play.

His Honour banged his gavel and called for silence, adding that if there were any more hoots and catcalls he would clear the court while Henry looked on wryly waiting for the disturbance to settle down. Then, looking straight at Maria he told her that the charges against her were real and had been substantiated by the evidence of the casino footman and others, so it would be wiser not to insult the court's intelligence further by these ridiculous histrionics! Further questions produced the same hysterical response including statements that the court had no right to try her as she was a foreign national and had broken no laws.

After a pregnant pause Henry said dryly. "Madame, you are well known in this city and in Bristol," and added menacingly, "… so if you do not wish to have this court know the full extent of your chequered history," At this point he lowered his chin and gazed at her menacingly from under his furrowed brow, "and beware Madame for my inquiries have been thorough, you would wise be to abandon this pathetic charade and tell us the simple truth."

Maria gave him a look of disdain and blurted "I do not know why I have been brought here. You have no right to arrest me on such a charge. It is ridiculous to even think I had any reason to be involved at all in the attack on Lord Trandon."

"Very well Madame, have it your way." Henry responded. "You will find that your rather foolish intransigence forces me to present another witness whose evidence will prove your deep involvement beyond any doubt. I call Melody Watson to the stand!"

Maria gasped and looked wildly around the court room as the luscious Melody, now dressed in her best clothes, was led by two stout wardresses who then stood behind her in the witness box. "You have no right!" She screamed..."You are bribing strangers to give false evidence against me. I do not even know this person and I find this treatment absolutely intolerable!"

This time, neither Henry nor the Judge took any notice of her outburst and the Clerk of the Court took Melody's oath.

Melody knew only too well that the lenience of the court depended on her performance so she was very forthcoming, telling the court in full about being approached by the casino footman and being told what to do. To bind her to go through with what was required he had given her an advance of five guineas saying that Maria di Siena would pay her the balance when the deed was done.

Maria roared in again with loud denials saying that it was all lies and that she did not know this tavern serving maid but lapsed into a sulk when Henry asked her that if she did not know the witness how did she know the girl's occupation but she put the final nail in her coffin when her uncontrollable temper led her to shout.

"I was told she had won prizes for her shooting... but she is a dolt who could not even follow my simple instructions"

This time the Judge simply rolled his eyes skyward for a moment before dismissing Melody and having her returned to the cells and gesturing for the trial to continue.

Clearing his throat, Henry asked Maria to explain her outburst but she refused to say anything more to the court and sat staring evilly at Alexander and Jessica sitting in the front row of the gallery. To all intents and purpose it was all over.

Priestly, the pompous defence barrister, very obviously conscious of his reputation, tried his best to make a fist of it, har'umphd and dryly quoted from obscure precedents in a vain attempt to present his client as being the dupe of more important people and that the evidence was flawed but after Maria's outburst it was all to no avail and after a short absence the jury returned with a unanimous guilty verdict.

Deciding that any more evidence at this juncture would overwhelm the jury and he wanted them fresh for the principal event, which was the trial of Rob Dacarius, the judge declared a ten day adjournment. This was accepted gratefully by all concerned with the possible exception of the main defendant who was languishing in a lonely cell at Grove Street gaol.

Rob had cleverly covered his tracks at the last trial and had been cleared but this time the evidence against him was overwhelming. In the dock he sneered at the jury and arrogantly shrugged off the restraining hands of the bulky warders and stared blankly at the court daring them to accuse him of anything.... In his mind he had every eventuality covered and was bolstered by the knowledge that he had one of the best barristers in England handling his case.

Like Maria he started off with indignant objections that he did not recognise the authority of the court and that he was now a Portuguese citizen and could not be tried under English law. The

Judge who been briefed thoroughly before reminded him that in spite of any family heritage, the fact was that he had been born in England and that the crimes had been committed in England, therefore the trial was legally allowed to continue with the case.

Henry stood up and in his quiet but determined manner wished Rob a good morning. It was a tactic that tended to give the accused a false sense of security and superiority and often loosened tongues that normally stayed silent. Rob Dacarius was no exception. Under cross-examination he blustered confidently and his advocate objected frequently but it was what Henry had been expecting and he rebuffed every interruption. Witnesses were called and their testimony was damning, involving Rob in everything that had happened.

The final crunch came the following day when Melody Watson took the stand again. This time she told the hushed court the full story from beginning to end, from her first acqaintence with him at Captain Brooks' camp in the forest to her part in the robbery and the subsequent plot between him and Maria to kill Alexander. Rob stared evilly at her and drew his hand across his throat. Melody turned white but took a deep breath and steeled herself to continue… after all, it was her or them. The thought of the transportation and branding frightened the life out her and this fear was her armour against the harsh accusations in the cross examination by his overbearing barrister.

The defence did their best but the few witnesses they

353

produced, which included Rachel who averted her eyes from the public gallery where Alexander with Jessica holding tightly onto his arm sat watching the case take shape. All the witnesses were weak and confused, with their statements crossing the evidence of earlier witnesses and they almost all collapsed under the cross examination by the astute Henry. During the presentation of prosecution's case the jury were silently paying wrapt attention as the story unfolded but when the defence took over now there were outbursts of coughing and bored yawning as Priestley blustered on and on, peppering the weak defence with dry unconvincing opinions and bouts of wild haranguing.

All in all, the trial did not run the expected three months and within six weeks it was apparent that all the suspects were guilty to some extent or other. A further week was taken up with the closing arguments and the judge's summing up. Finally the jury was sent out to consider their verdict... Two days later they gave unanimous guilty verdicts for all charged and the Judge adjourned proceedings for a further three weeks before the sentencing.

Eventually Rob, Maria and the three surviving gang members were sentenced to death (later commuted to transportation for life). Melody, because of the fullness of her evidence escaped the dreaded transportation and was given a lesser sentence to be served in Bristol, as were several minor players like the footman and other casino workers. No charge was brought against Ellis Starkey but he was warned that his conduct was suspicious and any further controversial behaviour would be noted.

If nothing else it gave Alexander an opportunity to get the measure of Barnes' accomplice in the Trandon Home Farm robbery.

Watching it all was the Clerk of the Court giving brief whispered instructions to his assistant. As the prisoners were bustled down to the cells he let out a sigh of relief and told the assistant to start packing his papers. As he walked over to speak to one of the guards the assistant took a bright green feather out of his pocket.

On his return The Chief Clerk was most annoyed to find that his man had disappeared

35

THE WEDDING

As the excitement of the trial subsided, things returned to normal in Bath, (or at least to as normal as they ever were in this eccentric city.) The hucksters packed up their stalls and side shows and one by one left to seek another location to re-create their rolling carnival The Upper Assembly Rooms again returned to its place as the centre of attraction and plans were being laid for the forthcoming winter diversions when a momentous event put the whole thing into reverse and another round of wild soirees, balls, fetes and celebrity breakfasts in the Sydney Gardens began again.

News had just reached the country of Nelson's stunning naval victory off Trafalgar on October 21st 1805 and the whole nation was going wild, albeit a little sad too at the loss of their hero. Bath re-acted as it usually did by making the most of any reason to celebrate and the air was thick with smoke from the fireworks in Sydney Gardens and Orange Grove. Groups of revellers in fancy dress roamed the streets singing popular songs and dancing with innocent bystanders as they wound their way to parties and dinner-dances.

Down at Maria's pleasure palace at Axfords Buildings above Walcott, Aimee, with Mendoza's encouragement and support had picked up the reins and was doing great business, particularly from the deviant patrons of the Saturnalia catacombs.

At the Assembly Rooms, Jessica and Alexander and all their friends joined in the celebrations to the full. Every night of the week there were parties and functions to go to. It was the perfect opportunity for a tired provost officer to relax awhile from the rigours of the investigation and the trial.

Trafalgar parties became the vogue at all the fashionable hotels and grand houses in town where the revellers dressed for the occasion in costumes with a nautical theme. The ladies wore all manner of complicated coiffures and the milliners were burning the midnight oil to produce hats like floating ships and frolicking mermaids and their ball gowns were festooned with ribbons bearing the names of the ships in the famous engagement off Cadiz.

Reinhart Butzbach, the enterprising manager of the Palatine Hotel in Orange Grove was Austrian and so the specialities of his restaurant were the dishes and delicatessen of his homeland. Superb light, crisp Wiener Schnitzels, spicy cooked meats, smoked sausages and the celebrated Weiner weis-bier, a clear strawberry tasting strong lager from the Tyrol... But the piece de resistance were his sweet cream pastries. Observing the current mood of wild patriotism, he

357

commissioned his supplier to produce an edible model of Nelsons famous ship HMS Victory which he displayed as a centrepiece in his restaurant.

Of course the redoubtable Mrs Edwards was in the forefront of these victory celebrations. Invitations to her famous soirees were like gold and she diplomatically let it be known that substitutions would be accepted for those finding themselves obligated to a prior engagement ... with her approval, of course... and as such approval did not come cheap, she profited greatly from this largesse.

Her experience in this field and her inherent sense of the styles, fashions and fads of the times stood her in good stead but this time it seemed that the Palatine Hotel had stolen a march on her. She was fuming and drawing on something she had once seen at a restaurant in Venice, she made Herr Butzbach's pastry supplier an offer he could not refuse. It was a contract to provide two model ships but somewhat bigger than the one at the Palatine, one of H.M.S, Victory and the other of the French ship Bucentaure.

Three days later they were delivered unseen in the early dawn and hidden behind screens on a specially decorated table in her large salon until it was time to present them. When she judged that everybody was well primed with liquor and the delicious dishes Mrs Edwards gave the signal to her Major Domo who called loudly for attention and while the string quartet burst into a jolly nautical air, she pulled a cord and the screens fell away.

Everybody gasped in amazement and applauded the

wonderful tableau with white paper wave tops on a dark blue cloth and smaller boats and sea birds dotted around them... The main models were perfection with white icing gun ports, thin white pastry sails with carefully crafted folds and delicate spun sugar rigging. The masts were of liquorice root and there were even moulded sugar cannons and rope coils on the decks.....But they were not there just to be seen.. Oh no, they were there to be eaten!

Two teams of five were chosen by auctioning off the places which went for as high as twenty five guineas each. Ironically Jessica and Cyrus got a place on the British team while Alexander had to be content with reluctantly attacking Lord Nelson's flagship. Both teams were issued with long handled kitchen spoons, (in deference to the occasion, Victory's team got bigger ones) and were lined up on their respective sides of the table and were to destroy the craft in front of them and the debris to be eaten by their supporters.

The Major Domo gave the signal to begin and with the crash of a gong the battle commenced while a band of shouting musicians played suitable patriotic airs with added drum and cymbal crashes imitating the roar of cannons. The competitors took to the task with gusto as they took their turns, chipping off large lumps of cake with each stroke and which the pretty hostesses handed back to their supporters to be gobbled up. Within ten minutes the ships were knocked to pieces with chips of cake and icing flying through the air. Finally there was a huge cheer as the French ship's liquorice mainmast fell and the model keeled over... The Victory had won again!

The evening was a roaring success, so much so that Mrs Edwards repeated the spectacle twice more in a week to make it the talk of the town. Her position in Bath as the leading society hostess was affirmed.... And the pastry chef could now afford to buy his daughter a pony for Christmas.

One of the wildest revellers was a young man dressed in a woman's fancy hat and brightly embroidered waistcoat who sang heartily as he bashed into the French ship with his spoon to which he had tied a small bright green feather

---

There was however one major change in Alexander's life. Since the botched attempt on his life he and Jessica had become very close indeed. Hardly a week went by without them being seen out dining at the best hotels in town and then sharing the night at either Trandon House or at Jessica's elegant home on Great Pulteney Street.

It was an even happier time for Jessica when she found out from Janet that Rachel had left for Portugal. With her off the scene there was little doubt that she could keep Alexander's mind on the business in hand...

They spent Christmas at Cyrus' elegant new house in North Stoke, a hamlet just below the landmark hill top circle of trees known as Kelston Round and barely a mile below his stud farm at Lansdowne, along with the radiant Alice who was looking radiant and Jeb who in contrast, looked drawn with lacklustre eyes and constant cough which he put down to a head cold. There to greet them were the members of Cyrus' extended family, most of them from up in the Cotswolds including Mary a pleasant faced buxom young widow whom Cyrus introduced as his new fiancé! This intelligence came as rather a shock as everybody assumed that he was a confirmed bachelor and much muttering and puzzled sideways glances were exchanged at the news.

In the event it proved to be a marriage made in heaven as Mary, who already had a nine year old boy and a six year old daughter was a natural born home maker and mother who was proud of her older husband but never interfered with his business and took his wild nights out in her stride. Within five years she had presented him with twin boys and girl and still looked as fresh and beautiful as she did on her wedding day.

There was also another little surprise waiting for Alexander.

By the time the Christmas festivities were over Jessica realised that there was little doubt that she was pregnant! In spite of all the enlightened Indian contraceptive techniques taught to her by her late father's mistress, she had just missed her second period so it was fortuitous that her rival had disappeared from the scene. She also thanked God that the lunatic Mahler was not here to take it as personal insult and start raving about more duels. She had persuaded herself that Alexander really had insulted her at the theatre but deep inside she knew that it had been her own jealous vanity that had triggered off all the trouble … But that was all water under the bridge now and she had to face up to the task of informing Alexander of the coming event..

It was at breakfast on New Years day that Jessica cast a cautious eye across the table, laid her knife and fork down and gingerly mentioned that she thought it just possible that she might be pregnant. She blinked her eyes and cringed at the expected reaction from Alexander…

Surprisingly he took the news with considerable aplomb, even enthusiasm. He talked at length about it, saying that he had always wanted a son, quite blindly refusing the possibility that it might be a girl! Jessica, for her part was quite relieved to find that he didn't insist on a termination... She had been terrified of having an abortion even though such matters were everyday occurrences in a pleasure mad city like this. Of course she would not have had to suffer the indignities of the Milk Street sisters where the street girls went but even the thought of a visit to one of the discreet nursing homes near Box that catered to the gentry in such matters, sent a shiver of horror down her spine.

As for broaching the question of marriage, in the event she did not even have to ask him. Alexander simply accepted that

362

nuptials would follow, particularly now that his paramour had gone away, and he enthusiastically told her go to ahead and make all the arrangements and plan the ceremony at Bath Abbey in six weeks time. Jessica kissed him warmly, hoping that by that time the lump would not be noticed.

It left her feeling rather confused and although she would never have admitted it, a little miffed as though the wind had been taken out of her sails. As she sat in her bedroom mulling things over she reasoned that like most sea-going men she had met, Alexander had lived for many years facing constant danger from nature and his enemies and had become fatalistic, accepting that which they cannot control.

The time passed quickly with a million things to do. Renewed activity in the war with Republican France kept Alexander busy checking security both at Warminster and Ensleigh so it was left mostly to Jessica to organise the Abbey service and the reception at the Upper Assembly Rooms. There were the bridesmaids and their dresses to order, the invitations to be designed and printed and a plethora of details to attend to from booking the caterers and coaches to the accommodation for the guests, some of whom would be coming from overseas. Janet was run ragged all day with errands to the shops and taking messages to various specialists.

On her big day Jessica was awoken by the sound of the wedding bells and her carriage was escorted from her Pulteney Street mansion to the Abbey by the Militia band and a section of

Hanoverian Dragoons. Awaiting her were the great, the good and her handsome bridegroom in his dashing uniform, plus a riotous cross section of the pleasure mad society that gave Bath its unique reputation. The formal wedding service was read by the Bishop of Bath and after the ceremony the open bridal coach led the procession of guests through streets lined with cheering crowds. Leaving Westgate Street they turned into Gay Street and wound up to The King's Circus and on to the lavish reception awaiting them at the Upper Assembly Rooms. Most of the onlookers had no idea who they were watching or what was happening. What did it matter to them anyway? It was another excuse to celebrate and pass that gin bottle round!

At the ornate doorway of the venue the greasy Captain Warmley, looking fatter than ever, greeted them and led the way into the foyer rubbing his hands at the prospect of the afternoon's takings at the tables and bowed obsequiously as they entered. As the bridal party moved on to the Yellow Room the big organ struck up a wedding march and the guests stormed the groaning buffet tables and the free drinks bar. For all the pomp and circumstance it was just like any old village wedding!

Old acquaintances and distant family milled around congratulating the bride and groom and adding their gifts to the large velvet covered table set up for this purpose at the rear, prudently guarded by two sturdy troopers from Ensleigh.

All their close friends came over to congratulate them but

Alexander was shocked by the appearance of Jeb. Instead of the hearty, robust horseman he once was, Jeb looked thin, pale and drawn and leaned heavily on a walking cane. His hands and voice were shaky and he seemed to be sweating profusely. Cyrus caught Alexander's anxious look and gestured him to one side where he explained that Jeb was seriously ill.

Apparently since they last all met at Christmas Jeb's doctor had told him that he had contracted a serious sexually transmitted disease and added in confidence that he thought that his beautiful Alice was possibly a carrier. Jeb did not inform her of the doctor's opinion and she remained blissfully ignorant of the tragic situation and within six months he had become a raddled victim of rampant syphilis. By contrast, Alice herself was immune to the condition and still looked just as beautiful as when they last saw her and except for her eyes which had a sharp glassy brilliance there was no indication that she was a carrier. Apparently, somewhere down the line the charming Alice had been a little too enthusiastic while making Mrs Edwards' guests at ease!

To lighten this sombre news Cyrus asked the newlyweds where they would be celebrating their honeymoon. In normal circumstances such an aristocratic wedding as this would be celebrated by a Grand Tour of European capitals or a cruise to Naples but with Napoleon's armies rampaging through Europe such a trip was out of the question, even in Portugal the situation was becoming sinister with the threat of a French invasion. In fact the only available thing left was a tour of the Highlands of Scotland or an extended stay in fashionable Brighton, which was rapidly becoming a serious rival to Bath. Pleading her pregnant state and not being exactly enthusiastic about shooting innocent stags or putting salt on her porridge, Jessica opted for the exclusive shops and comfortable hotels of the English south coast. Alexander gallantly put up no serious objection to her decision, even though he would have much preferred the machismo of the wild glens and an abundance of the single malt whisky.

On their return they settled comfortably at Trandon House, Jessica feeling at last that she was somewhere she really belonged. Mr Myatt's house on Pulteney Street was kept on as a town residence and it was there that the future Lord Trandon was born. They called him Terrance Alexander and had him Christened in Bath Abbey. It was the event of the season and was graced by their many friends in North Somerset & Bath. Some guests came from afar as London and two of Alexander's colleagues from his hard days in the Marines, even arrived from Gibraltar. Regrettably one old friend was missing. A week before the ceremony Jeb had died from his tragic infection.

The lovely Alice mourned him, mystified as to the real cause of his death. Three years later she married again with the same tragic consequences and still it did not even cross her mind that she might be somehow to blame. It was another four years later when her third husband, a Senior Royal Navy Flag Captain, also died at Valetta of the same disease.

The Fleet Surgeon who conducted the official inquest took a deep interest in the case. He had spent his whole career attending to the health of men at sea and had built up an almost encyclopaedic knowledge of sexually transmitted diseases. He had known the Flag Captain well and it was a most unusual case as the man had never had serious illness before and unlike many naval officers did not indulge in the social whirl when ashore. Knowing the incubation period of the disease and of its progression, he tracked the most likely time of the initial infection to the man's honeymoon on the isle of Minorca. Further checking of Alice's previous marriages confirmed his suspicions.

His final report stopped short of accusing the innocent widow but it caused Alice to review her misfortunes and the cruel truth eventually dawned on her. The monstrosity of this realisation affected Alice's mind and she turned her back on the world, passing the rest of her long life as a recluse in the Lansdowne house that Jeb had built for her, refusing to see any visitors, with just her maid and a manservant for company.

Postscript

ISLAND IN THE SUN

As the trial proceeded, Rachel realising the strength of evidence against her brother and the most likely outcome, went to see Mendoza and asked him to transfer her assets to Portugal and if he could arrange Rob's rescue. He was sad to hear her news about the trial but agreed with her decision and yes, he did have contacts who could possibly arrange Rob's escape but that it would be expensive. Without hesitation Rachel authorised the attempt. Mendoza then went on to hint that the ships often put into the Portuguese Atlantic Islands to get fresh water and provisions and that the harbour pilots were also Portuguese. He would see what could be done.

A week after the final verdict she left Bath without a farewell to Alexander or anyone and moved to Bournemouth to be near her brother. Mendoza had told her that it would be at least six weeks before the next move, till then she must be patient and not to visit him too often as this may look suspicious.

The prison fleet, mostly stinking ex-slave carriers, left three times a year. Until then the convicts were kept aboard hulks off Poole and other ports where occasional visits by relatives on compassionate grounds were allowed until their loved ones were shipped out to either the icy coast of Nova Scotia in Canada or the fever ridden island of Jamaica and its deadly plantations where the conditions were even more appalling. Usually here, after several years of backbreaking labour under the merciless tropical sun the burnt out prisoners were released to make their own way in the colony.... An opportunity which all too often proved too much, leaving them to beg on the dusty streets of Kingston until the grim reaper called them home.

In England, especially in periods of peace when thousands of discharged soldiers and sailors roamed the streets scratching a living by what ever means they could, these foetid hulls became crowded to bursting point. Under such pressure it was no surprise that there were often outbreaks of contagious diseases like cholera due to the breakdown of the already primitive sanitary conditions. At such times the Government would offer contracts to the captains of trans-Atlantic merchant ships to carry a number of convicts to penitential plantations overseas.

One of these vessels, a sturdy Portuguese ship called the Santa Clara, was currently in Bristol Docks loading a mixed cargo for Pernambuco in Brazil. Kingston, Jamaica was one of the ports of call and a group of felons it would be carrying into bondage there arrived at the quayside late at night in a black prison van. It consisted of four women and six men including Rob and Maria and was hustled aboard to be securely locked up below decks in the four barred compartments that served as the ship's brig.

Two days before it sailed one of Mendoza's representatives approached the ship's doctor in a dockside tavern and asked him to perform certain services. The reward was a sufficient sum of money to allow him to leave his stressful life at sea and set up a pleasant practice in Bath where his patients didn't regularly have broken heads and limbs to mend or obscure tropical diseases. He accepted the offer without further hesitation and was given a note and a mysterious packet of dark green powder.

The boat left on time hardly noticed in the flurry of a busy harbour and the voyage passed off without incident until on the morning of the eighth day at sea when the surgeon burst into the Captain's cabin and announced that he had found four of the prisoners, two women and three of the men showing symptoms of the plague. To prevent further contagion amongst the convicts he insisted that they must be put ashore as soon as possible. He emphasised that the crew also could be at risk.

Aghast, more at the prospect of not being paid on delivery for his charges than of the safety of his crew, the Captain immediately called for a chart and ordered a change of course to the nearest landfall, the small island of Porto Santo a few miles north of Madeira about six hours sailing time away. In the meantime he ordered that the victims were to be quarantined aboard the ship's longboat and towed fifty meters astern until they were in the harbour roads.

Arriving offshore the Captain waited for dark before giving

the signal for the boat to be rowed into the harbour and waited anxiously to hear from the Porto Santo authorities. Three days later a small cutter bearing the port pilot came alongside to report that two of the sick, one of them a woman, had died and that the others were in a critical condition in an isolated convent. After the messenger left the ship's doctor warned the Captain of the bureaucratic nightmare looming and it didn't take him long to agree and weigh anchor as soon as his water and stores loaded aboard.

The next day, on a cliff top in Porto Santo, a group of people were sitting in the warm sunshine happily enjoying a pleasant picnic and watching anxiously as a ship slowly slipped away over the horizon. It was Rod, Maria, Rachel, with her new husband, Rod's Portugese partner Diego and Mendoza's nephew Isadoro. As the last trace of their floating prison faded they drank an ironic toast to their floating prison wishing it a safe passage to Jamaica.

They laughed and joked together, ate roast chicken, fresh bread and fruit while young Isadoro brought them wine and told them proudly of his uncle's influence and power. As his stories of high places and exotic locations held them fascinated, they soon forgot their troubles and began to look forward to the future.

Maria's old predatory habits which had faded on board the prison ship began to stir again as she watched the handsome young man but she was confused at his total lack of interest in her... True, perhaps her recent hardships may have blunted her physical impact, but she felt that she still had an aura of sensual mystery and thinking that this was an ideal opportunity to test her power, she walked over to him smiling. She was surprised to find that her approach had a totally unexpected response from him when at the sight of her he turned and walked swiftly into a nearby clump of trees.

She followed him into the copse where at the sight of her he rummaged in his pocket for a small blue bottle and quickly drank the contents. There was a rustling in the undergrowth at her side and she glanced down too see what it was but when she looked up again the handsome Isadoro had vanished

----

News from the Circus

I'm just not sure what woke me up. I think it must have been an ambulance or a police car on the nearby Lansdowne Road but here I was, sprawled on the bean bag in the bright glow of the rare December sunshine coming through the tall window... I was dressed in my Jack Daniels T shirt and my old jeans while on the floor beside me was a crumbled green feather, the old parchment and lying on its side, the empty dark blue bottle... Last thing I remember was sitting on a cliff top on an Atlantic island with some woman coming on to me.

Outside my window a group of Japanese tourists were staring mesmerised at the majestic Georgian architecture and across the grassy green a group of well muffled up people were turning into Gay Street waving flyers about the Guildhall Christmas Market. Just then my mobile rang... It was Kitty asking if I could pick her up at Bath Spa station. Her train was just leaving Newport and would be there in about an hour. She said that she had quite a tale to tell me and I thought 'Well so have I'..... But wonder if she will believe it!

END